THE INTERN

Brooke Walton Series Book 3

JENIFER RUFF

THE INTERN
Copyright © 2018 Greyt Companion Press
Written by Jenifer Ruff
Cover design by Kim G Designs
ISBN paperback: 978-1724682000

ALSO BY JENIFER RUFF

The Agent Victoria Heslin Thriller Series
The Numbers Killer
Pretty Little Girls
When They Find Us
Ripple of Doubt
The Groom Went Missing
Vanished on Vacation
The Atonement Murders
The Ones They Buried
The Bad Neighbor

THE FBI & CDC Thriller Series
Only Wrong Once
Only One Cure
Only One Wave: The Tsunami Effect

The Brooke Walton Series
Everett
Rothaker
The Intern
Suspense
Lauren's Secret

Chapter One

Seven months had passed without another murder, and Brooke Walton intended to keep the streak going. She had too much to lose—her reputation as an accomplished medical student and her future as a surgeon—if she should ever get caught. And the drama that ultimately followed every death and disappearance exhausted her, carrying on for weeks and months after each incident. She wanted to focus on school and for everyone else to mind their own business.

Wedged against the door in the back seat of a small rental car with her two sisters, she stared at the disappointing scenery along Cancun's main road. Clumps of dry mangled shrubs and barren brown fields. Two rail-thin men on a decrepit front porch, tank tops exposing jutting collar bones. So far, Cancun bore no resemblance to the magical oasis touted on the resort's website. Still, it might be perfect. She shifted her gaze from the back of her father's head to her mother's. What they didn't know wouldn't hurt them.

Sydney lowered her paperback and squinted at Brooke. "What are you grinning at?"

Brooke avoided her sister's eyes. "Just . . . excited to be here." She lifted her long, blonde hair off her shoulders and rubbed her neck.

"She survived a grueling week of medical school final exams." Their mother gazed at a travel brochure about windsurfing, not bothering to look up. "She has every right to smile."

Brooke felt sorry for her father, who had single-handedly planned their four-night vacation, bought five plane tickets, and paid for the resort. She wondered how he had afforded it on his salary. Professors at Cedarhurst, a small private school, weren't exactly raking in a fortune. And now, in addition to helping with some of her medical school expenses, her parents were paying for Sydney to attend a special school for kids with learning disabilities. The tuition alone cost more than her mother's net salary as a social worker.

Brooke's legs twitched with pent-up energy. She'd been sitting still for too many hours, first on the plane, and now the car ride, attempting to ward off claustrophobia. She needed to go for a run.

After forty-five minutes of hoping the resort would be around the next corner, a large and colorful sign announced *Casa de Royale.* At the end of a long driveway lined with tropical flowers and swaying palm trees, a group of young men carrying colorful drinks sauntered by. The Waltons parked in the circular entry and a uniformed man approached. "Welcome Señor, and your beautiful family." He opened the passenger side door with a grand sweeping gesture. "If you will open your trunk, Ramon will unload your luggage."

"I'll get my own bag." Brooke leaped out and hurried to the back of the car. "I'll meet all of you up at the room. I'm going to take a quick look around. Check out the gym."

"Okay." Her mother glanced at the deepening shadows on the horizon. "Just be careful."

"Always."

"Welcome to our room," Sydney shouted when Brooke knocked on the door. "We're already unpacked."

Brooke glanced around. Clothes littered the floor, phone chargers trailed to wall outlets, and small piles of sand surrounded discarded shoes. All five of them together in one room. She dropped her bag next to a cot. "I need to go for a run."

"It's dark." Mrs. Walton zipped up her empty suitcase and turned to her husband. "Ian, do you think it's a good idea?"

Mr. Walton scratched his chin and peered out the window at the moon. "Just don't go far."

"I'm not being unreasonable." Mrs. Walton angled sideways so Sydney could pass by her. "People go missing. No one ever expects things like that to happen, but they do."

"I'll stay on the beach, near the resorts."

Mrs. Walton crossed the room to face her daughter. "How about this—just give me a few minutes and then we can all go for a walk together."

"Mom, I really need to run. I'll meet up with you later. I promise." She hurried into the bathroom and closed the door, ending the conversation. After changing into workout clothes, Brooke examined her reflection in the mirror. Gorgeous and perfectly approachable, if someone had enough confidence. She hoped no one would. She wanted to be alone. She left the bathroom attaching her running belt and slipping her phone into the pouch.

"Okay, I'm going." Brooke ignored her mother's frown. Halfway out the door, she turned and dipped her head back inside. "Oh, Dad. I need the car key. I left my cap in the car."

Mr. Walton tossed the car key. It was the old-fashioned kind, not a fob, but a long piece of etched metal attached to the rental company's tag. Brooke caught it with one hand and stuck it inside her pouch.

Sparkles of light in the flower beds illuminated the path down to the beach. She sprinted toward the breaking waves once her feet hit the sugary sand. Dance music, conversations, and laughter spilled onto the shoreline. She passed a man and woman with their arms wrapped around each other, and another couple holding hands and walking unsteadily. The lights from *Casa de Royale* petered out after a short distance, but another resort picked up where its neighbor left off, casting a glow over the beach.

Brooke ran faster, adrenaline fueling her body and focusing her mind, alert and invincible, like nothing and no one could stop her.

Eventually, she'd run beyond the long string of resorts to an unlit area. Small homes nestled beyond the dunes at the end of meandering walkways. Her phone alarm rang. Forty minutes had passed. Time to turn around. Not exactly the quick run she'd promised her father, but it was necessary. She stopped to stretch, mesmerized by the endless expanse of ocean hiding so much below the surface. She'd always loved the night. She closed her eyes and let her senses succumb to the salty breeze and the rhythmic roar of the ocean.

She opened her eyes when she heard voices. Loud voices. Obnoxious laughter shattered the tranquility as two young men approached.

"Ha, come on, man. No way!"

"I'm not making it up. She was amazing."

"Pff! Right! That's bull and you know it."

Americans. Two of them. Both looking fit and attractive, like they spent a lot of time working out.

Brooke moved farther away from the water, towards a walkway railing and the tall, thick plants covering the dunes. She would wait for whoever they were to move along. They almost walked past, until they spotted her.

"Wait, what's that?" The question came from a young man, early twenties maybe, in a hooded sweatshirt and rolled-up jeans. He stopped walking and craned his neck toward Brooke. "Is she real?"

"Yeah, she's real." His friend snorted with laughter. "What the hell do you think she is? A ghost?"

The guy in the sweatshirt expressed his approval with a long, low whistle. He gaped for a few more seconds before moving toward her. His friend stayed back, the waves lapping around his ankles.

"Hi there. I'm John." He turned his head toward his friend. "And that's Rico." Facing Brooke, he shoved his hand into his front pockets. "What are you doing all alone out here?"

He was more muscular than he appeared at a distance. And cute with his short and spikey blonde hair. "I *was* enjoying the peace and quiet."

"We're headed to a party. Wanna come?"

"No, thanks. But have a good time."

"We'll have a better time if you come with us."

Brooke met his gaze and said nothing.

"I'm worried 'bout you being out here alone." John tilted his head toward the hotels down the beach. "Come on. We'll walk you back to . . . where did you come from? Staying in one of the resorts?"

"Just go on to your party, please."

"Are you sure? We have lots of friends there and plenty of beer." He moved a few feet closer, smiling. The scent of his expensive cologne mixed with the faint smell of beer on his breath. He extended his arm.

"Don't touch me." Brooke stepped backward, the edge of the wooden railing dug into her back.

John's white teeth glowed in the moonlight. "Rico, get over here. We need to convince this pretty little lady she's lucky we found her."

Brooke glanced up and down the deserted beach. She could outrun them, couldn't she? If she got around them. Her muscles tensed, and her heart beat steady yet fast, as if she was already sprinting. Both men had stepped uncomfortably close, inside her personal space. Without warning, John's arm shot out and grabbed hers.

Brooke's eyes grew wide. She struggled to pull her arm out of his grip.

Rico glanced over his shoulder before grabbing her other arm.

"It's all good baby. Just relax. Damn, you're smokin' hot. You really are."

They grinned like crazed clowns. Their large and muscular hands tightened around her upper arms, digging into her biceps when she tried to shake loose.

"This way. Hurry." John pulled Brooke forward.

Brooke dug her feet into the sand and they half-dragged her down the path between the dunes. Her eyes darted around. Still no one in sight. An unfamiliar helpless feeling swarmed through her body, threatening to spiral out of control. Never had she been anyone's victim. Never. The situation seemed surreal. It couldn't be happening. Not to her. More adrenaline flooded her system, swirling up a frenzy of instinct and panic.

No one else on the beach.

No one to hear a scream.

No one to witness what might happen.

Lips pressed tightly together, the corners of her mouth edged up into a slight grin.

Meaty fingers dug deeper into her upper arms, cutting off her circulation. She could barely move her hands, just enough to reach her running pouch. Silently, she slid the zipper open, moved the car key into her palm, and squeezed her fingers shut around it.

The jet-black outline of a cottage loomed closer.

Blood pounded through her temples.

"In here!" They pulled Brooke toward an outdoor shower room, opened the wide creaky wooden door, and shoved her inside. She stumbled forward through sticky strands of a giant spider web and fell against the tall wood-planks in the corner. There was no one staying at the house. No one to see or hear or stop an inevitable crime.

Rico let go of her arm and positioned himself inside the doorway, spreading his legs and blocking the exit. "Why isn't she yelling for help? It's messed up. Don't you think it's messed up?"

"She's into it. Right, baby?" John took rapid, shallow breaths, leering like a predator about to pounce. Brooke recognized the steely determination in his eyes. She could feel his frenzied longing and the surge of power coursing through his muscles and veins. Seeing all of it for the first time in someone else sent chills down her spine like an electric current.

"It might be fun." She lowered her eyes with a sly smile.

"Close the door!" John told Rico.

Anticipation swirled into the heady rush of her already heightened senses as Rico latched the wooden door shut.

Brooke burst forward. She gouged the jagged metal key into his eye, turned it like a corkscrew, and yanked it back out. With a shriek, he collapsed to the ground, gasping, blood streaming down one side of his face. A low guttural moan escaped his lips.

"What the hell?" Rico stared at his friend's grotesque injury and then the chunk of eyeball Brooke flicked off the key. He lurched forward and gagged.

Brooke lunged at Rico. She zigzagged the key, tearing through delicate eye tissue, plunging it into his cheek, and ripping it out through his mouth. His hands flew to his face and he staggered backward into the corner before falling to his knees. "Oh, my God! You demented bitch!" He gurgled through a gush of blood.

"Shut up," she hissed.

One hand pressed over his gaping wound, Rico pulled out his phone. "I'm calling—"

"No, you're not." Brooke bared teeth with her smile. She kicked his phone out of his hand, slamming the heel of her shoe into the raw flesh of his torn cheek. He screamed in agony and turned around to shield his face, rocking forward on his knees.

John stared up at her from the ground, his lips trembling. He lifted a hand into the air as if to say he surrendered. "Get the hell away from me." His voice was shrill and hard to hear over Rico's uncontrollable whimpering.

"I don't think so." She laughed. "We're just getting started."

Quivering with a euphoric high, she glimpsed the ripped suspensory ligaments dangling from John's eye socket. She yearned to touch the bloody, fibrous elements glistening in the moonlight, but not yet . . .

John reached into his back pocket, his hand violently shaking, and pulled out a knife. In a heartbeat, Brooke pounced, tossing the key, and snatching the knife away. A crooked, unnerving smile appeared below her gleaming eyes as the blade sprung open. The pocket knife was nothing compared to the efficient tools she'd left at home, her favorite toys: a scalpel, a razor, and a bone saw, but it would get the job done.

"You're insane, lady! Just leave!"

She shook with laughter at the absurd thought of stopping now. She couldn't if she tried. There wasn't enough willpower in the world. Her heart pounded with excitement.

"Just go! We're not going to hurt you."

Her smile spread. "Oh, I guarantee you aren't. But you wanted to." She gazed at the moonlit glint of the blade. Long enough to reach through the thin bones behind their eyes and into their skulls. Long enough to lacerate their brains.

A lightning-fast stab, in and downward, destroyed John's ability to breathe. Rico met the same fate when Brooke leaped on him from behind as he struggled to leave. In utter fascination, she watched the men choke and gasp for snatches of oxygen, twisting and flailing on the ground until their remaining eyes shone up unseeing at the dark sky. She licked her lips, dragged their bodies together and lined them up side by side. They were big, but lean. Just perfect. Without the layers of fat that so often made dismembering a challenging task.

After removing her clothes, shoes, and running belt, she set them in a neat pile outside the shower. She turned on her phone's flashlight and propped it up against the shower wall, enhancing the moonlight, and then went to work, savoring the feel of the knife cutting across John's skull. Unable to stop smiling, she peeled his skin down over his face to reveal the well-developed muscles in his neck.

In room 212 at the Casa de Royale, Mr. Walton's phone pinged with a text. His wife glanced at the screen. "Ian, it's a message from Brooke."

"What does she say?"

"She said—I met up with some people my age. I'm having fun. Be back soon. Please don't worry about me." Mrs. Walton set down the phone and turned on her side. "Well, what do you think about that?"

"It's fine." Mr. Walton slid the phone back off the nightstand, typing. *Okay. Be careful. Don't trust a stranger. Don't go to anyone's hotel room. Text us in half an hour.* He hit send.

"I wish she hadn't gone." Mrs. Walton placed her hand on her husband's arm.

"She'll text us." Mr. Walton opened his novel. "She'll be careful. She's a smart girl."

"I know. You're right."

"Bottom line, she needs to get out more, not less. She starts that internship as soon as she gets back. Let her have some fun."

Chapter Two

Brooke dropped a messy armful of John and Rico onto the sand. She scooped up a forearm and hurled it into the ocean, watching it disappear under the churning black water. She chose a foot next, throwing each part as far as she could until the pile disappeared. Behind her, noisy and massive gulls dove into the outdoor shower for a fresh feast, squawking and fighting over choice morsels.

Getting rid of John and Rico would take a few more trips back and forth between the shower and the ocean. Each trip presented a risk. How would she ever explain carrying a bloody mess of body parts? How could anyone? And she'd already been gone much longer than she had planned. Her parents would be waiting up for her, worried. The seagulls and crabs could take care of whatever the sharks didn't. Most likely, the scavengers had already flown away carrying sections of the men's peeled-off faces.

She put her clothes back on, placed her phone behind a large piece of driftwood, and dug a deep hole to bury their wallets. With handfuls of wet sand, she began scrubbing her clothes, her skin, her shoes, and John's pocket knife. She wasn't taking any chances. Fully clothed, she walked into the ocean, through the crashing waves, until the warm water slapped at her chest. She lowered herself so she was fully immersed below the surface. The waves knocked against her, tugging and swirling at her clothes like a giant washing machine. When she could no longer hold her breath, she burst out of the water, closed John's knife, and threw it as far toward the horizon as she could.

Carrying her sopping shoes, she ran back to the resort wearing a grin of satisfaction. No need to worry. There was nothing to connect her to the mess she'd left behind. Those men deserved what happened. They wanted to rape her. She shuddered. Maybe they would have assaulted someone else tomorrow, and someone else the night after. Maybe they had already harmed others. Once a person acquired a taste for *certain things*, and the euphoric surge of energy that accompanied carrying out *those things* there was no stopping them. She, of all people, understood.

I didn't go looking for trouble. I didn't intend to kill them. It wasn't my fault. They all but begged for it.

Others might experience guilt. Like a wave deep in the ocean, it would start to build, surging forward, gaining strength, eventually washing over them, sucking them under. Her body wasn't wired for remorse like a normal person, and she was grateful for that immunity. Who needed it?

When she opened the hotel room door, every member of her pajama-clad family was still awake. Sydney was lying under the covers, iPad in her hands. Amanda was lying on her stomach with her phone. Her father had a book in his lap and her mother had a Kindle.

Amanda rolled over and sat up. "You were gone like practically forever."

Mr. Walton jammed his book mark between the pages and snapped his book shut. "What happened to texting in half an hour?"

"Sorry. My phone battery died."

"You went out like...*that*?" Mrs. Walton frowned, eyeing her daughter's wet hair and clothes.

"Yeah. We were swimming."

"Even your shoes are wet." Amanda pointed to a strand of seaweed stuck to Brooke's shoes.

Brooke grinned sheepishly. "What can I say? It was unexpected fun."

Mrs. Walton sighed. "I know you're an adult and I know you can be out whenever you want when you're at school, but when you're with us, we worry. We can't help it."

Mr. Walton nudged his wife's arm and they exchanged a look.

"Well, you can stop worrying now. I'm back." She grabbed a soft dry T-shirt out of her bag.

"We're glad you had fun." Mr. Walton got up from the bed. "Just put the car key on the dresser. Somehow, we forgot the bag with the sunscreen. I'm going to drive to a store early tomorrow and buy some." He opened his book, grumbling. "Costs a fortune at a resort. We could have bought three at Walmart for the price of one."

"Okay." Brooke unzipped her pouch. She swept her fingers from left to right.

Nothing.

She turned the pouch inside out.

Empty.

"Oh, no. Oh, no."

"What happened?" Mrs. Walton set her Kindle down.

"I can't find the key."

"You lost it?" Sydney's jaw dropped.

"Yes." Brooke gazed up toward the ceiling. A sick feeling spread from her stomach to her throat.

Mr. Walton stepped over the clothes and shoes strewn across the floor. "Maybe you left it in the car door."

"No. I didn't." Brooke sat down on the cot and dropped her head into her hands.

Amanda raised her eyes from her phone. "If you don't know where you lost it, then how can you know it's not in the car door?"

"It's not in the car door!" Brooke gritted her teeth to keep her body from trembling.

"Calm down. No need to get worked up. It's okay, we'll find it—ow!" Mr. Walton lifted his foot off Amanda's curling iron and kicked it out of the way. "Don't let losing the key ruin the vacation. It's not the end of the world. I'm sure the rental agency has an extra one. They can bring it before we leave. And I can suck it up and pay extra for the sunscreen." He laughed.

"I'll try to look for it tomorrow." Brooke crossed her arms, clutching and kneading her muscles.

"Relax." Mr. Walton put his hand on his daughter's shoulder. "There's nothing we can do about it now. This stuff happens. It's not like someone died."

"Yeah." Amanda's shoulders slouched as she returned her attention to her phone.

"I hope they don't charge a bunch to replace it." Sydney stretched forward, past her toes.

"I'm sure someone will find it." Mrs. Walton got out of the bed and headed toward the bathroom. "It has numbers on it, it's coded. So, when they do, it will be easy to call the rental agency and trace it back to us."

Brooke's heart was heavy. Worry and fear pulsed in waves through her body, leaving her nerves sharp and raw, and an empty vulnerable feeling in her stomach.

Chapter Three

Five Days Later

Brooke leaned against the wall of her new living room and slid downward until she sat on the floor. The student apartments were walking distance to the medical school buildings and all the other graduate and undergraduate buildings for those students who didn't mind a fifteen or twenty-minute walk and had sensible shoes for when the snow arrived. If she and her boyfriend, Xander, weren't splitting the rent, she would have stayed in the dorm.

Beads of sweat glistened on her forehead and trailed down between her breasts and shoulder blades. She hadn't had much to move: clothes, bedding, towels—lots of towels, hand weights, a couple of yoga mats, a broken toaster oven, and boxes of textbooks, although the books had weighed a ton. But then there was Xander's stuff. And he hadn't been around to help because he'd had to leave for Chicago right after his last final exam.

"Just like old times, being across the hall from you again." Jeff handed her a cold bottle of water. Since he was staying in East Dalton doing medical research for the summer, he was an easy mark for helping move heavy boxes. He cracked the plastic top on his own water bottle and raised it. "Cheers to us for surviving our first year of medical school. One down, three more to go."

"Some of us did much better than just survive." Brooke held the cold bottle against her forehead and closed her eyes. "I think I set the curves."

"That's right. Miss number one in the whole damned class. And you don't ever forget it." He glanced around at the studio apartment, empty aside from the cardboard boxes, suitcases, and bags. "Hmm. I just love what you've done with the place."

"Hey! Don't knock my apartment." She opened her bottle and guzzled half the water. "I like it. An empty room equals a yoga and Pilates studio. Plus, I happen to like being unencumbered. I could throw everything in the back of my car and go."

"Like if you had a car?" He laughed and scanned the space again. He glanced at a large cardboard box behind him, hitched up his pants and lowered his bottom a few inches toward it.

"Don't sit there!"

Jeff jumped up.

"That's not books. It's glassware. Belongs to Xander."

"Sorry, your highness. Glassware? You almost gave me a heart attack."

"Better a heart attack than spending the night picking glass out of your rear. Here." She patted the floor. "Grab a seat on the linoleum. It's safe."

"I'll just stand. Anyway, your place just leaves much to be desired."

"You're in the same exact space across the hall." She took another long chug on the water bottle, almost emptying it.

"My apartment doesn't look anything like yours, thanks to a concept most people employ, perhaps you've heard of it. It's called furniture." Jeff chuckled. "God, what a—"

Brooke's empty water bottle bounced off his chest.

"Ooof." He bent over as if he'd been injured. "Before you hit me, I was about to offer my help. Let's go get you some stuff to decorate with."

"I need a bed and a chair. That's all. And there's a Goodwill store a few miles from here."

"Ha!" His brows shot up. "Oh my God. You're not kidding." His mouth hung open. "I get that you can't afford real furniture, but have you ever heard of Target? Ikea?"

"Still too expensive. I'm going to Goodwill. You wouldn't believe the stuff people get rid of. I'll find something."

Jeff bit down on his lip but let out a spurt of laughter anyway. "Okay. Whatever you say." He threw his hands up. "This is going to be an experience. Let's go."

"I absolutely dread shopping, you know. I hate it."

"If you only shop at Goodwill, I can see why."

Brooke grabbed her bag and they walked outside to Jeff's SUV in the parking lot. He clicked his key fob to unlock the doors. "Does Xander know he'll be living in an empty apartment with some Goodwill specials?"

"He served in Afghanistan. I would hope he can handle it. Besides, we have three months to make improvements."

"We, as in me?"

Brooke opened the door and sat down. "Crank up the AC."

"How is Xander anyway?" Jeff started the car and leaned over to get the AC going.

"He's fine. He already started his PTSD internship in Chicago."

"Do you miss him?"

"Yes." *I guess you could call it that.* She worried Xander might still make a connection between her and Rachael Kline's disappearance. Fortunately, her classmate's disappearance six months ago was no longer huge news. The whole investigation had apparently lost steam, down to its last few puffs. Soon, she hoped, it would go down in history as one of those mysterious unsolved disappearances and she could forget about it entirely.

She smiled at Jeff. "He feels bad he couldn't help. My parents wanted to help too, but my sister had a recital today."

"Eh. We got it done. So, you start working on Monday?"

"Yep." The job offered unlimited learning opportunities—fresh cadavers coming in every day—and an amazing stipend.

"You're really lucky you got that position. Everyone wanted it."

"My interview was strange though. The Chief Medical Examiner hired me, but I got the feeling he resented me."

"Obviously not, or why would he pick you?" Jeff peered sideways at her. "You know, a few months ago, you said the Medical Examiner's Office would be the ideal place to work—"

"It is."

"But, you said you had to find a paid summer job."

"I did. I have a ton of loans already."

"Then suddenly, sort of last minute, the Medical Examiner's Office has a huge chunk of cash to offer a student from Rothaker? Strange coincidence, don't you think?"

Brooke shrugged. "Not really."

The closest Goodwill was about twenty minutes away. When they arrived, Brooke marched toward the back of the store, where the furniture resided.

Jeff followed, his nose in the air. "Good god. It's a yard sale with cash registers."

Brooke opened her arms wide with a flourish, as if she was a game show host presenting the prizes. "See, I told you, there's some good stuff here."

"Hmmpf. Just make sure you disinfect everything." Jeff pointed to a leather armchair. "Once upon a time, this was a decent leather chair. It's a little worn, and could possibly be infested with who knows what, but otherwise it could work."

"No, it's too big. Here's a perfectly good lawn chair."

"You're not going to get a plastic lawn chair for your room."

"Why not?"

"Because, adults just don't do that. Whoa!" Jeff lowered his voice to just above a whisper. "Check that out." A man wearing jeans and a T-shirt had emerged from the back of the store carrying a small upholstered armchair. He was over six feet tall with a chiseled jaw, muscular tattooed arms, and stylish short hair.

Jeff whistled. "Do you think he got all those muscles on a no-carb diet working out in prison? What do you think? Looks like it." His eyes followed the man across the store. "I'm all for giving criminals a second chance, but did he get arrested for being too hot? He's like a sexy movie star. In a not quite civilized way."

"He looks civilized to me."

"Shh. Don't ruin it."

"Never mind the prison fantasy. Check out the chair he's carrying. There's our compromise." Brooke hurried over to get a better look at the chair he set down. "Looks clean. But I can't find the price."

"Oh, uh, the price?" The muscular guy laughed. "I don't know."

"Can you find out?" She tried to mask her annoyance. She couldn't stand people who didn't do their jobs well.

"Uh, Sure." He laughed again. "I'll go ask someone. I'll be right back." He turned and left through the doorway in the back of the store.

"You're right, Jeff. This one is perfect."

Jeff rolled his eyes. "What am I going to do with you? Are you still going to buy used crap at Goodwill when you're a renowned surgeon?"

"Maybe. Who knows? I could be paying you to shop for me some day. If you don't pass Microbiology."

"Ow. That hurts. I got that grade up to a solid C."

The man returned with a sticker on his thumb. He eyed the chair for a moment, before attaching the sticker to the top. "It's going to cost fifteen dollars."

"Hmm. More than I wanted to spend." Brooke placed her hands on her hips, only partly joking. She turned to Jeff. "So, in your expert opinion, you think this one is good enough for the Spring Creek apartments?"

"It will do for yours."

"Consider it sold."

"Let me help you carry it." The man with the tattoos stepped forward.

"No. I've got it. But thanks." Brooke turned her back on him, hoisted the chair, and walked toward the register. "My workouts come in handy occasionally. It's all been so I could go shopping and carry my own chair out."

Jeff lagged, looking over his shoulder. "That guy was so handsome. Sort of reminds me of Xander."

The man's gaze traveled past Jeff and followed Brooke to the checkout counter. He hovered around a shelf of outdated appliances, watching her until the front doors closed behind her. Less than a minute later, he left the store through the back, thanked the employee who was collecting donations, and drove away in his truck.

Chapter Four

Two months ago, Brooke had seen the massive Medical Examiner's Building for the first time. Resembling an old museum, with an unusual blue roof, it must have once been impressive and stately. Now, it was a challenge to overlook the cracked concrete, the crumbling edges, and the dirt and mildew coating the surfaces. But she imagined the building was full of dead bodies waiting to be eviscerated and examined. In other words—it was heaven.

A glance at her phone confirmed she was early, as always, for her interview. Early and well prepared. She smoothed her hair, adjusted the collar of her blouse, and took a deep inhale to fortify her confidence, although that was hardly necessary.

Inside, there was little natural light. The water-stained entryway desperately needed fresh paint. She had expected more of a sleek, modern building like the ones in the movies. This was not it.

There was no one around to greet her, so she moved further into the interior on her own. She spotted a closed door with a tarnished plaque announcing Human Resources. She tried the handle. Locked. Under a flickering fluorescent light, she crossed the giant hall and saw a hand-written sign. *Rothaker Summer Applicants* was scrawled in half-print, half-cursive and barely legible. An arrow under the lettering pointed through a maze of hallways. She followed the arrow, passing room after room, each with closed doors. The building was eerily silent, aside from the occasional creak of pipes hidden behind the dingy walls. The click-clack of her heels echoed in the corridor. A faint but familiar smell—disinfectant mingled with the sharp stench of internal organs—permeated the air and grew stronger as she headed deeper inside the building.

Halfway down the hall, a metal folding chair sat outside yet another closed door. The plaque screwed into the wood bore the name of her interviewer, *Dr. Gold, MD., Chief Medical Examiner.* Light spilled out from under his office door, unlike the other rooms she'd passed. Muted voices indicated the room was occupied, so she sat down. She practiced for the interview as she waited, crossing and uncrossing her legs at the ankles. It was difficult to relax knowing someone might be in Dr. Gold's office interviewing for the position she so desperately wanted.

When the Chief Examiner's office door opened, out stepped one of Brooke's medical school classmates, Connor, a bodybuilder with considerable size and strength.

He broke into his typical good-natured smile and winked. "Hey, Brooke."

"Hey." Brooke did her best to smile around her clenched jaw, resisting the urge to slap his amiable grin.

"Brooke Walton?" a graying old man wearing a white lab jacket called from behind a large desk without standing up.

"Good luck." Connor probably meant it because he was *that* kind of person. Nice through and through with no ulterior motives and a desire to enjoy each day. He was her competition at school, and now for the internship, even if he didn't view himself that way.

Brooke stepped past Connor and into the office, closing the door behind her.

"Have a seat. I'm Dr. Gold." His face was deeply wrinkled, his eyes weary under thick eyebrows. His voice matched his appearance, crackly and dry.

Brooke sat. Her interviewer placed gnarled hands on his desk. *Rheumatoid arthritis.* His fingernails were groomed, ugly but clean stubs with smooth, intact cuticles, unlike her own. A cane leaned against the wall behind him, within reach. His frailty offered an explanation as to why he might want an intern. And that meant Connor might have an advantage.

"So, you're *the* Brooke Walton." Dr. Gold's face held no trace of a smile.

"Uhm, yes." *Huh? What does that comment imply?*

"I've read your school transcripts and resume. I'll admit, I am impressed. You come highly recommended." His words didn't match the tone of his voice. He spoke with a hint of disdain.

"I do?" She tilted her head. "Who recommended me?"

"I can't remember. One of your professors."

Brooke suppressed a smile and sat up even taller.

Dr. Gold put on his reading glasses, adjusting them on his nose a few times before lifting her resume from his desk and holding it inches away from his nose. The paper trembled slightly in his hands. Brooke averted her gaze and scanned the room. The empty, peeling walls were covered with newspaper articles, some so faded and yellow they were impossible to read.

"So, what should I ask her?" he muttered to himself. "Tell me, Ms. Walton, what do you think we're looking for in an intern?"

Brooke edged forward in her seat. "You're looking for someone craving experience and willing to work at a relentless pace to thoroughly examine each cadaver without missing a single thing. Someone who wants the truth, who wants to find out what each body has to tell us. Someone like me."

Dr. Gold folded his arms across his chest and stared, his face unreadable. No smile. No frown. Nothing.

Brooke intertwined her fingers in her lap. "You also need someone strong enough to help you lift and turn bodies. I'm much stronger than I look."

She rose from her chair and removed her suit jacket. In one graceful movement, she dropped into a plank position at the side of his desk and did five one-arm push-ups. *Take that, Connor.* She returned to her seat, her porcelain skin flushed pink.

Dr. Gold leaned back in his chair and pulled on the corner of his bowtie. "I wasn't expecting a side-show performance. We already have strong assistants." His eyes moved to a brown stain on the wall near the ceiling. "What we do here, handling unattended deaths and determining cause of death, is incredibly important. If we aren't thorough, families can be denied life insurance and killers can get away with murder." He placed her resume down and leaned forward, glaring. "Some people are hiding secrets in death. It's our job to uncover them."

Hairs stood up on the back of Brooke's neck. The interview's direction was hitting a little too close to home. She swallowed. *Don't be paranoid.*

"This is a high crime area, as I'm sure you know. We're always busy. And quite honestly, we're grossly underfunded. Although," he coughed, "you wouldn't know that from the stipend we're suddenly able to offer." He cleared his throat with a raspy grating sound. "We have more bodies than time to examine them. It's that simple. And that's where you come in."

Brooke pressed her hands against her legs, forcing her body to stay still. *The possibilities! I must have this job. It won't even seem like work. It's going to be amazing. So amazing.*

"If we have you, or someone like you, handling our paperwork and reports, entering all of it into computers, the other medical examiners and myself will have more time to conduct examinations and autopsies."

An unlimited number of fresh cadavers arriving every day full of diseased organs. Wait? What? What did he just say? Data entry?

"Is something wrong, Ms. Walton?"

"Ahh, no, it's just . . . well, I thought I would be helping with the autopsies, you know, since I'm a medical student."

"Oh, I see. Well, I'm sure some of that can be arranged if you can keep up with the reporting. The amount of paperwork we're required to complete is staggering. It gets worse every year. And all of it needs to be entered into the computer system. It's called IP Data App, no . . . IP Med Data. Something like that." Dr. Gold scowled.

"Okay. I'm sure I can figure it out." *He just hammered my excitement down a few notches.*

Dr. Gold blathered on about the reports in need of filing and the data in need of entering. He stumbled awkwardly through vague explanations of the computer system, leading Brooke to conclude he hadn't kept up with technological trends over the years and was now intimidated by the systems created to facilitate his work.

Now it makes sense why he needs someone. A wave of disappointment swept through her.

"You can start full-time as soon as your school year ends."

Brooke raised her eyebrows, but Dr. Gold's gaze had settled on a paper on his desk and he didn't notice. She glanced over her shoulder toward the door. "But, don't you still have other candidates to interview?"

"Bodies don't stop coming and, as you so eloquently stated, I need to find out what they have to say. I've only so many hours in each day. Stop into our payroll department later this week—it's in the building across the street now. There's one woman, part-time, she'll get you set up. As I'm sure you're aware, the amount you'll be receiving is exceedingly generous." He lowered his voice. "Possibly absurd."

Huh? "Okay. Thank you so much. I look forward to working with you." *Yes, nailed it!* She rose and offered her hand, but Dr. Gold's hand was occupied pushing himself up from his chair. When he stood, the curve of his stooped back was evident under his lab coat.

"Oh, I almost forgot." She clasped her hands. "I have a family commitment the last week of May, right after my final exams, but it's only for four days."

"Fine. Start whenever you get back. We'll certainly be expecting a lot from you."

"Of course, I understand."

Brooke practically skipped down the hallway, the rattling pipes sending her off with a chorus of creaks and moans. The interview was strange for many reasons. Nothing was as she expected. Dr. Gold was surprisingly old and unfriendly. The building was deteriorating almost as fast as he was. Yet she stepped outside grinning. Regardless of her official responsibilities, she planned to take full advantage of the opportunities there.

Those two months had passed quickly—studying, finals, the family vacation, the move to her new apartment. Only one day remained. Any nagging worries about the lost rental car key had been pushed aside and forgotten. She couldn't wait to start her internship.

Chapter Five

igh from two white lines and his first string of wins in a long time, he strutted out of the dim, hazy basement room where a select group of "invited" guests, none as pleased as him, were leaving. He did a mini-fist pump down by his hip, out of sight.

My luck returned! Didn't I know it would come back if I was patient?

With a stack of money stuffed into the inner pocket of his sport coat, a proper celebration was in order. Once he was inside his car, the tinted windows and locked doors allowed for a wide, private grin. He tapped his phone, searching his recent calls for the number of the blonde who'd had sex with him on their first date. After a few rings the call went to voicemail.

Sherry. Might want to update the contact with her name.

Undaunted, he scrolled through his phone until he found another prospect. Dianne was, if memory served, on the high end of the attractive scale.

After two rings, the phone picked up. "Hello?"

Her voice was low and wispy. Obviously asleep.

As if he cared. "Hey, baby."

"Huh? What the—" The phone relayed some shuffling and bumping. "It's three in the morning!"

"And I just hit it big. Want to help me celebrate?"

"I want to sleep, asshole. Did you forget you hit on my friend after we went out? Do me a favor. You won some money tonight? Good. Pay me back what you borrowed, then lose my number."

He decided not to call anyone else. It was too late at night, or early in the morning, for people stuck in boring day to day routines, afraid to take risks.

But he hated being alone, always had. And after such a great night, he craved company. Well, there was always the "escort" option. For a few thousand dollars a gorgeous girl would arrive at his house and behave however he wanted her to behave. But he'd be out at least five grand by the morning. Unfortunately, he needed most of his win to pay back creditors. He wasn't going to blow it all on a gorgeous girl. Not this time. Although, thinking of blowing things reminded him he'd better track down Fabulous Jack and get some more cocaine while he had the cash. He'd need a steady source of uppers if he planned to stay awake night and day.

He started his Mercedes and pulled away from the shadowed lot, still unsure of his destination. He didn't want to go home. Not when he was feeling so damn good, so damn invincible, so on top of the whole world!

He pounded the wheel, bobbing up and down on the seat. "Yeah, yeah, yeah, yeah, yeah! I'm back! The king is back!"

Believing he was smart for fearing the possibility of getting pulled over, he cruised down side roads that traveled past the train station on the outskirts of the city. Thinking about how great everything would soon be, now that he was on a roll, he drove slowly, or at least he thought he was until he noticed the speedometer. No matter, he thought, not letting up on the gas. If he got stopped by the cops, he could always say he had been rushing to a crime scene.

Not far from the train station, under the cascading light of a street lamp, two women in stiletto heels smoked cigarettes as they leaned against a building. The too-short skirts and extra low cut, tight tops did more advertising than any billboard ever could. For rent. By the hour.

One waved. "Hey sugar. Wanna party?"

He ignored them, not wanting to give them the satisfaction. Street walkers weren't his style. Especially not these. One was way overdone. Big hair, short skirt, too much make up. The other...

The other caught his eye.

Young. Petite. Long, straight dark hair, not teased or fluffed or whatever women did to poof their hair up. His preferred look. Even dressed like a slut on a street corner, there was something about her. She had potential. Wipe off her make-up, change her clothes, and she would look a lot like one of his former college girlfriends.

He stopped his car against the curb and lowered his window halfway. The overdone woman sauntered over.

"No." He pointed to the petite brunette. "I want her."

The brunette strode to the passenger side and leaned forward through the open window. A tattooed butterfly graced her front shoulder. She was in her early twenties, maybe younger, it was hard for him to tell. With big brown glassy eyes, she looked as high as he felt. She ran her tongue slowly over her red wine-colored lips. "Good evening. I'm Alyssa."

Chapter Six

Wearing a scoop neck T-shirt under a lightweight jacket and a silver cross around her neck, private investigator Jean Thompson picked at a hangnail while the middle-aged woman seated across from her desk dabbed her eyes with a tissue.

"I'm sorry. Just give me a second." The woman pressed her fingers against her lips. Her husband reached over and put his hand on her shoulder. Tears welled in his eyes, threatening to slide down his cheeks, but he bit down on his lip and they stayed put.

Jean glanced away out of courtesy and noticed the long thread trailing from the cuff of her jacket sleeve. She pulled her arm out of sight. "It's okay. Take all the time you need. I'm in no rush." She had another hour before she had to pick up Millie from the after-school program. She tried to imagine Millie twelve years from now, at aged twenty-two. What if she was an energetic and accomplished medical student? Someone, who, by all accounts was responsible, liked, and admired. How would she feel if her daughter vanished from her dorm without a trace? And, if after six months, there was still no evidence of what happened to her. No traces of her body. Jean shuddered. She would lose her mind. Go completely off the grid with despair. She almost lost it when Millie was five and had played hide and seek at Target without telling her. Five minutes of frantic searching seemed like an hour. They were seconds from a Code

Adam when Millie popped out of a rack of dresses. She couldn't imagine functioning for the rest of her life, never mind the first year, if she had experienced the same tragedy as the couple seated on the other side of her desk. Her heart ached for the Klines.

"It's been a challenge to cope since Rachael went missing." Mrs. Kline pressed her lips together. "If she's not out there, I mean, if we can't find her . . . we really could use some closure."

"I understand completely. What you're going through, it's a parent's worst nightmare, and I will do all I can to help make it stop. When I was with the NYPD, I was the lead detective on five different disappearances. My team found two missing teens, one of them after two years.

"Two out of five?" Mr. Kline slumped backward in his chair.

"And we found the perpetrators responsible for two of the others."

"And the fifth? The fifth remains unsolved?" His grim expression reminded Jean of someone who had already prepared for the worst.

Jean leaned forward. "I will do everything in my power to find out what happened to your daughter. I've read over police files and all the interviews. I can get started working for you as soon as you're ready to hire me."

The Klines exchanged glances. Mr. Kline reached into his pocket and removed his check book.

After she escorted the Klines from her office, Jean sank into her chair and let her head drop back. The meeting had left her emotionally drained. Part of that was the reality of the situation.

I don't expect to find Rachael Kline alive.

Too many months had passed. But she hoped to uncover the truth behind the young woman's disappearance. It was like another high-profile unsolved mystery. Two years ago. Everett College. Jessica Carroll. Another promising young woman. No concrete explanations for her mysterious disappearance. Her body had been found the following spring, once the New Hampshire snow melted, but no one knew how she wound up so far from the campus, or why. Carroll's family had given all the information obtained from their private investigator to the Klines, and the Klines had given it to Jean. Tomorrow, she would ask the New Hampshire State police for the files from the Everett case.

There were possible explanations for Rachael's disappearance, some accepted scenarios, but no proof. And heartbroken parents needed concrete evidence, not just plausible speculation. Exploring the similarities between the two disappearances was a good strategy.

She had already thought a great deal about the Kline case. Thank goodness they hired her. Her daughter's medications weren't cheap, and neither was their rent, and now she'd gone and told her daughter she could start the horseback riding lessons she'd been begging for. Hoping her ex would finally send the child support payments he owed was a waste of her time and energy.

It wouldn't be easy, or the Klines would already have answers, but Jean aimed to please. Nothing would be more professionally satisfying than to find Rachael Kline. But, if that wasn't possible, the next best thing would be bringing whoever had harmed her to justice.

Needing a mental break, she turned on her computer. A scan through her internet updates confirmed that people did indeed disappear, and not just young women. One of the top headlines read: Two American, male tourists currently missing in Cancun.

Chapter Seven

Wide awake, Brooke rolled out of bed and sprang to her feet before her alarm chimed. The first day of her internship had arrived.

Pressing her lips together to suppress her smile, she rode her adopted bike to the Medical Examiner's Office. The old Schwinn had sat abandoned outside for months during her senior year of college. No sense letting it go to waste. When she graduated, she took it with her, buying a lock at Walmart for her new acquisition.

Cars passed menacingly close, buffeting her as she pedaled the rusty ten-speed. A car horn blared nearby, sending a jolt of fear through her. Under her breath she swore and wished she could have had a good look at whoever had nearly caused her to lose her balance.

She dismounted at the back entrance where deliveries and pickups were handled. A tall fence blocked the transport area from public sight, so no one could see the business of the office—body bags—going in and out throughout the day. She locked her bike to a pole, smoothed her wind-blown hair, and hurried inside.

"Good morning." Brooke leaned against the doorway of Dr. Gold's office.

He grunted, wrapped a gnarled hand around his cane, and rose slowly from his chair. He shuffled past Brooke, forcing her to step aside so he could gaze down the corridor. "Where is Jerome?"

Brooke's smile faded fast at the lack of welcome. "I don't know who Jerome is."

"One of our assistants. He's going to give you a tour."

With a low swishing sound, an electronic door opened a few yards further down the hallway. A man around her age meandered into the hallway wearing blue scrubs.

"There he is. Jerome, come over here."

Jerome could not be described as fat or muscular, but an odd combination of both—just big. He was wiping his nose with the back of his hand when his eyes met Brooke's. He froze, staring as if he'd discovered a mermaid sunning herself on a rock, something one never expected to see. She returned the stare and his gaze flew to the empty wall. A flush of red appeared on his cheeks.

"Jerome, this is Brooke Walton. Our new intern. Give her a tour of the building. I have calls to make before I start examinations."

"A tour?" Jerome rubbed his chin.

"Show her to the office you set up."

"Oh. Okay. It's this way." He still didn't make eye contact. He more or less spoke to her neck.

Brooke followed in silence, containing her disappointment. Not much of a welcome. This was not how she imagined her first day.

Down the hall from Dr. Gold's office, on the opposite side of the hallway, Jerome stopped walking. "This here's your office. Most of the old rooms don't have a swipe pad, they've got the old locks and you need a real key, but this one does. You got an access card?"

"I do. I haven't tested it yet. Let's see if it works."

Brooke swiped her card—success—and opened the door. She stepped inside the dim space and Jerome followed. She turned to look for a light switch and discovered Jerome only inches from her face. Brooke flinched and threw herself backwards, away from him. His arm extended toward her face. She ducked to the side, raising her arms in defense.

Jerome stared, his brow furrowed. "Ah, sorry, about that. Just turning the light on here." With a click, the fluorescent lights rattled and hummed to life.

Brooke straightened. "Yeah. Lights." She cleared her throat as heat burned her cheeks. "Of course."

Yellow artificial light struggled to fill the space, blinking a few times as the overhead fixture sputtered. A small windowless office presented itself to her, reeking of mildew and a thrown-together-at-the last-minute effort. A chair and a metal desk, circa WWII surplus, and stacks and stacks of papers were practically the only things in the room. An old computer sat idle in the center of the piles.

A sense of claustrophobia crept over Brooke. At her side, her massive companion breathed loudly like he was attempting to suck up all the available oxygen.

"Lovely." Brooke smirked. "Sort of like a cozy dungeon room."

He glanced at her, but immediately looked away again, dragging the back of his hand across his face.

A round clock on the wall ticked loudly as the hand snapped forward.

He pointed to a large monitor and keyboard on the desk. "That's your computer."

"Oh. I thought it was a boat anchor."

"Huh?"

"Joking." She turned to him. "What do you do here, Jerome?"

He cleared his throat, not making eye contact. "Oh, I'm, uh, an assistant medical examiner."

"Uh huh. You know, if we're going to work together, it would be nice to make eye contact."

"Oh, sure. Sorry." He slowly raised his eyes to meet hers, his cheeks turning red as he did.

"Better. Now, assistant medical examiner—did you need a special degree for that?"

"Yes." He returned his gaze to the floor, but he recovered faster this time. He swallowed hard. "I mean, yes. I have a college degree in health sciences." He stood up a little straighter and puffed out his chest.

"Oh. From where?"

"Oops. That's supposed to be plugged in. Here, I'll get it." He bent under the desk and took his time pushing a plug into the wall socket.

Brooke sighed. "What does a medical examiner assistant do here, exactly?"

"Whatever the medical examiners need me to do."

"For example?"

"Disinfect the autopsy tables. Calibrate the scales. Check the x-ray equipment." He gazed up at the ceiling and stretched his fingers out one at a time like he depended on them to come up with his duties. "I transfer bodies from storage to the autopsy room and back. And I assist with the autopsies." He sounded unnatural when he spoke, like someone trying to affect a refinement they didn't possess.

"Great. Show me the storage room and the autopsy room." She blinked, reminding herself not to come across as so demanding, and let a small smile cross her face. "Please."

"Okay. Sure. This way." He lumbered down the hall ahead of her. "There's two of 'em. One is the isolation autopsy room. It has its own refrigeration and deep freeze. It's for decomposed bodies and ones with contagious diseases."

Brooke followed him past doors for record storage, male and female locker rooms, a meeting room, and a viewing room for families. All appeared unoccupied and dark.

"Where is everyone?"

"During the day it's mostly just me, a few other assistants and medical examiners, and Dr. Gold. Sometimes it's just me and Dr. Gold. The administrative people have been moved to another building for now." He pointed to an air vent hanging down from the ceiling and surrounded by dark splotches. "This one leaks. And it's got mold."

The overhead lights flickered on and off, casting creepy shadows around the walls. With a hissing, spitting noise, the entire corridor went dark.

"What the—" Brooke's gaze flew upward. The lights hummed back to life again.

"Electrical problems." Jerome stuffed his hands into the pockets of his lab coat. "Old building. But we caught most of the rats. And there's generators in the cold storage rooms so they won't ever lose power. Can't have the bodies warming up." He stopped outside a door, newer than the others. "This here's the main autopsy room."

Brooke swiped her key card again. A green light flashed on the door panel. The door swung open to a large room with metal tables, collection buckets, scales, and microscopes. A petite Asian woman with a thin neck was busy conducting an autopsy. Large, dark-rimmed glasses covered most of her round face.

Jerome tilted his head toward the woman. "That's Mya. One of the medical examiners." He pointed to another door at the back of the autopsy room. "Through those doors is the cold storage room for bodies and tissues." They walked to the storage room and he pressed a second button. Double doors groaned as they inched open. A blast of cold air followed. Brooke wrapped her arms around her body, bracing herself against the chill, and shuddered.

Jerome went in first. "Dr. Gold never comes in here. It's too cold for him. Makes his arthritis bad. He can't pull the drawers out or move the bodies anyway."

Stainless steel refrigeration compartments covered two walls. A tall table with a laptop and charts sat in the center. "New arrivals go on the left." Jerome walked a small circle in the center of the room. "After they're examined, they get put back on the right side. We move the labels on the outside of the doors, like this here, so we know who is in which compartment. Then they get picked up by the funeral homes or a crematorium."

Jerome backed up and held up a hand, closing his eyes and opening his mouth. The sneeze that emerged was an ear-shattering blast, amplified by the tile walls and floors. The spray cloud dissipated in a downward trajectory, fading away before it reached the tile floor.

Brooke cringed, backing away. "Do you have a cold?"

"Allergies." He sniffled. "I think it's the mold. Not in here, but in the rest of the building."

Shivering, Brooke scanned the labels on the right side of the room. Robert Moore, Edna Jones, Marianne Hernandez, John Doe . . .

The doors opened with a low swoosh sound.

Dr. Gold stood with his cane just outside the open doors. "There you are." A scowl etched itself onto his face. He narrowed his eyes. "When you've finished wasting time on this little tour, your paperwork will be waiting—if that's all right with you, Miss Walton." The old man turned and shuffled off, grumbling to the hallway. "It's not going to do itself, you know."

Brooke took a parting glance at the right side of the room, sighed, and followed Dr. Gold back to her office. Tap, step, step, tap, step, step. Walking behind him was like moving in slow motion.

When they reached her office, he held out one of his knotted fingers, pointing at the chair in front of the computer. "Did the HR people set you up with a login?"

"Yes. I've got it." She sat, and he hovered above her.

"The information can only be entered and edited from this location. Something to do with the server and security."

"Okay." She doubted it was true.

Dr. Gold clutched a piece of paper listing instructions for using the computer and the Medical Examiner Office's information system. His face scrunched up with concentration. He frowned, dropped the paper onto the desk, and squinted at the computer monitor. "Here." His finger lingered in front of the screen, shaking slightly. "Click on that picture there. That one. The black square with the red thing in it."

Brooke couldn't help but wonder at his uncertainty. She clicked on the icon.

"No. That's not the one."

"This one here?" Brooke chose another and clicked again.

"Wait, I can't—yes, that one." His finger dropped away. "Now you enter the name and password they gave you."

He stared intently at the screen, his relief evident when Brooke entered the information and proceeded into the application. Above them, the light fixture on the ceiling buzzed, threatening to extinguish at any time.

"Look for something that says, um—" He rubbed his chin and moved closer to the screen. His eyes roamed from the paper he'd set down to the pile of documents on the desk. "What I need is for the information on those papers to be entered into this system."

Sensing his frustration, Brooke explored the application without waiting for his instructions. "Got it. I'll figure it out. I can let you know if I have any questions. Or . . . is there someone else you'd like me to ask?"

"One of the other examiners can help you, since I'll likely be busy. There's Mya. And Greg. Dr. Draven is always on the computer doing something when he's here." He snorted. "But that's not often. Not during the day." He pointed to the stack of papers again. "You need to take care of all those."

Brooke nodded and Dr. Gold left, grumbling under his breath about procurement procedures and budget cuts.

She scrolled through the application and took note of the data necessary to complete each entry. Next, she sorted through the documents piled on her desk. Autopsy and toxicology results. Insurance company requirements. A slew of names, dates, and CODs – causes of death. Most of the forms were written by hand and contained Dr. Gold's barely legible mix of scrawling print and cursive writing.

Most of the information could have and should have been in digital format from step one.

Her phone beeped a few times. A text from Xander. Two calls from an unknown number. She set the phone aside and plunged into her work.

When she was entering data, she spotted a familiar name on a list of recently completed autopsies. Edna Jones. Edna's autopsy, a full evisceration, had been conducted and signed off by Dr. Morris Draven. Clinical details included fluid build-up in her lungs and other organs, ventricles thickened from high blood pressure—typical signs of heart failure. All the necessary documentation was complete in the computer. But Brooke remembered a door labeled Edna Jones on the left side of the storage room. Jerome had told her the left side was for new arrivals. Either Jerome got confused—a very real possibility—or Edna Jones was on the wrong side.

Brooke put her fingers on the keyboard and scanned the next file but halted. She sighed, placing her hands in her lap and leaning back in the chair. Her job wasn't to question the data, only to enter it. But her deep intolerance for mistakes and incompetence made the issue impossible to ignore. In addition, she was exceedingly anxious to escape her dreary office. The autopsy and storage rooms were practically calling her name from down the hall.

Holding her breath and tiptoeing down the corridor, she took the same route she'd taken earlier with Jerome, passing Dr. Gold's closed office. She scanned her card outside the main autopsy room and entered. Two medical examiners were working inside. She froze. *Are they going to ask me what I'm doing?* A short, bearded man with a nametag that read Greg picked up shears. His lab coat fit tightly around his doughy arms and back. He turned toward Brooke and raised his arm.

He's signaling for me to leave.

Greg adjusted the microphone and began his dictation, making Brooke feel invisible.

The female examiner was still in the room. What was her name? She was easy to forget. Oh yeah, Mya. When she leaned over the table she pressed a gloved finger against the bridge of her glasses. *Gross. I hope she just put on new gloves.* Jerome stood across from her, next to a tray of instruments. He alone acknowledged Brooke's entrance by following her with his eyes as she passed.

Brooke nodded at him and kept walking.

It must be okay. I am authorized personnel after all.

Inside the cold storage room, she ran her eyes over the labels on the left. Sure enough, Edna Jones was in the same slot Brooke noticed earlier. None of the bodies on the left had been examined yet, so there were no CODs on the labels.

Through the two square windows in the doors, the medical examiners were busy, but Jerome appeared to be looking right into the storage room.

It shouldn't be a big deal if I check on one of the bodies. I work here now. It's my job to be accurate, especially for insurance purposes. And with this Edna Jones scenario, the accuracy of the data is in question.

Still, she checked again, making sure no one was coming before she opened the door on the storage unit. A puff of chilled air escaped like smoke. She grabbed the thick shelf handle and pulled. It was heavier than she expected. She placed a hand on the unit for leverage. With the grind of metal, it inched forward.

Is anyone coming?

She pulled again. A low groan escaped the drawer as the rollers gave up their cargo. The shelf was halfway out. Brooke contracted her biceps and pulled the rest of the way.

With a familiar surge of anticipation, she unzipped the body bag. Edna Jones resembled a statue, her expression set in stone. Her hands were crossed over her abdomen and her bright red nails, unusual with squared edges, stood out against her wrinkled, colorless skin. Brooke lifted Edna's head to search for stitches behind the neck. None. No signs of evisceration. So why had Dr. Draven signed off on an internal autopsy? Brooke placed her hands on her hips and frowned. Someone had screwed up. She zipped the bag, shoved the drawer in until it clanked shut, and went in search of Dr. Gold.

The Chief Examiner's door was halfway ajar, but she knocked anyway. "Excuse me. Do you have a minute?"

His frown indicated his frustration at being interrupted. "What is it? I thought young people knew everything about computers these days."

Brooke pursed her lips, holding back a sigh. "No, I —"

"Then what? Can't you see I'm busy?"

"I found a mistake. A discrepancy with one of the cadavers currently in the storage room."

"A mistake? How would you know it was a mistake?"

"I noticed a cadaver was listed as having been examined with a full autopsy. But she hasn't even been examined yet. She was still on the left side of the room. I mean, maybe a visual examination had been done, but not an autopsy."

"And you know this because?"

"I just happened to see her name on a door when Jerome took me into the storage room this morning. She was on the left. I went back to the storage room to find out why the data didn't match what I saw."

"You took your own look at the body?"

"Yes. I did."

Dr. Gold turned to look out his office window. Brooke held her breath, expecting a reprimand.

"Who conducted the autopsy?"

"Dr. Draven."

Dr. Gold's head started toward her but stopped. For a split second, he viewed her out of the corner of his eye. "I see. I'll take a look tonight. I must leave in a minute to visit a crime scene. Rarely happens but this one is important. You can change the data that's already in the computer. Can't you?"

"Yes. I can delete some of the fields for now and fill them in once you have the correct information."

"Yes. Do that."

"Okay." She turned to walk away.

"Brooke."

She stopped, turning back to him. "Yes?"

He was staring out the window. "Don't mention this to anyone else. Not yet anyway."

"Uh, sure. No problem."

He returned to scribbling on his notepad. She waited a few more seconds before leaving again.

At the end of the day, Brooke returned to the autopsy room. Greg was working alone, poking around inside a chest cavity, earbuds in his ears. Brooke opened her mouth to ask if he wanted help but said nothing. He was in his own world, removing the internal organs. She knew the feeling.

Greg moved from beside the cadaver, reaching for a tool from the stainless-steel tray. The body was more visible now. Gray skin and wrinkled flesh, an elderly person of nondescript stature, female. The old woman's slender arms had been positioned at her sides. Square-shaped, bright red fingernails rested against the metal autopsy table.

At least the Chief Medical Examiner was trying to get it together and make sure things eventually got done correctly.

Or he was covering his ass . . .

Chapter Eight

He tossed his car key onto the table and slapped his phone down, ignoring the incoming call. The steady, incessant ringtone made him want to scream. A glimpse of his reflection in the hall mirror revealed feverish, blood-shot eyes. His mood had changed from euphoric to agitated in the time it took to drive home. He was in no state to talk to her, but she wasn't giving up. He finally answered with the energy of a much older man who had just finished a double shift of manual labor. He did work unusual hours, but it wasn't his job that had left him spent and his nerves raw and shaky.

"It's me. Alyssa."

"I know. What is it?"

"Are you home?"

"I just walked in. I need to sleep. I'll call you to—"

"No. You need to get out of there."

"What are you talking about?"

"You have to go. He has men coming. Two big guys. Monsters. They could be there any minute."

"How do you know?"

"Just trust me, baby, please."

He hated it when she called him "baby." He knew it was a term of endearment, but to him it implied weakness.

"If you don't disappear . . . I really don't know what they might do to you, but it won't be good. Unless you have the money."

"If I had the damn money I wouldn't be in this situation, would I?"

"Can't you borrow some from your family? They're rich."

"No! Don't even talk about them."

His family was no longer an option, not after his last encounter with his father. His father's harsh words were easy to remember.

"Enough. You're not a child anymore! You're an adult! You don't even have a family. You have only yourself to take care of. Why can't you do it?"

"I just made a bad investment. This will be the last time, Dad. I promise. It's really important."

His father shook with anger. "That's what you told me last time. And the time before that. It's what you told your sister, too. We're not going to keep enabling you while you decimate our retirement funds. Get yourself together before you lose the job I went out on a limb to get you."

"Yeah, great, Dad. You got me a job as a coroner."

"The only reason you're still a coroner is because you don't have the board certification to be a pathologist! What's stopping you from getting it?!"

Draven had kept his eyes glued to his feet, unable to come up with an excuse.

"Get whatever help you need. We've done all the research for you. We've given you the phone numbers of exactly where you should go. I'll even pay your bill when you get there. But don't come back here ever again if you're only going to ask for more money."

His father's disgusted expression was the last he'd seen of his family in almost a year. Nothing had improved. Things had become worse. Much, much worse.

"If you don't have the money, then get out of there. Hurry." Alyssa's urgent pleas grated on his frayed nerves.

He rushed to the front door to make sure it was locked. *How did my life come to this?* He'd been wrenched from a promising future to one barely escaped fiasco after another. Too many close calls to count. "How do they know where I live?"

There was no answer on the other end of the line.

"Alyssa! How do they know where to find me?"

"I don't know. Maybe they don't. Maybe they're just looking. But don't be there in case they come."

The last time they found him was terrifying. They had guaranteed a next time would be far more unpleasant. He shuddered. He didn't want to find out why. He hurried into his bedroom, tossed the phone on his bed, and grabbed a duffel bag. He stuffed in clothes, a toothbrush and toothpaste. He wasn't sure where he would go. He'd probably end up sleeping in his car, wouldn't be the first time, until he got the money.

He grabbed the phone again. "You still there?"

"Yes. What—"

"I'm gonna need you to help me."

"Yeah. What can I do?"

"I have to raise some cash. Get rid of some things for me. Sell them to some of your friends and clients. Can you do that?"

"I can try."

"Okay." He was sweating even though it was cool inside his home. "Where are you?"

"I was going to work tonight. Unless . . . unless you don't want me to."

"No. That's perfect. I'll meet you near the train station, where we first met." He dropped the phone from his ear and closed his eyes, before lifting it back up. "Alyssa, I'll make it up to you. I promise."

"I know you will. Be careful. I love you."

"Yeah." He hung up and snuck out his backdoor like a burglar even though it was his own home.

Chapter Nine

The pile of papers on Brooke's desk steadily grew smaller. With each COD, she tested her knowledge by coming up with the symptoms, means of diagnosis, and known methods of treatment—the same way she would prep for a quiz. *Almost done.* The tap of Dr. Gold's cane announced his presence in the hallway. She swiveled sideways in her chair and took a sip of her water, waiting for him to reach her door.

"Where are all the forms that were on the desk this morning?"

Brooke rotated the last few inches to face him. "I filed them in the records room."

"You've already entered the data and filled out the online reports?"

"Yes."

"Hmmm." Dr. Gold removed his lab coat. "I'm going to take my daily walk. It's a relatively cool day. I recommend you go outside for some fresh air."

"Sure. Just as soon as I finish these." Kudos to him for taking a walk, in spite of his arthritis. At least he was trying to get some exercise. More than she could say about most people.

After a few more minutes, she put on her cap to protect her skin from the sun and left the office with the lunch she had packed earlier in the day. The first few breaths of air outside the building seemed remarkably fresh. She strolled to a nearby park, where others on lunch breaks walked laps around a pond and ate at picnic tables. Taking a break was an unusual concept; she was always go-go-go. She really couldn't say why she had agreed to come outside and eat in the muggy summer air when she could have eaten her lunch inside and saved at least twenty minutes. Maybe her dreary office with the flickering light was starting to bother her.

Unable to find an unoccupied table, Brooke wove through flower beds to sit on a rock under a giant Oak. She opened her lunch bag and took a bite of her sandwich. Sunlight peeked through the branches and baked the top of her head through her black cap. The sun made her insides feel like a pot of water close to boiling on a stovetop. The antsy, escalating sensation made her angry.

Her phone buzzed. She reached into her backpack and removed it, checking the screen. Robert Mending. He was a classmate from college who still had a crush on her. He called often, pretending to be interested in friendly conversation even though he knew she and Xander were a couple. Robert claimed he was dating someone, but it was obvious that if Brooke asked him, he would jump in his car and drive from Boston to East Dalton, breaking up with his current girlfriend on the way. He'd already called Brooke several times during the past week, although he hadn't left a single message.

With a sigh, she answered. "Hi, Robert."

"Hi. Calling to see how the summer is treating you."

"Fine. I'm on a lunch break because there's a first time for everything." Her eyes followed a boy's frisbee sailing through the air toward a black dog. "What are you doing these days?" Her question felt fake, rehearsed, because she didn't really care how or what he was doing, but that's the kind of thing people said and so she supposed it sounded normal to everyone else.

"Oh . . . you know, a little of this and that."

She huffed. *Your only responsibility is to figure out which causes are worthy of your family's philanthropic gifts.*

Frisbee in his mouth, the dog galloped back to the boy.

"How is your work at the morgue?"

"Call it a medical examiner's office. Sounds more professional." The dog was jumping now, intent on racing toward the next catch. Brooke sighed. "It's not exactly what I expected."

"How so?"

"I thought I would be doing autopsies, examining bodies. I was excited about it. But instead they have me sorting through paperwork, submitting reports, data entry. Stuff almost anyone could do."

"What? You're doing paperwork? That's not . . . I mean, I can't believe that's what they have you doing. But, don't worry. Maybe it's just for the first few days."

"Yeah, I hope so. I mean, I'm grateful for the job, it pays really well, but I was hoping to learn a lot there this summer." She switched the phone to her other ear. "Any particular reason for your call?"

"Well, I do have some news to share. Did you hear that Rachael Kline's family has just hired a private investigator?"

"What?" Brooke froze with her sandwich a few inches away from her mouth and clenched her jaw. "How would you know?"

"I still keep in touch with Jessica's family. The Klines have spoken to the Carrols a few times."

"Why would they do that?" Brooke put her half-eaten sandwich down.

"Since Jessica disappeared at Everett and Rachael disappeared at Rothaker. Two unsolved mysteries at Ivy League schools near each other.

They're hoping to find a connection. I mean, I guess they're desperate for answers."

"What type of connection?"

"Maybe someone who knew both of them."

"Do Jessica's parents still think someone harmed her? Are they ever going to accept that she wandered off drunk and died of hypothermia in the blizzard?"

"Well, we don't know that's what happened for sure. I mean, how did she end up so far from the school if no one else was involved?"

"Yeah . . . I can't answer that." *Or your next call would be to 911, unless you like me far more than I can imagine.*

Brooke chewed on her lower lip. Technically, Robert was a friend and she didn't have many, by choice. But . . . he annoyed her. Always making a big deal about Jessica's disappearance, and Rachael's disappearance too. How many times had he said, "I know you must be a little traumatized about Jessica and Rachael, since they were both classmates of yours when they disappeared."

Brooke rolled her eyes. Jessica and Rachael had paid the consequences for threatening her.

She took a carrot out of her bag and snapped it in half. "So . . . what do you have planned for the weekend?"

"It's the regatta at the club. I'm crewing for Dad. What about you?"

She put the tip into her mouth and crunched while she spoke. "I'm teaching four exercise classes, and Saturday is my long run day."

"Nothing social planned?"

"No, nothing social."

"You should come to the regatta! Or to the dinner after. You know Dad's club. The party will go on until dawn. We could see a show, go to some clubs maybe, just to get you away from East Dalton for a few days. I mean, if you can get someone to cover your classes."

"No, I can't. But thanks for asking. I have to go now. Say hi to your girlfriend for me."

Brooke hung up and tossed the rest of her sandwich in the trash. She lifted herself to her feet and began the walk back. Twice she shivered involuntarily. Somewhere, a private investigator was comparing names on lists and making connections between the two women who had given Brooke no choice except to kill them. How long until her name was mentioned?

Across the park, the jogger switched directions, so he could keep his eyes on Brooke Walton. She pumped her arms and took long strides while she walked.

On her path, a man in a business suit approached. His head turned to her as she passed, but he continued to walk forward, eyeing her over his shoulder and nearly walking into a trash can.

Ha! Way to be super obvious. You got what you deserved!

As Brooke approached, a woman walking at a slower pace moved to the side of the walkway. She sized Brooke up and down. Brooke passed without giving anyone even a sideways glance.

The jogger wiped the sweat from his forehead and slowed to a walk. Mouthing the words to the music streaming into his ears, he stayed a safe distance behind the young woman all the way to the medical examiner's building. Once she disappeared inside, he could stop watching her and return to his office.

Nothing to report today.

He changed the channel to get his daily—no, hourly—fix of news update.

Ukraine paid the president's lawyer for a private meeting. Amazon announced its newest location. And in Mexico, a fishing trawler discovered body parts in Kabiscey Bay, near the resort city of Cancun.

Chapter Ten

Brooke shifted her weight back in the creaky office chair, intertwined her fingers and raised her arms overhead to stretch. She yawned and glanced at the wall clock. With a forced exhale that made her lips trill, she leaned forward to lift the top paper off her pile. Dr. Gold's messy writing again. Almost all the forms were his at first, but others were dropping them off now, too.

Why do the work yourself if someone can do it for you?

The yellow paper in her hand told her a man named Robert O'Donnell had spinal bulbar muscular atrophy when he died. Now that was interesting. She had yet to see the condition in real life, or death. She patted the pile of forms on her desk and left to see for herself.

As usual, the corridor was empty. She still wasn't sure if she had permission to go wherever she pleased in the building but asking was not in her best interest. She knew better than to ask and risk receiving an undesirable answer.

Inside the autopsy room, she could no longer detect the strong disinfectant chemicals or the sharp scent of viscera immediately apparent to anyone visiting the area for the first time. But she couldn't imagine ever becoming immune to the storage room's icy coldness, a feeling she now associated with death. Alone in the refrigerated area, she crossed her arms over her chest to ward off the chill before it crept into her bones to stay.

She scanned the labels up and down the doors until she located Robert O'Donnell.

She had her hand on the latch, about to pull, when the swoosh of the storage room doors indicated someone was coming. Brooke instinctively stepped back toward the center of the room. A man in his late twenties or early thirties entered, wearing grey slacks and a dress shirt so perfectly fitted it had to be custom made. His expensive-looking attire accentuated a lean body. At closer look, he was too lean, with sharp features and hollowed out cheeks. His dark hair and widow's peak reminded Brooke of Count Dracula. His eyes were hidden behind dark lenses, but Brooke could tell he stared directly at her, without apology.

"Hi." She tucked her elbows to her sides and clasped her fingers together. She shifted on her feet and prepared an answer in case he asked what she was doing there.

The man removed his sunglasses, revealing striking green eyes and dilated pupils. His gaze traveled down her body. "Who are you?"

"I'm Brooke Walton. The intern . . ." She flipped over the authorization card on her lanyard. "From Rothaker Medical School?"

"I heard Eugene hired someone."

"And you are?" Her tone was exceptional in its politeness, in case he had the authority to tell her to leave.

"Dr. Draven."

The error he made with Edna Jones rushed to her mind, along with the urge to point it out, but she held back. "Oh. It's nice to meet you." He was younger than she expected. And there was something else unusual about him—a sharp, unnerving vibe that was hard to describe but impossible to miss.

She twirled her authorization card. "So, you examine bodies at the crime scenes?"

"When they call me."

"What sort of work do you do the rest of the time?"

"I'm a physician."

"Yes, I know. But I've never seen you here during the day. So, I meant where else do you work?"

Dr. Draven stepped forward. "I need to check on something. Excuse me."

Brooke moved aside, allowing him a straight line to the computer. He jiggled the mouse to bring the screen to life.

She took a final glance at the door where the cadaver of Robert O'Donnell was lying inside with his unusual disease. She didn't feel comfortable satisfying her curiosity with Dr. Draven in the room. Robert O'Donnell would have to wait.

"What are you checking on?" *If I get to know him, I might be able to do more autopsies.*

"Work." He answered without taking his eyes off the screen.

Brooke raised an eyebrow. Maybe he already knew she had brought his error to the Chief Medical Examiner's attention. Perhaps Dr. Gold had told him.

She left without saying goodbye. She felt Draven's eyes on the back of her head, watching her walk out. What did he need to do on the computer that he didn't want her to see? Fix another one of his mistakes? She left but couldn't help from stopping outside the storage room and peering back in through the window. Dr. Draven poked at the keyboard. Half his frown was visible in profile. In that second, he turned toward the door and caught her studying him. His eyes locked on Brooke's and narrowed, sending a chill through her body that wasn't from the cold. She hurried away with an irritating I-have-to-do-something-feeling about Dr. Draven, the same way she felt about the broken toaster oven in her apartment—she either had to fix it or get rid of it.

By three thirty, the only remaining forms were the ones with handwriting so messy they were completely indecipherable. Brooke scooped them up and took them to ask Dr. Gold what they said. A few steps away from his office, voices streamed out through his open door. She stopped.

"Yes. The arrangement is unusual, perhaps not unlike your own." It was Dr. Gold's gravelly voice.

His comment was followed by a huff from whoever was in the room with him. "How much?"

"It's confidential. And the donor wants to remain anonymous."

Another huff.

"It costs us nothing and we benefit." Dr. Gold's voice was firm. "She's a smart girl. She learns quickly. She's very attentive to detail. So, enough about that. Sit down. We need to talk."

With a creak and a click, the door shut.

Chapter Eleven

Jean deleted the message from the Klines, tucked a stray hair behind her ear, and took another sip of her lukewarm coffee. They were just hoping she'd found something related to their daughter's disappearance. She returned to studying the files on Rachael Kline's investigation, hoping for inspiration. Praying was more accurate. Truth be told, Jean was getting desperate. She'd become an expert on Rachael's case files, but how much longer would her new clients pay her if she didn't come up with a new lead? She had no new information to offer the Klines. That wasn't good for bringing a perpetrator to justice. Nor was it good for her business reputation. And Millie was so thrilled about her first riding lesson, scheduled for next week. Jean needed some success if she was going to continue to pay for them. How she would hate to tell her daughter that the lessons might have to wait. Again.

The police reports from the days and weeks following Rachael's disappearance were thorough. Jean had to give them that. Hundreds of searches and interviews were documented. Once Rachael was officially missing from her medical school dormitory, detectives had spoken with every single person who lived or worked in the dorm. Many people thought Rachael's death was somehow related to her volunteer work with domestic abuse and HIV prevention because it took her through some dangerous areas of the city. Lots of thoughts. Lots of ideas. Lacking were actual clues. Evidence. Anything useful.

Rachael's purse had been picked up by thugs who used her credit cards to purchase stereo equipment but knew nothing of Rachael. They found the purse in Greenwood Circle, a park where derelicts and drug-users congregated at night. The location suggested an opportunistic crime by a drug user or a gang member. Possibly an assault that ended in her death. But where was Rachael's body?

The city of East Dalton did have a major crime problem. Jean had combed through the police files for several other local deaths that had started out as missing person cases. Two other young women were drug overdoses, their bodies eventually found. A few cases turned out to be suicides. And then there was the girl who went missing, disappeared in New Hampshire at Everett College. Her body was discovered months later. Her wealthy family had provided the Klines with copies of all the files from their private investigator, hoping their extensive investigation might somehow help with Rachael's. The Klines had provided the copies to Jean.

With help from Rothaker University, detectives working on Rachael's case had run background checks on anyone who was deemed suspicious, like the thugs who found her purse. But not on her fellow medical students. With no other route to follow for the moment, Jean gathered background information for each of the people Rachael had been closest to at school: her friends, her lab partners, and the men and women who worked at or visited the clinic where she volunteered.

Rachael's anatomy project partners were first because Rachael had spent a lot of time with the group.

First there was Rakesh from India. His father died unexpectedly in early November. He had to leave school suddenly and return home to be with his family. He wasn't even in the country when Rachael disappeared.

Next was Xander Cross. A former football player from University of Nebraska, then a veteran with a tour in Afghanistan. She pictured a big, tough guy with lots of testosterone. Potential anger management issues. Unfair stereotyping? Too bad. She had to work every angle or say goodbye to the horseback riding lessons.

Last was Brooke Walton, a graduate of Everett College. *Everett? Wait, what year did Jessica Kline disappear from Everett?* She flipped back to the Everett file and confirmed both women would have been there at the same time. *Hmmmm.* Jean moved Brooke to the top of her list.

Chapter Twelve

Calmness settled over Brooke like a soft blanket as she took in the grey morning sky, the raindrops sliding down the windowpane. As much as she loved the rain, it wasn't good for bike-riding. Her tires would fling mud up her back. Running would be less messy.

With a light rain drizzling down her neck and keeping her cool, she pounded her feet against the pavement, leaping over pools of water. Her legs were long and lithe, but she saw them as agile, powerful, and unstoppable.

Less than a half-mile from work, a bolt of lightning sliced through the dark sky, followed by an alarming crack of thunder. She raced across the street and into the Medical Examiner's building as the rain turned into a torrential downpour.

Shivering in the entryway, she shook her head and shoulders like a dog, relieved to have missed most of the storm. The precipitation outdoors intensified the reek of mildew inside the changing room. She wrung water out of her ponytail, changed into the available scrubs, and placed her wet clothes in a locker. Her lean body was lost in the too-large scrubs, but at least they were dry. A damp chill followed her to her office, where a new mountain of reports waited to be filed. She sat down at her desk, crossing one ankle behind the other, and logged in before grabbing the top paper and taking a cursory read to see what she needed to do.

Tap, step, step . . . tap, step, step . . . TAP, STEP, STEP.

The distinctive sound of Dr. Gold and his cane grew louder as he approached her office. He stopped in her doorway. "Good. You're here."

TAP, STEP, STEP . . . TAP, STEP, STEP . . . tap, step, step.

He didn't stay long. Guess that was just his way of saying hello.

"Don't dawdle," he grumbled from down the corridor. "Busy day ahead. Meet me in the autopsy room. I can use your help."

"What?" She shot upright, hoping she'd heard correctly and wasn't misinterpreting his words. "Coming in a second!" She logged out of the system as fast as she could and leapt out of her chair, racing to catch up.

In the autopsy room, Dr. Gold stood under a fluorescent light and raised a piece of paper, holding it at arm's length. "We'll start with . . ." He frowned, adjusted his reading glasses, and moved the paper farther away, leaning his head back. His hand shook as he squinted at the page. ". . . with Mrs. Gretchen Ackerblom."

"I'll go get her." Brooke hurried to the cold storage room and pressed the button to open the doors. She marched to the left side of the room and was searching labels for Ackerblom when she heard the whoosh of the doors opening again. Jerome entered, along with the faint smell of aftershave, his hair recently cut and washed.

"Morning!" She was unable to disguise her excitement. "For whatever reason, I'm getting a break from reports. I'm supposed to get Gretchen Ackerblom." The combination of damp hair and thin scrubs in the cold room made her teeth chatter involuntarily.

Jerome cleared his throat. "Um, would you like a sweater?"

"No." Brooke walked down the left side of the room a second time, scanning labels. "I meant, no, thank you."

"Because I have an extra sweater you can wear. Well, a sweatshirt. It's clean."

"I'll be fine once I get out of here."

"Let me see if I can help you find her." Jerome reached across the computer for the computer mouse. Instead, his thick fingers sent it sliding across the desk. His second attempt sent it crashing to the floor.

Brooke read the labels again, rubbing her hands vigorously around her upper arms. The sound of the rain echoed on the roof, mixing with the sound of the mouse dangling from its cord and swinging into the side of the table while Jerome fumbled to set it back in place.

"If you can't find her, are you sure you heard the name right?"

"Yes, of course, I'm sure."

"And you still can't find her?"

"No. Can't you find her in the computer?"

"It's still warming up."

"Well, look around the room for yourself."

Jerome stood up and walked to the right side of the room. "Hmm. She's over here. She's already been autopsied."

"Are you kidding me?" Brooke tossed her head back and then glared at Jerome.

"Says she died of natural causes. Are you sure Dr. Gold asked for her?"

"Yes, I'm sure. I don't get confused. Someone messed up, but it wasn't me. Who works at night?"

Jerome pulled the drawer out with a grating scrape like fingernails on a blackboard. "Any of the medical examiners might come in if they get a call. But mostly it's Dr. Draven, or Greg. And Paul. And sometimes me."

A crack of thunder boomed through the room. Their eyes locked as the overhead lights flickered.

She swept her hand over her pony tail. "This isn't the first time this had happened, and I've only been here a week. I mean, seriously, either a body has been examined or it hasn't, how hard is that?"

Jerome swallowed. "Yeah, I didn't—"

Brooke unzipped the body bag just enough to reveal the head, neck, and upper torso. "No sign of an autopsy."

They slid the body onto a gurney and Brooke walked behind Jerome as he wheeled it into the autopsy room. Dr. Gold leaned against a table, reading a report.

She waited for him to look up. "Dr. Gold, I just wanted you to know— this body was on the wrong side of the room, just like last time. Someone listed the cadaver as having been autopsied when it wasn't."

"Is that so?" Dr. Gold shifted his gaze to Jerome, who studied his shoes. "Mr. Ackerblom, husband of the deceased, called me this morning requesting an autopsy. He had some concerns. Where's the label?" Dr. Gold looked straight at Jerome. "I want to see who signed off on it."

"Uh," Jerome scuffed his sole against the floor. "She might have been on the wrong side of the room, but I didn't see anything to indicate she'd already been examined."

Brooke whirled around to face Jerome, her hands on her hips. "What? You said . . . it would be in the computer, wouldn't it?"

The doors to the autopsy room opened and one of the nurse examiners called from the doorway. "Dr. Gold, there's a family here hoping to speak with you."

He threw his hands up in frustration. "I'll be back." With a snap, he peeled off his latex gloves and dropped them into the waste container. He took hold of his cane and shuffled out of the room.

Brooke clenched her hands and glared at Jerome. "What was that about? Why did you make me look like a liar?"

Jerome tucked his head like a turtle trying to hide in a shell. He stepped backward and bumped his side into the metal edge of a table, put out a hand to steady himself and accidentally sent a pair of scissors sailing to the floor.

"Tell me," she hissed. "Why did you lie?"

"I just . . . we don't . . . I don't want to get Paul in trouble. He works the nightshift. He might have made a mistake. He needs his job. He has a kid to take care of."

Brooke dug her nails into her palms. "That's very kind of you, Jerome, but do not, ever, ever, again make me look like I don't know what I'm talking about. Are we clear on that?"

"Yeah. I didn't mean to make you look bad." He rubbed the side of his hip. "I just, you know—I didn't want anyone to be in trouble. Sorry."

"Fine. Where's the label?"

"It's gone. I'm sorry. I didn't—"

"Want anyone to get in trouble. Right." She nodded. "So you've mentioned." Brooke exhaled through teeth clenched so tightly she had to consciously let up before she cracked a molar. Jerome's visible discomfort only fueled her anger. He was practically cowering. "Who signed off on the cause of death?"

"Uh . . . I don't remember. We'll need to write a new one anyway."

"I'm going to find out as soon as I log into the computer system."

Swoosh.

Dr. Gold hobbled back into the room, muttering. "Unfortunate . . . more documentation. Where were we?" He grabbed another pair of gloves from the box on the wall and stepped close to the table. "What do we have here?"

"We don't know yet." Brooke squeezed her hands together. Her eyes darted to the tray of autopsy tools a few feet away. "Our job is to tell Mrs. Ackerblom's story and determine what killed her."

"Sounds like a line from *CSI*." Jerome smiled.

Brooke scowled at him.

"Well—" Dr. Gold covered his mouth and waited until his ragged cough subsided. "I spoke with her husband. She was in an assisted living facility. Her family requested the autopsy. They were rather insistent and I'm glad we're able to comply today." He gulped, and coughed again, causing both Jerome and Brooke to look his way. "You can both stop staring at me. I'm fine. Grab the UV light, Jerome. Swing it over to Brooke."

Brooke adjusted the light. Dr. Gold crossed his arms and rocked back on his heels. "Let's see what they're teaching the first years at Rothaker. What does the external examination tell you?"

Brooke moved the light slowly over the body. Purplish black areas appeared on skin mottled with age spots and crisscrossed with prominent veins. Jerome took pictures and irritated Brooke by getting in her way.

"Abrasions on her torso, bruises on her upper body, including her face." Brooke nudged Jerome out of her way with her elbow. "I'm going to turn her now."

Dr. Gold nodded.

"Patches of discoloration on her back side as well." Brooke grabbed the measuring tape. "A bruise six cm in diameter located one cm from the L2 vertebra."

Brooke continued the examination, sharing her observations until there was nothing left to tell.

"Fine." Dr. Gold shifted his weight and winced. "Let's begin the internal investigation."

"Can I?" Brooke reached for the scalpel.

Dr. Gold leaned against the gurney. He stroked his chin and eyed Brooke. "Be my guest."

Brooke made her first incision, firmly piercing the papery skin. Every other image, sound, and smell in the room fell away from her consciousness. Only her work, the tools, and the cadaver existed. At first, she worked silently. Tiny lines of intense concentration appeared on her forehead and a slight smile curled the corners of her lips as she processed her observations. Dr. Gold stood close by. After a few minutes, Brooke straightened. "Hemorrhaging of her esophagus and tongue."

"Correct." Dr. Gold continued to stare.

"It appears that she may have died from lack of oxygen."

"And?"

A powerful crack of thunder shook the walls. Brooke didn't flinch.

"No evidence of an asthmatic attack. No contusions along her neck muscles. No broken hyoid bone."

Jerome scratched his nose. "Why are you saying what you don't see?"

"I'm just thinking out loud."

"I believe she's ruling out strangulation." Dr. Gold lifted his chin and watched Brooke.

"Hold on. I need to check a few more areas. Nothing in her windpipe. Hmm . . . I'm going to open her abdomen."

"Go ahead. I must say, you're surprisingly comfortable with this work." Dr. Gold spoke with a hint of something that sounded more like suspicion than praise.

Brooke made a clean slice into the abdominal cavity and then into the stomach, releasing a putrid stench. She manipulated the organ while Jerome mopped up fluids alongside the body with a sponge.

Dr. Gold leaned forward. "And what do you think now?"

"There's nothing in her stomach."

"So, what can we conclude from that?"

"She didn't eat before she died?" Jerome suggested quietly.

Brooke set down the forceps and turned to Dr. Gold. "She was suffocated."

"I concur. Asphyxia is the official cause of death for Mrs. Ackerblom." Dr. Gold dipped his chin. "Things don't always present themselves the way we expect them to. Shine the light over her head again. You'll find petechia under the eyelids. Jerome, make sure to take pictures."

"Someone abused her at the nursing home, maybe?" Brooke put her hand around her chin. "Suffocated her with a pillow?"

"It's not our job to speculate." The doctor tapped his cane. "I'll notify the police when we're finished. We need to clip and scrape her fingernails. Then take samples of head, eyelash, pubic and eyebrow hair to compare with any foreign hairs. Which you should have done first, but I didn't expect to find anything suspicious. Then you can go ahead and close up the body."

"Can you, I mean, do you know how?" Jerome fumbled in his pocket, yanked out a tissue, and sneezed.

"Of course." *I've been slicing things open and sewing them back together since I was a toddler.*

After the specimens were collected, Jerome cleaned the incision area and Brooke sewed the skin flaps together with meticulous, even stiches.

Dr. Gold struggled to remove his gloves. "Nice job. I know, the family won't see it. Doesn't mean they won't appreciate their loved one being taken care of with respect."

The smile on the Chief Examiner's face nearly floored her. A half-smile, corners of his mouth just barely lifted, but it was enough to count.

"Thank you."

"Still not worth so much money," he mumbled.

"Excuse me?" Brooke stopped sewing.

Dr. Gold turned to Jerome. "Remember when you tried to do the stitching?"

Jerome's face and neck flushed crimson.

Dr. Gold's laugh morphed into a cough. "You can finish cleaning up once Brooke is done, and then we'll move on."

"Sure." Jerome kept his eyes down.

After teaching two evening exercise classes, Brooke returned to her new apartment. She peeled off her sweaty clothes. Each sock had a hole in it. The damp chill she'd carried with her throughout the day finally disappeared after she took a shower, letting the hot water cascade against the curve of her lower back.

Dressed in one of Xander's extra-large sweatshirts, as the blender turned her kale and frozen bananas into a smoothie, she let out a deep sigh of satisfaction. She'd made the most of her opportunity to impress Dr. Gold. He now knew she was capable of more than entering data and filing reports.

The data entry work hadn't been a complete waste of her time. She now possessed some interesting insight, and none of it reflected well on the people who worked there. She'd discovered two mistakes already. Professional health care providers shouldn't make mistakes. Good thing the employees at East Dalton's Medical Examiner's Office only worked on people who were already dead. To be fair, she didn't know who was to blame besides Dr. Draven. Maybe it wasn't any of the doctors or nurses. Maybe it was the mysterious Paul who worked the night shift. Or maybe the technologically-challenged Dr. Gold had entered data incorrectly.

Or, maybe the discrepancies she found weren't mistakes. Maybe someone had a reason for entering inaccurate information. In any case, the system was a mess. As the Chief Examiner, Dr. Gold needed to make some process improvements and become comfortable using the computer before the state was hit with a bunch of lawsuits.

Stepping around Xander's television set, which Brooke had yet to plug in, she set her half-finished drink on the floor and plopped into her chair, curling her legs beneath her. She took a second to appreciate the peaceful silence in her apartment before waking up her laptop, entering her password, and typing *Medical Examiner's Office* in the browser. She scanned a series of articles.

Most medical examiners are moonlighting doctors and nurses supplementing their income. They are paid by the state for each body examined. A set fee for driving out to the scene of death for a visual exam, more for completing an autopsy.

Medical examiners receive approximately one hundred dollars for a visual exam. About the same pay as the men and women who drive the vans to deliver the bodies from the site of death to the morgue or Medical Examiner's Office.

Brooke strummed her fingers on the arm rest. Xander's unpacked boxes sat stacked against the wall. The pitter patter of rain continued outside. She rolled her shoulders forward inside the cozy warmth of his sweatshirt.

Four possible explanations surfaced to explain the mix-ups. The first, and most innocent—gross incompetence. Sloppy mistakes from overworked and overtired employees. Paul, the night-shift guy Jerome was trying to protect, might have a day job and then work at night when he has the opportunity, never getting adequate sleep, going through the motions of his job in a sleepy haze of fog, unaware he's mislabeling bodies. Or, he might just be an idiot.

The second possible explanation—Dr. Gold's ego. Was he too old to do the autopsies but pretending he still could? Was he getting confused? Losing his faculties? Making mistakes right and left?

Brooke wrinkled her nose and contemplated the third explanation—greed. Was one, or more, of the medical examiners maximizing their on-the-side source of income by collecting money without doing the work? Could they be logging in to the computer and taking credit for exams and autopsies that never occurred? If the patients were elderly or didn't have close friends and family following up and asking questions, who would know? The apparent lack of oversight, thanks to Dr. Gold's aversion to computers, might present someone with a tempting opportunity.

Brooke unfolded her legs. Which of her possible explanations were correct? Stupidity? Ego? Greed? A combination? Or, a fourth explanation. Something else. Something far more interesting and sinister. Perhaps someone didn't want people to know what really happened to Edna Jones, or that Mrs. Ackerblom had been suffocated.

The tingle of goosebumps spread across her skin.

Had the discrepancies been occurring for months, or years, or had they just started? And why had no one else noticed? *I mean, of course, I'm smarter than all of them put together, but still . . .*

Was everyone there *in* on whatever was happening?

Chapter Thirteen

Jerome jerked and twisted his phone between his hands before he got shot and died.

"Crap. So close to the next level."

He shoved the phone in his pocket and resumed his duties, gathering up a large container of sodium flouride. Turning to shove the storeroom door open with his butt, he leaned back and stopped with a thump.

"Oops!"

He whipped around at the sound of a woman's voice. Heat rushed to his cheeks. "Oh, I'm sorry."

"I should have been watching where I was going." The stranger had curly hair, pulled back and knotted at the nape of her neck. She wore jeans and a snug fitting T-shirt under a light jacket. The thousand or so fabric pills covering it indicated a lot of use. "Maybe you can help me. I'm looking for Brooke Walton."

Jerome shifted the heavy container. "She's in the autopsy room."

"Is it possible to speak with her for a few minutes?"

"Um, are you a friend?"

"Jean Thompson." She flipped open a small wallet to reveal an ID, a picture of herself ten pounds lighter, and closed it again before Jerome had a chance to figure out what he'd seen.

Her smile and confidence influenced his decision. He placed the container on the ground and wiped his nose with the back of his hand. "She's this way."

Jean followed Jerome down the dingy corridor and stopped outside the double doors. He scanned his card, stepping back as the doors opened. "Brooke? A woman named Jean Thompson is here for you."

<hr>

Brooke stood alongside Dr. Gold, happily dissecting the thoracic cavity of a middle-aged man. She'd spent most of the day filling out computer forms, hoping for the chance to work in the autopsy room. Dr. Gold hadn't asked for her help until the afternoon, and now she was being interrupted. She winced, not looking up. "For me?"

Dr. Gold huffed. "I'd prefer you didn't have friends visit you while you're working."

"I don't have any . . . I mean, I don't know anyone named Jean Thompson."

"She's with the, um . . ." Jerome turned to Jean. "Who should I say you're with?"

"Tell her I'm a private investigator and I've been trying to get hold of her for some time to talk about Jessica Carrol and Rachael Kline."

Jerome tilted his head, frowning.

Jean nodded in the direction of the autopsy table. "She'll know who they are."

Jerome stepped inside the room and repeated Jean's words.

Brooke's heart skipped a beat. With tense muscles, she placed a dripping set of lungs on the scale as if it was a fragile baby bird and recorded its weight.

"Authorized personnel only." Dr. Gold released a heavy sigh. "Tell Brooke's friend she can see Brooke in the meeting room in about ten minutes."

"All, right." Jean waved. "Thank you. I appreciate it."

"I'll show you where you can wait." Jerome turned and walked past her.

Jean stood unmoving, viewing the autopsy room and its occupants.

"This way, ma'am."

"Right." She turned and followed him.

In the autopsy room, Dr. Gold grunted. "Do you know why she wants to speak with you?" He pressed one knotted finger against the bridge of his glasses and squinted into the body cavity from the other side of the table.

Brooke swallowed hard, rallying the patience she would need to survive the meeting with Jean. "My guess is that she's investigating the disappearance of two women, both from schools I happened to attend."

"Hm. The young medical student who disappeared last winter? Terrible shame. I hope you can be of some assistance. And try not to have any other visitors when you're here working."

"I didn't exactly invite—" Brooke stopped herself from saying anything else about the matter. She had more pressing issues to deal with than Dr. Gold's grouchiness.

She hurried down the main corridor to the family room, adjusting her ponytail. Flickering lights led the way. Might as well get the meeting over with as quickly as possible. Her mouth was dry, and out of nowhere, cramps tightened her stomach. Did she have time for a quick stop to the restroom?

Greg with his omnipresent earbuds walked her way, preoccupied with his phone. She wanted to scream "Hello!" Normally, she wished people would mind their own business and leave her alone, but she wasn't accustomed to being ignored. He glanced at her just before passing. Unless she was imagining things, his stare turned into a glare.

What is wrong these people? Am I the only normal person who works here? She brushed off her sense of discomfort and stepped into the family meeting room where Thompson waited.

Jean held out her hand. "Hi, Brooke. Jean Thompson. I'm a private investigator hired by Rachael Kline's family."

Brooke offered a slight nod and shook Jean's hand. She glanced at the couch, her eyes drawn to the dark stain on one of the cushions. They remained standing.

"Sorry for interrupting you at work. But you haven't answered my calls, so . . . "

Brooke tried to mask her irritation, kneading her hands. She imagined grabbing Jean by the throat and smashing her head against the edge of the door, then telling everyone Jean had a weird seizure and fell. But she knew better. The drama would be endless. And the Klines would just hire a new investigator. "It's okay." She smiled. "How can I help?"

"You're one of nine people who were studying or working at Everett when Jessica Caroll disappeared, and then at Rothaker when Rachael Kline disappeared."

"So many?"

"Yes. I obtained lists of students and staff from both schools."

Brooke reached for her authorization card and remembered she had taken it off before the autopsy. She rested her hands by her sides. "And you're hoping one of us might be able to help?"

Jean lowered her voice and stared into Brooke's eyes. "One of you might be the reason two women disappeared."

A chill shot along Brooke's spine. *Darn, this woman is direct.* She forced a pensive expression. "Really? Gosh."

"You seem to be the only one on the list who had actual known contact with Rachael and Jessica."

Brooke's pulse pounded in her temples, but she forced her face to stay relaxed. "I didn't know Jessica well, but I was interviewed by detectives. Unfortunately, I wasn't of any help. But Rachael, I did know Rachael. She was in my anatomy group with two other students. All of us have racked our brains to come up with relevant info to share with the detectives."

"I've read all of the interviews. I'm going to speak with your other anatomy partner later today. Xander Cross."

"Oh. Well, you should know, he suffered from Post-Traumatic Stress Syndrome during the year. He was often confused. Paranoid. Keep that in mind when you talk to him."

"Is that common knowledge?"

Brooke shrugged. "I couldn't say. Maybe not. Xander is also my boyfriend. That's the only reason I know."

"Hmm." Jean wrote something down on her small spiral pad. "Was there any kind of jealousy between the three of you? Being lab partners, you worked closely together . . ."

"No." Brooke shook her head for emphasis. "Definitely not. Rachael was seeing one of our classmates. Sleeping with him, anyway. And Xander and I weren't even a couple until long after Rachael disappeared. I suppose the situation brought us closer together. Tragedies can do that." Brooke lowered her gaze and placed her hand over her mouth, trying to appear hurt by the recollection.

"Tell me what you think about Rachael's disappearance."

"Her death—I mean, I guess we don't know if she's dead or not—but her disappearance had something to do with Greenwood Circle. Her purse was found there. A matter of being in the wrong place at the wrong time. A crime of opportunity. That's what I think."

Jean's phone rang. She took it out of her jacket pocket, glanced down at it and frowned. "Excuse me." She poked her finger on the screen for a few seconds. Her breath was rushed. "It's my daughter. I'm going to have to leave. Thank you for your time and cooperation. I do have more questions for you, but I can come back, or we can set up a time to talk."

"Sure. You've got my number." She sighed with relief and watched Jean hurry from the meeting room.

"I miss you." Xander's voice on speaker phone filled the quiet kitchen.

"Same." It was sort of true. She didn't mind having Xander around. He was a good study partner, a great running partner, and excellent at several other things she appreciated. "How are you doing? Any nightmares recently?"

"I'm doing okay. It helps to be around people who know exactly what I'm going through. Listen, I talked to a private investigator today."

"Yeah, one came to speak to me, too. Right in the middle of an autopsy."

"She asked if there was some love triangle between you and me and Rachael."

"I told her you and I weren't even together when Rachael disappeared."

"Yeah, I told her that too. But..."

"But what, Xander?"

"She mentioned your connection to the woman who disappeared at Everett."

"My connection?" A sharp burst of anger radiated through her veins. "Jessica dated my ex-boyfriend's friend. I barely knew her. We didn't have anything in common. I wouldn't call that much of a connection." Brooke didn't appreciate the way Jean Thompson was planting ideas in Xander's head. She didn't like it at all. "Honestly, sometimes I wish all these unpleasant disappearances could be left in the past, so we could just move on."

"Me, too. But first, I want to finally learn what happened to Rachael. Don't you?"

Brooke picked a rubber ball off the counter, crushed it in her hand and then slammed it against the wall. She took a deep breath and let it out slowly, closing her eyes and gritting her teeth. "Of course I do."

"Hey. Check out the new report about those missing tourists in Cancun. I still can't believe it happened when you and your family were there."

"What? Oh . . . okay. I will."

"Call me tomorrow?"

"Sure."

She opened her computer browser to the page covered with photos and sensational news headlines, each vying to be opened and read. *NFL quarterback addresses divorce rumors. Governor joins fight on tax repeal. Obesity linked to twelve cancers.* She didn't have to scan for long before she saw an article that caught her interest: *Missing Cancun Tourists Possibly Slain in Shower.*

She clicked on the photo of yellow police tape around the outdoor shower.

Owners of a Cancun beach villa returned to their vacation home to discover a shocking and confusing situation—remnants of a brutal death scene inside their outdoor shower. According to detectives, the human remains had been there for several weeks and were mostly picked apart by domestic animals and wildlife.

The state's deputy attorney general was unable to say at this time if the remains were in any way related to the two American tourists who went missing at the end of May, but they have said that it is a possibility. Several body parts were recently collected by a fishing trawler and positively confirmed as the two missing Americans, Rico Vega and John Peters. Authorities are investigating their deaths. Anyone with information related to the finding is encouraged to come forward.

A variety of crimes in Mexico have made recent headlines, plaguing a country popular with foreign visitors. Explanations for the eruption in crimes include an escalation in gang activity, specifically, the Black Shadows, as well as drug cartels, and the opioid crisis. Mexico had the most murders on record last year. Authorities are under increasing pressure to reduce drug and gang related violence before their tourism industry is permanently affected.

Brooke finished reading the article and laughed.

Chapter Fourteen

The Chief Medical Examiner stood near Brooke with his phone against his ear. A few minutes ago, he had been about to tell her which corpse to get next. Instead, he held up a finger, devoted his full attention to whoever was on the other end of the line, and left Brooke waiting.

Brooke placed one hand on the cold steel of the autopsy table. She stretched through the crown of her head, like a ballerina, lifting her chest and contracting the muscles around her core. To pass the time that would otherwise be wasted, she performed quick sets of tendu exercises, extending her straight leg sharply to the front and drawing it back toward her body.

She hated being idle and she had to leave soon to teach at the gym. Her irritation led to thoughts of other vexing issues related to the Medical Examiner's Office. She considered mentioning the need for a complete overhaul of internal control procedures once Dr. Gold finished his call, but that would only slow their progress even more and she was anxious to do another autopsy before she had to go. Perhaps she would raise the topic once they had the next autopsy underway, if that time ever arrived.

Dr. Gold finally stuffed his phone into his pocket, frowning. "Change of plans. Bring Mrs. Violet Simpson in." The unpleasant smell of afternoon coffee breath wafted from his mouth. "She'll be our seventh examination so far today. I suppose that's progress."

Brooke rushed from the autopsy room to the storage room. *How much more would be accomplished if I were in charge?*

She entered the room and Jerome straightened from his slouched position in front of the computer, sucking in his gut.

Brooke strode past him. "I'm getting Violet Simpson."

His large fingers pounded the keyboard. "Wait. She's already been examined. She didn't have an autopsy though. COD is natural causes."

Brooke twirled around, nostrils flaring. "*This* is ridiculous! Why bother recording data if all the information is going to be wrong! Who did the exam?'

"Uh, Dr. Draven."

She stormed out of the storage room. When Dr. Gold turned her way, her anger kicked up a notch. "Violent Simpson is listed as already having an autopsy and this is—"

"Calm down." Dr. Gold held up a hand. "I know. We're taking another look."

"Oh." Brooke stopped, the tension draining out of her neck and shoulders. She wasn't used to being scolded. She pivoted halfway around and returned to the storage room, sighing. "He does want Violet Simpson," she told Jerome, "even though she's already been examined."

"Oh, okay." Jerome grabbed the handles of a gurney.

The jarring buzz of an electronic bell filled the room.

"Isn't that your signal? A new delivery at the loading dock?"

"Yeah. Can you get this by yourself?" He glanced down at the gurney.

"Of course I can."

Jerome left through the back door to help move newly-arrived corpses inside. Brooke tugged and slid Violet Simpson's body from the drawer to the gurney and pushed it into the brightly-lit autopsy room. Dr. Gold was tapping his pen against the table. He huffed when Brooke entered the room.

As if I'm the one slowing down the process. She positioned the gurney in line with the steel table and transferred the body once again.

"Why are we taking another look?" She unzipped the body bag and looked to Dr. Gold.

"I just received a call from the police about an anonymous tip."

"I see. Anyway, it doesn't appear there was an internal exam done previously." She scanned over the body under the glaring overhead light. Violet Simpson was a black woman in her late fifties. Not especially over or under weight. Normal stretchmarks and a few scars. Nothing about her seemed unusual.

Dr. Gold made hand written notes on paper. Brooke rolled her eyes. *We have a Dictaphone.* More work for her later.

"I'm turning her over." Brooke placed her hands beneath the cadaver's shoulder and lifted. The coolness of the skin came through her latex gloves. "Perhaps this is a good time to speak to you about some—" Brooke's mouth dropped open. A short, jagged gash ran between Mrs. Simpson's shoulder blades. "Holy crap! Is that . . . it looks like a stab wound." She finished turning the body but couldn't pull her gaze away from the torn black and purple tissue. "Since when is a stab wound a natural cause?"

Dr. Gold pushed his glasses toward the bridge of his nose and leaned forward, observing the wound as if it was something as mundane as a paper cut. Brooke studied his reaction, her face tightening, silently urging him to demonstrate a stronger response to their discovery.

"Hmmm." The old man pursed his lips.

"Dr. Draven got this one really wrong." The pitch of Brooke's voice rose with every word, her earlier excitement and exasperation returning. *No one could miss a stab wound.* She fidgeted with her hands, waiting. Dr. Gold still hadn't offered a single comment on the situation. After a few more seconds of silence, she couldn't suppress her outrage any longer. "What are you going to do about it?"

"I'll amend the death certificate and open an investigation. We need to take pictures and collect trace evidence. This is . . . unfortunate."

Why isn't he fuming? Why isn't he stomping around complaining about Dr. Draven's incompetence and the need to fire him immediately? What is going on around here?

After Violet Simpson was subjected to a comprehensive examination, Jerome returned her body to the storage room. Brooke followed. She crossed her arms and rubbed her shoulders for warmth. "Hey, Jerome."

He pushed the drawer the final few inches until it clicked into place, then turned to face her. "Yeah?"

"I need to talk to you,"

"Uh." He tugged at the collar of his lab coat. "N-now?"

"Yes. Privately." She glanced at the door behind her. They were already alone in the storage room, but she grasped his elbow and led him toward a corner.

Jerome let his arm stretch as far as it could before his body followed.

Brooke lowered her voice to a whisper, not releasing his arm. "There's something going on here."

"There is?"

"Come on. Isn't it bothering you, too? How can you stand it?"

Jerome gulped. His gaze dropped to her hand on his elbow.

"The question is, what's to be done about it?"

Jerome swallowed hard and closed his eyes. He leaned toward Brooke, his lips on course for her own.

"Wha—!" Brooke slammed her hand against his chest and shoved him hard. "Jerome! Oh my God! What are you thinking?"

Jerome stumbled backwards. Red splotches formed and spread across his pale skin. Brooke could almost feel the heat of his embarrassment. "I . . . I thought . . . I'm sorry, I—"

She put her hands on her hips. "I'm going to pretend that didn't happen. Jeez. Try to focus here. This is important. Something is going on with the autopsies, or lack of them."

Jerome still looked embarrassed and uncomfortable, like he had just been stung by a swarm of bees. He barely nodded.

"How long have you worked here exactly?"

"Um, almost a year."

"And it doesn't bother you that there are so many mistakes?"

"I, uh, I haven't really noticed."

Brooke tilted her head. "You haven't really noticed?" *Maybe I shouldn't have said anything since I don't know exactly who is involved.* But she couldn't stop her irritation from rolling off her tongue. "Can you imagine if this was a hospital?"

"It's not like bodies are being lost." Jerome shrugged.

"Not that we know of." She sneered as she paced the floor. "There's something broken and suspicious about this system. It's way too easy for things to fall through the cracks. Maybe if Dr. Gold would use the computer system instead of writing everything down . . . anyway, why isn't he retired?"

"Because he's good at what he does. And it's hard to hire people here. This place doesn't pay a lot for doctors. They can do better at a hospital or in private practice." Jerome spoke as if he was repeating something he'd heard many times before. "And his wife died. I guess he doesn't play golf. He needs this place."

"Then he needs to do a better job with it." She twirled the end of her ponytail around her finger.

"I don't even think he takes a salary. Or he gives it all to charity. I heard something like that. He lives in a small townhome somewhere. I mean, I heard it's really nice, but he moved out of a big doctor type house into the townhome after his wife died."

"Hmm. Still, not an excuse. We need to find out what is going on."

"Right." Jerome gulped with a loud squelch. He dropped his gaze to the floor and a new flush of red flooded his cheeks.

Not that I don't have enough problems of my own. She spun around and marched out of the storage room, glancing at the clock. "Crap!" Less than half an hour until her class, and it took almost that long to get to the gym. While helping Dr. Gold in the autopsy room, she'd lost track of time. Grabbing her belongings from a locker, she ran out the back entrance.

Her phone rang from inside her backpack, escalating her stress. She ignored the ringing and spun the dial on her combination lock. After coiling her bike chain below the seat, she walked her bike down from the loading dock and into the secluded back area used for deliveries and pick-ups.

The ringing had stopped, but an annoying *taadaa* of trumpets announced incoming texts. *It can wait. Whatever it is, it can wait.* But in spite of her own instructions, she straddled her bike, yanked her phone out of her bag and read the messages.

I need to talk to you when you have a chance.

It was her mother. She would call her later.

Important. Please call me as soon as you can.

Her mother again.

We're all okay. Didn't mean to worry you. I need to talk to you because the missing rental car key was found in Cancun. Police have questions.

A vein pulsed in Brooke's temple after she read the last text from her mother. She wanted to tilt her head up to the sky and scream at the top of her lungs. Instead, she glared at her phone, clenching her fingers tight around the edges until her knuckles turned white.

First Jean. Now this.

A car accelerated nearby, unexpectedly loud and sudden. The back end of a black sedan was flying straight toward her in reverse. She gasped, rooted to the spot, unable to move as the tail lights came closer. At the last possible second, she leapt from her bike. Her head hit the edge of a retaining wall and she slammed to the ground a few feet away.

The car crushed her bike with a nasty crunch and screech, then shot forward and sped away leaving Brooke splayed across the pavement.

Chapter Fifteen

Brooke was lying on the cracked pavement beside the loading dock, legs spread awkwardly apart in front of her. Stars and zig zag bolts of light danced across her vision when she forced her eyes open. She immediately squeezed them shut again, but the shapes and flashes of light remained. Cautiously, she propped herself up on her elbows. Grit and a slimy substance coated her hands.

"Are you okay?"

She blinked to clear her blurring vision. A big guy was rushing in her direction. The corners of his lab coat flapped open as he ran. Jerome. He stopped at her side and stared down, his face awash with concern. "Are you okay?"

"I . . . I don't know . . . what just happened?" Fear flooded her body at the prospect of broken bones or anything that would prevent her from exercising. Without a major dose of daily exercise, she couldn't cope. She conducted a mental assessment of her body parts and slowly moved her legs so that she was sitting on them, but intuition told her not to get up yet. Shaking inside, she extended each arm and then rolled her neck gently forward. None of her movements elicited pain. Only her head hurt.

"I was near the back door when I heard a noise and ran out here." Jerome moved his hand toward her mangled bike. "I think I heard your bike getting crushed."

"It happened so fast." Brooke's confusion gave way to anger and her hands balled into fists. "Some idiot backed into me when I . . . when I . . . I was reading a message." Her stomach turned. She'd just remembered the last text from her mother, the reason she hadn't seen the car until it was almost too late. "He didn't even look! If I hadn't jumped off my bike when I did . . ."

"Your bike is ruined."

Brooke followed his gaze and frowned. Her overturned bike, her sole means of free transportation, looked pathetic. One of the pedals was bent backwards and the frame was twisted. Sharp pain radiated from the back of her head. She touched the area and her fingers came away covered with blood.

Jerome stared at her hand and his face turned whiter than usual, as if he didn't spend every day surrounded by bloody innards. "You must have hit your head. You need to see a doctor."

"Any more good news you want to tell me?" Feeling a little shaky, she stood and wiped dirt and debris off her hands, smearing one side of her pants with streaks of blood.

"There's a lot of blood." He rubbed the back of his own neck. "Come back inside and have Dr. Gold check it out."

She reached for the back of her head again to determine the size of the painful laceration. "It's not a big deal. A small cut on the head can bleed profusely. It will stop. What I need is a ride. I'm supposed to be teaching a class in ten minutes."

"You shouldn't—"

Her voice rose. "I need to be at the gym in ten minutes."

"Okay, okay. I can give you a ride. Just let me—"

"It has to be now. Please."

"Sure . . . okay. I'll get my keys." Jerome hurried away, but when he looked back, he stopped walking, did a 180, and focused on an area beyond her.

"What are you doing? You need to hurry."

"Did you see that guy?"

The motion of turning, even slowly, made her feel woozy. "What guy?"

"I swear I saw someone. He just disappeared behind the fence."

She squinted in the direction Jerome pointed. "I don't see anyone. Hurry up and get your keys. And grab me a towel for this cut. Please." She placed her hands on her thighs, transferring more blood to her pants, and leaned forward, struggling against a wave of dizziness. Her thoughts raced, sorting through the ramifications of a possible concussion.

Jerome kept moving, muttering, mostly to himself, "I think there could be someone following you."

She straightened herself to look around. "No one is following me," she snapped. Eventually she focused her attention on the door Jerome would come back through, willing him to hurry. "I can't believe this is happening. I'm never late," she murmured aloud through gritted teeth. Her anger and frustration kept her from realizing how much worse things could have been, if not for her quick reflexes.

Jerome returned, huffing and puffing like he really had run to get his keys. He pointed to his car and opened the passenger side door for Brooke.

"Speed if you can, okay?" Brooke got in, slammed her door, and they drove away.

Chapter Sixteen

It was almost five thirty. East Dalton's rush hour traffic would be at its peak. According to the schedule he was given, Brooke was expected to leave her day job and head straight to Peak Fitness. He didn't anticipate anything interesting would happen on her way from one job to the next, but he didn't exactly mind watching her. She either ran, walked, or biked to wherever she was going. No matter how she traveled, she looked good doing it. Everything she did seemed purposeful yet effortless, so that he now thought of her as a graceful machine. He finished his espresso, tossed the cup into the trash can, and drove his motorcycle over to the Medical Examiner's Office. Several vantage points there allowed him a good view of the back of the building without being seen.

She must have been held up doing something inside the office, because it was nearing six o'clock and her bike was still locked to one of the support beams in the back. He was about to take off, figuring she had left early, gotten a ride from someone and left her bike behind, when she finally rushed out the door. She unlocked her bike and straddled it, eyes glued to her phone. A car backed up, faster than normal, heading straight for her. She leapt out of the way and took a brutal fall. Thank God she had quick reflexes. His first reaction was anger at the thought of her being hurt. He was torn between going after the car and running to her side. She wasn't supposed to know who he was yet, but he couldn't leave her there alone when she might have been seriously hurt. He started toward her, to check on her, then held back when he saw a big guy in a white lab coat run out of the building and over to her side, looking very concerned. She yelled at the guy in the lab coat, refused medical treatment, and insisted on a ride. No crying. No signs of panic or fear.

He shook his head in disbelief. And by that time, it was too late to go after the car that almost hit her. He replayed the scene in his mind. It could have been an accident—someone so preoccupied with getting out of there that they forgot to look before backing up. But he thought not. The timing was too perfect, as if the car had been waiting for just the right moment. He was so lost in thought he didn't realize he had moved from his original position and was in plain sight as the lab-coat guy unexpectedly turned his way.

Oh, crap.

He ducked and spun around, making sure he wouldn't be seen again.

At his townhome, he hacked into the Cancun police department's database and researched all the information available on the murders of the two American tourists. If the others were right about Brooke, she was something else.

He called his connection again.

"So, Brooke Walton really had that rental car key last?"

A siren started wailing on the other end of the phone.

"She took it with her for a run on the beach. According to her parents."

"Wow. Jeez." He whistled his exhale. "It's hard to believe, but . . ."

"Just keep watching and keep us posted. We'll take care of the rest and get confirmation."

"Will do."

Chapter Seventeen

The exercise studio was packed, each person close to a mat and sur-rounded by his or her own collection of equipment. A few were stretching or doing crunches. Several were preoccupied with their phones. More than one of them had forlorn expressions, shifting their gaze from the clock on the wall to the doorway. When she rounded the corner, someone yelled, "She's here!" Cheers erupted when she entered the room.

A young woman in the front row jumped up to greet her. "I'm so glad you came!"

"You're never late." Tom, a lean and muscular workout addict, stretched his arms overhead while he spoke. "We were worried. Oh." He pointed to her leg. "Is that blood?"

Brooke glanced down at the dark stains on her legs and grimaced. "I'm so sorry, everyone." She plugged her phone into the stereo system. "I had a little accident with my bike when I was leaving my day job. But don't worry, I'll make it up to you during class."

"We don't doubt that," laughed a man to her right.

"Are you sure you're okay?"

Brooke wasn't sure who was asking. She attached her microphone. "Yes. Thank you. I'm fine." She moved her gaze across the room. "Looks like everyone has a ball, a band, and a set of weights. So that's what we'll use."

She pushed the button to start her play list and a steady beat filled the air. "Let's get going."

She began the class by warming up with squats and lunges. After only a few repetitions, her head pounded like someone was banging away inside it with a small hammer, confirming what she already suspected. She had a concussion. She stopped lunging but kept counting as she turned around to face everyone. "Keep going! I'm just going to talk you through the work out today. That's right. Good job. Spine long. Sit back into your heels. Four more."

There was nothing to be done for her concussion, aside from allowing it time to heal. She hoped it wouldn't take more than a week or two. At least the external bleeding had stopped, and her cap covered the dark, damp mess in her blonde hair. She cringed at the notion of backing off her workouts for a while. The thought of a few days without intense exercise made her nervous. Exercise kept her calm and sane, kept her from losing control. She needed it now more than ever. Unbelievable, all that was happening. She hated all this . . . drama. But she would get through it. All of it. One annoying dilemma at a time.

"Concentrate on what you're doing. Nothing is moving right now except those glutes! Last set of eight. Don't give up now. Make it count." She wove through the mats, correcting form and encouraging everyone to work harder.

After class, three different people offered to drive her to her apartment. She graciously accepted a ride from a woman headed in her direction. Once she was dropped off, she unlocked her apartment door, stepped inside, and made a bee-line for the bathroom cabinet. She grabbed the bottle of ibuprofen and popped four into her mouth. Then she called her mother.

"Hi, Mom."

"Brooke! I left you messages hours ago."

"Sorry I couldn't get back to you until now. I saw your messages after work but then someone ran over my bike, by accident. I had to get a ride to the gym and I was almost late for my class."

"Oh my gosh! Someone ran over your bike? Were you on it? Are you okay?"

"My bike isn't, but I'll be fine. What did you want to tell me?" She grabbed a half-full water bottle from the refrigerator and gulped it down.

"I know you're busy, but this is important. You're not going to believe it when I tell you."

"What happened? You said someone found the rental car key."

"Yes. The key was found with, well, remember those young men who disappeared in Cancun when we were there?"

"Yeah, of course I remember. It was all over the news." Brooke sat down and tried to focus, massaging her temples. The pain wasn't unbearable, just enough to make her desperate to go to bed and shut out the rest of the world.

"It still is all over the news. You'd know if you ever watched TV. Well, the key was found with parts of their remains."

Darn it! Her heart rate spiked and her headache reached a new height. *Breathe. Just breathe.* "Really?"

"The police have the key, and apparently it had blood from the victims on it. You know how they can tell that in their labs? Of course you do, you're a doctor. Almost a doctor. So, your father gets a call from the police, because they traced the key right to him through the rental agency."

"What did they say to him?"

"Well, they had all sorts of questions."

"Like?"

"I don't remember exactly—"

"Please try. I'd like to know."

"Basically, your father told them how we had lost the key our first night there while you were running on the beach."

"Oh. So is that—"

"Whatever happened to those boys happened not far from wherever you were running. It makes me ill to think about it. I should have never let you run alone at night, especially in a strange country. Remember that I didn't want you to go? And believe me, the police weren't impressed with us for letting you run in the dark alone. It was embarrassing. We felt like inadequate parents."

A wave of nausea was slowly but surely building. She didn't know if it was from the ibuprofen dissolving in her empty stomach, or a symptom of the concussion, or just a stress reaction. She wasn't thinking clearly, thoughts and implications flashed through her mind, and she laughed.

"What's funny about any of that?"

"Nothing. Nothing. I guess I'm just relieved that nothing happened to me. That I'm okay. And it's not like you let a twelve-year old run alone at night. I'm twenty-three." She focused on the rise and fall of her chest with each breath.

"It's my job to protect you. So, the main reason I wanted to speak with you is to let you know that the police will be calling you."

Her jaw clenched. "Why?"

"You're involved in this terrible situation now, like it or not. We told them that if you'd seen anything suspicious you certainly would have mentioned it to us. Still, they think it's possible you might have seen something when you were out there. We shouldn't have let you go."

"I know. Believe me. I know."

"We told them you met up with some people your age and went swim-ming."

An uncomfortable lump was forming in Brooke's throat. She gulped.

"We didn't even know if they were young men or young women or how many or from where. I don't think you told us. Did you remember their names? Maybe they saw something."

Stress and frustration swirled to a crescendo inside her. This was one of those times when she needed to go for a hard run. But she couldn't. Getting her heart pumping like mad would be terrible for her head injury. "Hey, mom, sorry, I've got to go."

"Oh. Well, all right. Be careful. Take care of yourself."

"Always."

"Call me if the police talk to you."

"I will."

She said goodbye to her mother and considered asking Jeff if he had any food, but the tight, troubling sensation around her head made her want to close her eyes and be alone more than anything else. She lowered herself into her chair and powered on her laptop to do a little research. Her eyes and brain rebelled against the glare from the screen. She reduced the brightness, but her pupils still reacted to the light. She snapped her laptop closed with frustration.

It's not the end of the world. This will pass, and you will be fine.

She took slow, measured breaths to stay calm. Thankfully it was sum-mer, not the school year when she had to be on her laptop constantly to complete her assignments and prepare for quizzes and tests and couldn't spare a few days off. She sighed. A week or two of taking it easy on her workouts and not spending too much time on the computer should be all her brain required to heal.

I can do it.

I can do anything.

Her phone rang. Xander. She ignored his call and texted him instead.

I have a bad headache. I'm going to sleep.

On the sagging mattress she'd purchased from the previous apartment owner, she stayed in bed for longer than usual, her mental energy whirling as she tried to devise a plan. She tried not to think about her concussion because it made her feel weak and vulnerable.

Her phone beeped with an incoming text. She rolled onto her side and scooped it off the floor.

Hi. It's Jerome. How is your head?

She scowled. "How did he get my number?" she said aloud, typing—*I'm fine.*

She wasn't fine, but her persistent headache wasn't her biggest problem. It was the mounting pressure from Jean Thompson and all the other people still demanding to know what happened to Rachael and from the key that was no longer lost.

I need to permanently take care of a few things, and fast, before my whole world falls apart.

Chapter Eighteen

Yesterday had been a hell of a day. His little burst of rage was no surprise. But when he peeled out of the parking lot, he hadn't been thinking clearly at all. The drugs made him act on impulse. And then when he got home, and Alyssa showed up, high as a kite and acting like they had a real thing between them, well, it was one interfering chick too many.

The sun had risen hours ago when he stepped outside onto his back patio. There she was, still asleep on a chaise, exactly where he'd left her at three in the morning, after he'd given her a hard shove, shouted at her to leave, and stormed inside. He had locked his door behind him and assumed she'd go away. What more of a hint did she need? Even with her smudged makeup channeling a racoon, the make-up he hated because it reminded him that she was a whore, her expression was peaceful. That pissed him off. Her, looking all relaxed when she was causing him a ton of stress by crashing on his back patio. This wasn't a slum house.

"Alyssa," he hissed. "What are you still doing here?" *Big mistake letting her think we were more than business associates who also had sex.*

He drew his hand through his rumpled hair, thinking how best to deal with the current situation. Telling her to F- off yesterday was obviously ineffective, so a different approach was in order. Last night, he dreamed she was begging him to open the door and let her in. Although, in hindsight, since she'd never left, had it really been a dream?

"Alyssa." He didn't even try to mask his displeasure.

He was first surprised by the limpness in her arm when he grabbed it. He tugged her forward and her whole body collapsed.

She's still passed out. Or is she? Yes, she must be. She's just passed out. This probably happens to her all the time. Passing out wherever for the night. That's what happens to whores and drug addicts.

He touched his fingers to her throat. She had no pulse and her skin was cold.

Crap.

He pressed his fists against the side of his head.

Oh, crap!

He dragged her off the chaise and started CPR as soon as she flopped to the ground. Pressing. Pumping. Pressing. Pumping. Sweat rolled down his temples and dripped onto her chest. He continued after five minutes, then ten. A painful, fiery sensation flared through his arms. He didn't let up until the burning subsided and his muscles succumbed to a numbness that rendered them useless.

This is not happening. This is not happening.

He collapsed back on his heels, slick with sweat and trembling from exhaustion.

Panic hit him at once like an unexpected freight train barreling down the tracks. His gaze darted over the stone wall dividing his backyard from his neighbor's. The woman sometimes came outside early in the morning to water her plants. He prayed they were damp enough from yesterday's rain and she'd skipped a day.

With despair, he stared back down at Alyssa's lifeless body.

No, no. She's dead. She's really dead.

He rocked forward and back on his knees, covering his mouth with his hands. He encountered the dead every single day, but this was different. This dead body, at his house, had the capacity to destroy him. An investigation would mean bad business for him. His stomach lurched. He'd probably lose his job . . . again. And then what would he do the next time Scope sent his men for their money?

He hoisted Alyssa off the ground. Her head hung backward, swaying from side to side with each hurried step toward his house. He willed his neighbor's door to stay closed until he was safely out of sight.

Inside his kitchen, he paced around, still holding Alyssa in his arms, unsure of where to put her. He couldn't bear to look at her. His hands were clammy with perspiration. His legs grew weak and he was breathing too fast, not taking in enough oxygen. He needed to sit before he hyperventilated. Waves of nausea rolled through his body.

What am I gonna do? Make her disappear? Leave her somewhere? Call the police? No. I can't call the police.

After a crazed rush of desperate ideas, he sent Alyssa's body tumbling into the empty closet of his spare bedroom. He tore off his clothes and stuffed them in the washing machine. In the shower, his face contorted with anguish, he wrestled with the best course of action, the one least likely to end with his ass in jail. Dressing, he struggled with each shirt button because he couldn't stop his hands from shaking. He locked up his home and drove to work to get a body bag.

How had it come to this?

On a few rough nights he had turned to Alyssa for comfort and she had stayed until the morning. Maybe he'd asked her to. She said he had pleaded. But only because he was feeling down, couldn't bear to be alone, and didn't have enough money to pay for her time. And then there were the days when he slept at her awful place, when Scope's men were looking for him. Still, that alone shouldn't have led her to believe they were actual partners or equals in any way. They weren't. Far from it. He wasn't as messed up as her. Once he got through this rough patch, he had planned to clean up and start seeing someone more like him—ambitious and educated, from a supportive family. But, until then, he hadn't wanted to be alone. Couldn't stand to be alone. Especially after a big loss. He had needed someone else by his side, someone who could make him feel like he was still okay, and the most appealing thing about Alyssa was that she hadn't dumped him like all his other so-called friends.

He shut off the vacuum and sat down, dropping his head into his hands. He got a whiff of himself—alcohol and sweat—and cringed. When had he last brushed his teeth?

Now that she was gone, he missed her. As he eliminated all traces of her existence from his place, his loneliness followed him around, piercing him with sharp, incessant jabs. If Alyssa were there, she could have been a big help with the situation. She wouldn't have panicked. Maybe she would have prevented him from getting all-out drunk while he figured out what to do. Maybe he wouldn't have passed out for God knows how long. But more likely, she'd have gone out to buy more booze to carry them through the ordeal.

He searched Alyssa's coat and found an interior pocket. A roll of hundreds and twenties sat nestled inside. Thousands of dollars.

That bitch!

She knew he was desperate for money. She could have helped, instead of watching him sell his Rolex, a gift from his grandfather and the last decent thing he still owned besides his AMG. He pocketed the cash before he tossed her clothes into his firepit, doused them with lighter fluid, and dropped a match on top. Flames shot up and he jumped back. Tears rolled down his cheeks as he watched her clothes burn and ashes float up to the sky. He wasn't grieving so much for her, as for himself. Her death was an inconvenience. One more nasty complication in his life. He wanted nothing more than for the nightmare to end.

Why haven't I gotten a call about the body? Surely someone has found her by now. What's taking so long?

He reached into his pocket to check his phone and came up empty handed. *Oh my God! I left it in the car!* That was hours ago. Nausea welled up inside him. He rushed away from the firepit, feeling like he might vomit. *No. No. No. This can't be happening! I missed the call!*

He paced around, pulling at his hair.

Pull yourself together. It might not be too late.

He needed to drive back to work and make sure the situation was under control.

Chapter Nineteen

Police in Mexico, working on the murder investigation of Rico Vega and John Peters, say they have their first break in this disturbing case. Authorities have been under increased pressure to find justice for the victim's families and to prevent a massive revenue loss for their tourist industry. Resort owners and locals agreed that someone must have seen or heard something. They expect the lack of tips stemmed from fear of retaliation from gang members like the notorious Black Shadows.

According to Police Chief, Ramon Garcia, the tides have now turned. The nature of the evidence had not been released, but authorities claim they have found something to directly link someone, or, most likely, multiple persons to the crime.

Jean turned away from the television, leaned her elbows on her desk, and dropped her head into her hands.

I could use a little turning of the tides about now.

Rachael Kline's case once had the full attention of law enforcement and the media and went nowhere. What had led her to believe she could discover new leads for a six-month old case when a city full of detectives had failed? Possibly her opinion that a woman couldn't simply disappear without a trace, even when it appeared she had.

How long could she keep billing the Klines if she didn't have any solid new information? How long would they keep paying her? This was her only case. Aside from her occasional work retrieving and analyzing criminal records and doing background checks for a few attorney friends, she had no other current income aside from her small pension. Good thing Millie's favorite food was mac and cheese, usually on sale for ninety-nine cents.

She'd been over and over the files and reports, peeling back the layers of the investigation, looking for anything that stuck out.

Think! Think! Think! She ran her fingernails through her hair and over her scalp. *What do I have? What am I missing?*

If the perpetrator was a complete random stranger, Jean might not ever find the connection. But most disappearances and deaths weren't random. More often than not, the guilty party came from within the victim's inner circle.

Jean picked up the records of Rachael's anatomy group partners. Only two had been in the country when Rachael disappeared. Brooke Walton and Xander Cross.

Something about Brooke Walton seemed off during their first interview. Brooke was an uber-educated, driven and accomplished young woman. She maintained her poise exceptionally well when Jean spoke with her. Jean didn't know many people like her, and that alone could explain why she just seemed different. But she believed there was something else. Call it a gut feeling, or ex-cop intuition, Jean couldn't put her finger on it exactly, but she had a sense Brooke might know something she wasn't sharing.

The records indicated Xander was a former college football player and ex-military. He must be big and strong. More than capable of overpowering a young woman. But why would he? Did he have too much testosterone for his own good? Was it drugs? An accident? Brooke Walton and he were now in a relationship. Was Brooke covering for him?

What a shame she'd barely had a few minutes to speak with Brooke before she got the text about Millie. But Brooke was here in East Dalton. One more call or visit to see her wouldn't hurt anyone.

Chapter Twenty

Brooke strode into the storage room, arms wrapped around her chest, hugging herself to ward off the chill. Jerome sat at the computer station in the center, fingers poised above the keyboard. He turned to her with puffy, bloodshot eyes. "Hey."

"What happened to you?" Brooke shot him a sidelong glance. "Too early for you?"

"Huh?"

"Looks like you missed a night of sleep."

"Oh. Uh, I was playing Fortnite until the morning. I had just leveled up —"

"Yeah, I'm not a gamer."

Jerome's pale skin flushed with pink. "How did you get here? I saw your broken bike still locked up out back."

Brooke circled the perimeter of the room. "I jogged. Slower than I would have liked, I still can't run because . . . never mind. Anyway, I've got to take my bike somewhere to get it fixed."

"Do you need help getting it to a bike shop? I mean, I have a car and—"

"Yeah. That would be great. Maybe tomorrow around noon. If we're both available. Thanks for the offer."

"You're not doing data entry today?"

"Not today. Dr. Gold requested my help." She stood in front of the drawers, reading labels. "I'm getting Jane Doe."

Jerome yawned and tapped on the keyboard. "She's in drawer P-32."

"Got it. Why is she unidentified? Or did someone who works here just happen to lose her name? That wouldn't surprise me." She heaved the drawer out from the wall. "Is there any information about her in the computer?"

"She was discovered in the early morning. Alone. No identification. No clothes. No fingerprints in the system. Suspected drug overdose."

"No one examined her where she was found?"

Jerome shrugged. "No medical examiner available. The police can't wait around all night. If no one can come, they have the body transported here. I know because one of the guys who delivers bodies is my buddy. He works the night shift. He got me this job."

"Paul? The one you were protecting the other day?"

Jerome pulled at the collar of his lab coat. "Well, I wouldn't say, I mean, we don't know that—"

"You're right. Just forget I said anything."

"Here, let me help you." Jerome stood from the chair.

Brooke held up her hand. "I've got it. I don't need help."

Jerome grabbed one end of the body bag anyway. Together, they transferred it onto the gurney, into the autopsy room, and onto the table next to where Dr. Gold stood, tapping his infernal cane.

Brooke clasped the zipper, peeled the body bag partway open, and gasped.

"What is it?" Jerome leaned in.

Brooke kept staring, one hand covering her mouth.

The petite woman's long brown hair laid across her fair-skinned shoulders, with a single stripe of deep red color on the left side. Her health had been recently neglected, but she was still attractive. Remove the nose piercing and dark eye make-up and the dead woman could have been Rachael Kline's identical twin. The same Rachael who departed the Rothaker Medical School dorm in pieces spread throughout six heavy-duty garbage bags. Or was it seven? If Brooke hadn't cut her up and single handedly tossed those bags into the dumpster, someone could have convinced her that Rachael had spent the last six months living an entirely different life than that of a privileged medical student, a rough life, and now here she was lying in front of them.

"What's wrong?" Dr. Gold crossed his arms. "Do you know her?"

"No. I . . . I don't know her." Brooke steadied herself against the table. "She looks a lot like someone I used to know at school."

"Might as well use this thing today." Dr. Gold mumbled before speaking into the Dictaphone. "This is the autopsy of an unidentified, Caucasian female conducted by myself and intern Brooke Walton. The subject appears to be in her early twenties. Butterfly tattoo on the frontal side of her left shoulder. She wasn't wearing any clothes when she was found. Body temperature, rigor mortis, and lividity indicates estimated time of death as twenty-eight hours ago. A man discovered her in Greenwood Circle. It's an abandoned park in the city."

Greenwood Circle? The same run-down park where I planted Rachael's pocketbook. "She couldn't have laid naked in Greenwood Circle all day without someone noticing her. Could she?" Brooke moved around the table to get a different view.

"Not likely. No. I wouldn't think so." Dr. Gold shifted his weight. His knees cracked loud enough for everyone to hear. "Go ahead and tell me what we need to do, Miss Walton."

Brooke finally regained her focus. "Well, a blood sample for analysis, to see if she did overdose, and make an impression of her teeth in case we can match them with dental records. Then we'll examine her body to confirm that there isn't a different primary cause of death."

Dr. Gold nodded. Jerome finished removing the body bag and circled the table, snapping pictures with the digital camera.

Brooke spread Jane Doe's toes apart. "Fresh needle tracks between her toes. Older, barely visible tracks on her arms."

Jerome set the camera down. He flicked a sheet into the air and let it float down over the body.

Brooke checked the nasal passages and ear canals. She moved part of the sheet aside and rotated a slender arm, so the palm faced up. "Bruising on her wrists." She adjusted the sheet and the light for further examination. "Deformities in her chest wall." She ran her gloved finger around the area and lapsed into momentary silence before saying, "An uneven step off in ribs below her heart. Possible fractured rib. Like someone was pounding on her chest? I'm going to turn her over."

Jerome stepped up, sliding his hands under the corpse.

"I got this." Brooke angled her body so Jerome was unable to help.

With Jane Doe in a prone position, Brooke stretched forward, hovering over the cadaver. "She has a triangular shaped abrasion on her lower back, and there's a strange indentation inside it. Two small depressions in her skin."

"What do you make of it?" Dr. Gold cupped an elbow with one hand.

"Whatever it was punctured the skin, but there's no sign of bleeding to—"

"It happened after she died." Jerome nodded.

"Right. There are traces of a gray powdery substance in her hair, across her shoulders and back. It's faint, but smeared into her skin, like she was dragged through it."

Dr. Gold turned to Jerome. "Take samples and label them. Scrape under her fingernails. And then you can go and do something else. I don't need both of you here."

Jerome yawned again, covering his mouth with the back of his gloved hand.

Brooke moved down the table. "I'm examining her genitalia." She lifted the sheet covering Jane Doe's lower body and folded it over her torso. She repositioned the light and the cadaver's legs. "Visible tears and abrasions. Evidence of a recent sexual assault, or rough sex. And healed abrasions. Jane Doe is possibly a prostitute."

"She looks like the type of girl that hangs out near the train station." Jerome nodded. "Some of them are young."

Everyone stopped working to stare at him.

"What?" His face turned a deep pink like he was overheated. "I drove by there once with friends. We didn't stop or anything."

Brooke smirked, returning her attention to Jane Doe. She swabbed for seminal fluid. "There's no semen, but it's strange. I think she's already had an internal cleansing."

Dr. Gold frowned. "That's not unusual for a prostitute, Miss Walton. If she was, indeed, a prostitute."

Brooke grabbed a fine-toothed comb and ran it carefully through the pubic hair. "Nothing."

"There's nothing under her nails either." Jerome lifted Jane Doe's hand toward his face and sniffed. "Her hands smell like bleach."

Brooke set down the comb. "I'd say that's unusual for a prostitute."

The door to the exam room opened. The team turned toward the sound of heavy breathing. For a few seconds, no one spoke, and no one moved.

Dr. Draven stepped inside, panting like he'd sprinted down the hall. He avoided eye contact with everyone in the room and stared at the body on the table. With pale skin, red-rimmed eyes, and sunken cheeks, if he were to lie down on a gurney he could be mistaken for a cadaver.

"Hey." Jerome was the first to break the strained silence.

"Dr. Draven?" Dr. Gold cleared his throat. "Well, this is a surprise."

Draven rubbed a hand through his disheveled hair and rolled his shoulders back. He stared at them, then patted his pockets and glanced around. "Oh, uh..." He grabbed a lab coat from the wall. "Yeah, I was, uh..."

Brooke refrained from asking if he had received a call to examine Jane Doe in Greenwood Circle last night. Obviously, he missed it because he was partying all night. Out of the corner of her eyes, she stared at him with disgust, resisting the powerful urge to tell him what she thought of him. His complexion was a washed-out gray, and it wouldn't have surprised her if he threw up at any moment.

"We have an unidentified female," the elderly doctor told Draven. "She was delivered as a suspected drug overdose."

It's more suspicious than that now. Brooke didn't say so aloud. She didn't want to involve Draven. She wanted him to go away.

Dr. Draven slid his arms into the lab coat. "I can take care of it. Since I'm here."

Brooke held her breath, afraid of what Dr. Gold might say, worried she might not get to examine Jane Doe after all.

"We've got this." Dr. Gold waved a gloved hand. "Why don't you go home and rest up in case you get some calls tonight." Dr. Gold's eyes remained on Draven. "You can proceed, Brooke."

Draven scowled. "You're letting the intern do the autopsy?"

Dr. Gold didn't answer.

Draven threw up his hands. "If there's no reason to believe it's a homicide, all you need is a blood sample. Why collect the data? Especially if there's a backlog. That's the kind of thing that slows everything down. That's why there always *is* a backlog."

"I'll worry about that." Dr. Gold glowered.

Jane Doe's body offered up an intricate puzzle waiting to be solved. Less than a minute after resuming the autopsy, Brooke forgot about Draven hovering close by. All signs of life around her— Draven breathing and fidgeting, the occasional crack of Dr. Gold's knuckles, the electronic bell indicating the arrival of new bodies, Jerome trudging across the room, the hum of the air conditioning system, and the rattle of creaky pipes—fell away. Everything except the cadaver faded into the background like elements of an insignificant dream.

Brooke pinched the cadaver's skin between her fingers. "Add dehydration to the list of findings."

Dr. Draven scratched the side of his neck. "Another symptom of drug addiction."

"I know." Brooke frowned. *Why is he still here? Is he waiting for me to make a mistake because he knows I reported his?*

The internal examination revealed recent sternal and rib fractures. Brooke scrunched up her mouth. "With this many injuries, maybe she was taking drugs for the pain. Addictions sometimes start with pain killers."

"So, it's a drug overdose then," Dr. Draven wrung his hands. "As originally suspected."

"The tox report will make that determination." Dr. Gold winced, massaging his knuckles. "Get her teeth, Brooke. Then you can go ahead and put her back together."

Brooke turned to get the dental imprints. "Whoever wiped Jane Doe's hands and insides of trace evidence made a big mistake. I mean, otherwise no one might have suspected foul play."

Clang! Bang! Clang!

Brooke jerked her head around at the sound of steel instruments crashing to the floor.

Dr. Draven stood with his hands raised, the utensils at his feet. A stainless-steel cup continued to twirl, spinning on its side until its momentum slowed and it rolled across the floor. He muttered something and bent over to collect everything. The hand that remained on the counter bumped against a pair of scissors teetering on the edge. They dropped with another loud clamor.

Dr. Gold coughed and turned away.

Brooke waited for the Chief Examiner to look at her. "When do you think we'll know Jane Doe's identity?"

"Maybe never." Dr. Draven looked paler than when he first joined them. "That's how it is with some of these drug addicts and prostitutes." He moved closer to Brooke. The smell of liquor floated off his breath.

Brooke took a step to the side, away from Draven. "We need to find out who did this to her. I mean, who wiped her nails and washed her insides clean? And why."

Draven's head whipped around. "That's not your job."

Brooke concealed her anger behind a disingenuous smile, and then, much to her own surprise, her smile broadened. Dr. Draven had given her an incredible idea. An idea that might erase the connection between the two women she had killed. An idea so wonderful, it might make most of her current troubles disappear.

She stepped back and lifted her chin, assuming perfect posture. "You're absolutely right, Dr. Draven. That's for the police to figure out."

Chapter Twenty-One

Brooke carried a package from her mailbox to her kitchen counter. Wetting her lips, she used her apartment key to saw through the packaging tape and open the small box inside. The switchblade gleamed in the morning light streaming through her window.

The family vacation had taught her the importance of being prepared for every opportunity. Unfortunately, she'd also learned that even the most intelligent, most thoughtful people could experience moments of carelessness. Because of the rental car key, she still didn't know what the final consequence of her mistake would be. She hated mistakes and she hated people who made them. She set her jaw, determined to make up for her error.

She opened the knife and lightly ran her finger along the blade. Not as sharp as a scalpel, but it wasn't like she could go running around East Dalton with one of those in her pocket. This little gem would fit neatly inside her running belt for easy travel. She slipped it into her backpack and headed to work.

In the locker room, she changed into scrubs before stopping at Dr. Gold's office.

Mya stood in his doorframe in her much-too-big lab coat, her hands clasped together in front of her chest. "Could you come to the autopsy room for a consult, please?" Mya's meek, timid voice irritated Brooke.

"I'll be there as soon as I can." Dr. Gold rummaged around in a desk drawer. "You'll have to be patient."

Mya thanked him and walked away, passing Brooke without giving her a second glance. In fact, it appeared Mya went to great lengths to pretend she didn't see her. Shrugging off the insult, Brooke wished she could be the one to figure out whatever it was Mya needed. She loved a challenge.

"Good morning." *I hope he needs me to work in the autopsy room.*

"Hmmff. I'm glad you got here early. The paperwork is piling up on your desk. You must be way behind."

"I'll get right to it." She held back a sarcastic retort. She imagined peeling Dr. Gold's weathered skin off his swollen knuckles and studying his gnarled bones.

Sure enough, the pile of papers on her desk had multiplied since the previous morning. She sank into her office chair and gulped down water from a plastic bottle, waiting for her computer. Pipes rumbled and vibrated inside the stained walls. After logging in, she clicked through prompts, headed straight to the intake inventory list. She scanned down the list of cadavers currently at the Medical Examiner's Office. Rachael Kline's doppelganger was still listed as a Jane Doe.

Brooke tapped her fingertips on top of her desk, still staring at the screen. How was it possible that Jane Doe hadn't been identified yet? No one had reported her missing? Jane Doe and Rachael Kline had an eerily similar resemblance, and they were around the same age, yet Rachael's disappearance had instigated a flurry of police work. Detectives had flooded campus and the areas where Rachael volunteered, interviewing everyone. "When did you see her last?" "How was she acting?" "Where were you last Friday night?" The media soon followed, swooping in just like the hungry seagulls in Cancun, hoping for any morsel they could twist into a story. And now, six long months later, a private detective was breathing down Brooke's neck, still attempting to uncover the truth. How different things were for Jane Doe.

Brooke rested her elbows on her desk, hands forming a steeple.

So far, it's as if Jane Doe never existed.

Good.

If no one else cared about Jane Doe, all the better for Brooke. She needed to get the ball rolling out of her court and into one where it belonged.

Someone murdered Jane Doe. And whoever did it could have easily killed Rachael, too.

She scooted her chair closer to her desk. The more she considered the situation, the more she convinced herself that Jane Doe had indeed been murdered and that Jane Doe's killer and Rachael's killer were the same person.

She rose, feet planted in a wide stance, hands on her hips.

Somewhere in East Dalton, a killer is hiding. A killer who goes after a specific type. I must find him, or her, before the police do, and get Jean Thompson off my back. And maybe then, when the murderer is apprehended, everyone will forget about Rachael, once and for all.

With a look of stone-cold determination, Brooke bit back a smile. She had a lot of work ahead of her, but she was confident in her ability to accomplish whatever she set her mind to doing.

She hustled to the storage room and the drawer with Jane Doe inside. With a glance at the doors behind her, she pulled the drawer open and unzipped the body bag. The resemblance to Rachael was more pronounced now that the heavy make-up had been washed off and her face was clean. Her skin was tinged unearthly-blue yet appeared fresher than when they first examined her. A clear image of Rachael's crumpled body flashed into Brooke's mind. Rachael doused in blood. Copious amounts of blood. What a mess it could have been. *Could anyone else have kept it contained like I did?*

Brooke stood with her back to the entrance, blocking the view from the door. She grabbed her phone out of her backpack and snapped a picture of Jane Doe's head and the butterfly tattoo. She dropped her phone into her backpack and removed a plastic sandwich bag. She pinched a strand of the cadaver's long, dark hair between her fingers, yanked it out, and placed it in the bag.

She was leaving the autopsy room as Jerome entered. His eyes lingered on her as she passed, the corners of his lips just starting to curl up. He walked right into the open door, stubbing his toe on the bottom edge. "Ow." He jerked his foot off the ground and winced. "I'm okay." He straightened himself, limping toward the center of the room. "All good." He winced with each step. "Yep. I'm fine." The words were more groaned than spoken.

"Hey." She lowered her voice. "My login isn't working. Can I borrow yours?"

"For the computer?"

She rolled her eyes toward the ceiling. "Yes. For the computer."

"Why isn't yours working?"

She sighed. "I don't know. But I can't log in and I can't do my job. So, can I borrow yours?"

"Oh. Um—"

"Jerome!" Dr. Gold's yell turned into a cough and soon enough he was bent over hacking and coughing.

"Coming." Jerome hustled down the hall.

Darn.

She followed Jerome to Dr. Gold's office and stepped in front of him. "Excuse me. I noticed Jane Doe's tox report isn't back yet."

Dr. Gold coughed a final time and straightened, his eyes watery. "We won't have that for another week. Maybe two." He lifted a few pages from the stack of papers in front of him, lowered his head and peered into them, lifted a few more, frowned, dug into another pile. "Forget about what I said earlier, Brooke. I'd like you to help with examinations again."

Help? I'd say I was the one doing them. But inside, she was thrilled he had changed his mind. The pile of papers on her desk could wait.

Jerome shifted from one foot to the other. "Um, what did you need me for?"

"Never mind now." He rose slowly from behind his desk like every movement resulted in a little pain. "Brooke can do it."

Chapter Twenty-Two

*I*s this slutty enough?

She slipped a black workout tank over her head and pulled on black yoga pants.

Maybe.

Standing on her tiptoes, she checked herself out in the mirror over the bathroom sink.

Nope.

Dressing like a prostitute wasn't working out too well. None of the clothes in her closet looked the part. She didn't own any jewelry - much less gawdy, flashy stuff - and her only high heels were her very sensible interview pumps.

Brooke bit off a piece of her protein bar and set it on the nightstand. She leaned on the wall beside her closet, coming to the only possible conclusion: she was searching for an outfit she didn't own.

She had pretty much given up when the doorbell rang.

Through her peep hole, Jeff stood outside with a brimming grocery bag from Healthy Food Planet in his arms. She opened the door.

"Hey." He popped a grape into his mouth. "Just stopping by to see what you're up to. About to go for a run?"

"Actually, I'm trying to find a costume for a party, it needs to be sort of slutty."

"French maid. You'll look great. Trust me."

"It needs to be more like a prostitute."

"Be a high-class call girl and go looking like yourself. Perfect." He ate another grape. "Wait, who is having the party? Why costumes? Why wasn't I invited?"

"It's not really a party, more like a dress up thing for work."

He frowned and leaned back on his heels. "The morgue is stranger than I thought. Take my advice, don't dress sexy for work, *especially* if they tell you to. In fact, that's not acceptable. Especially not—"

"I promise, it's not like—listen, there's nothing to worry about. Can you just help me?" She stood aside so he would come in. "See if I have something that could work."

He followed Brooke to her closet, took a quick glance, and scrunched up his nose. "You barely have any clothes. Wait." He pulled a pair of red skinny jeans off a hanger. "These might work."

"What about a top?"

"Like I said, you've got no clothes. Now this is a time when it is actually appropriate to go to Goodwill and buy a shirt. If you need a costume sort of thing."

"Forget it. I changed my mind." She didn't need to look like a prostitute to talk to one. In fact, what had she been thinking? Dressing like a prostitute might make her unwelcome competition. She'd have more luck obtaining information from prostitutes who might know Jane Doe if she went as herself.

Jeff ran his hand over one of the sweaters hanging in her closet and grimaced. "Have you heard from Xander?"

"Oh. I need to call him back." *To make sure he hasn't spoken to Jean Thompson again.*

"You shouldn't need a reminder to call him. You know, I don't understand what goes through that crazy gorgeous little head of yours."

Thank God you don't, because I don't have time to make anyone else disappear… "Sorry, Jeff. I just remembered I have to be somewhere." She led him toward the front door and opened it. "Thanks!"

"Thanks for what? I didn't do anything except insult your wardrobe." Jeff laughed as he left.

Outside, the crickets were chirping an evening chorus. Brooke left her apartment wearing black running pants and a black tank with the words, "Meet me at the Barre." Blending into the darkness like a svelte Ninja, she hit the ground running as soon as she stepped into the night air. A fast pace was natural for her, particularly with her determination in high gear. She had to force herself to slow down to prevent her headache from returning. She shouldn't be running at all, but it was so much faster than walking. She'd thought of only one location where prostitutes might be found. She planned to head straight there.

In less than forty minutes, with sweat glistening across her forehead, chest, and arms, she was close to her intended destination. A dark, deserted area beneath a bridge, close to a highway overpass and not too far from the train station.

What would my mother say if she could see me now?

She slid her fingers along the fabric of her running belt and the outline of her new knife nestled inside.

At a secluded intersection, a lone motorcycle coasted to a stop at a red light a block away. The forest green color of his tight shirt rang a bell. Hadn't she seen that same male driver on a bike before? A tremor of uncertainty spread through her body. She turned the corner with less conviction about being alone. *Am I imagining things?* She shook out her hands, pushing her nerves away.

Most of the street lamps lining the abandoned storefronts were broken, courtesy of well-aimed rocks, but three scantily clad women wearing spiky heels stood together under the dim light of an intact streetlamp. The tips of their cigarettes glowed red.

Perfect.

Brooke slowed to a walk, watched by three sets of jaded eyes mounted in caves of eye shadow. A screeching police siren escalated in volume, drawing the women's attention away until the vehicle passed over the highway bridge and the sound receded. Brooke was just as relieved that the police hadn't come their way and forced the women to leave before she spoke to them.

"Excuse me." Brooke kept moving toward them. Their unfriendly faces checked her up and down. She took a deep breath and plunged into the cloud of smoke surrounding them. "I'm hoping you can help me. I'm trying to find someone who knows a woman with a butterfly tattoo on her shoulder. Dark hair with one red stripe. Petite."

A woman with dyed-red hair and a super short skirt tilted her head and eyed Brooke. Her pupils were dilated and her eyes moved in a rapid, unnecessary way.

A tall raven-haired woman smacked a wad of gum. She was thin, but not fit, with no muscle tone. She appeared young and old at the same time. She glared at Brooke. "What are you doing here, missy? You're too fresh for this, you're going to get your sweet little ass handed back to you and it won't be pretty."

Brooke covered her nose with her hand in a futile attempt to filter the smoke. "I can take care of myself. Do you know who I'm asking about? She has a butterfly tattoo on her left shoulder."

The red-haired girl turned around and gazed beyond the street. She reapplied lipstick and smacked her lips together. After a second, the three women exchanged glances until one finally nodded.

Brooke shifted her weight, taking the time to look at each of them. "Do you know her or not?"

The third woman was thin with long stringy blonde hair. She stepped forward and blew smoke into Brooke's face. "We don't know her. You need to leave." Her voice had a twang to it, like she might have come from the South.

Brooke held her breath, unwilling to inhale the smoke. Her nails dug into her palms as rage invaded every muscle. She hated cigarette smoke and she hated being dismissed.

The blonde-haired woman stepped closer, pursing her lips like she was about to spit.

"I would really appreciate your help." Brooke spoke through clenched teeth. She took her phone out of her running pouch and tapped the icons. *Roll the dice.* "I know you know her."

"Alyssa has a butterfly tattoo. And I haven't seen her in a few days." The red-haired girl took a puff of her cigarette. "Why you asking 'bout her?"

The blonde stepped closer and glared at Brooke. "Yeah. Why you lookin' for Alyssa?"

"Take a look at this picture. You'll see I'm not looking for her. I know exactly where she is. She's dead in a body bag inside a drawer. I'm trying to find out who she is."

They gathered closer all at once, hovering over Brooke's phone and the picture of Jane Doe with a stitched-up Y-shaped incision. Brooke turned her face to the side and coughed.

"That's Alyssa." The blonde bit into her lower lip. "I've seen her before without makeup. That's Alyssa."

"Alyssa who?" Brooke fanned the air in front of her face and turned to the side to breathe.

"Candle?" The red-head met Brooke's eyes.

"Cable." The blonde suddenly sounded young and afraid. No trace of the Southern accent. "Her name is Alyssa Cable. What happened to her?"

"She was murdered."

"Damn."

"Who killed her?" The red-head's voice came across as genuine, her attitude having disappeared.

"That's what I'm trying to find out. Do you know where she lived?"

"Yeah, Holly Gardens. But lately she'd been staying with that dealer, called him her boyfriend. He weren't no boyfriend. He just wanted her to find him new customers."

Excellent! "Do you know who the boyfriend is?"

"She told me he works at a morgue. Real creepy."

Really? A spark of excitement shot through Brooke's body. "Do you mean that he works at the Medical Examiner's Office?"

The blonde scoffed. "I don't know what you call it. Where the dead bodies go. That place."

"Do you know his name? What he looks like?"

Heads shook. The red-head dropped her cigarette butt and ground it into the pavement with the toe of her platform shoe.

"Thanks for your help." Brooke took a few steps back. "And, you might not have heard the news yet, but smoking also kills you."

"Being a pushy know it all will kill you, bitch." The red-head tossed her head, eyes defiant.

"Yeah. And Alyssa didn't smoke, bitch." The black-haired woman flicked her finished butt towards Brooke.

"Thanks for your help." Brooke let out a final cough before leaving. Across the street, she took a deep, satisfying breath of smoke-free air. Perhaps she'd had a big stroke of luck, but, assuming there weren't other women who resembled Jane Doe and had butterfly tattoos on their shoulders, it had been all too easy to identify the mystery cadaver as Alyssa Cable. And she was one step closer to finding out who killed her. She jogged back to her apartment, planning her next move.

Chapter Twenty-Three

Brooke sat on the floor of her living room, feet propped up on one of Xander's boxes, scrolling through the internet on her laptop. She found no one named Alyssa Cable in the right age range in the news or on social media. No arrests. No Facebook or Instagram pages. Maybe Alyssa Cable wasn't Jane Doe's real name. But according to the street walkers who identified her, it was the name she used, and the only one Brooke had to go on.

Just for fun, Brooke typed her own name into the browser. A long list of links came back. Results from local 10ks, half marathons, and marathons, which included her name amongst the top female finishers. She saw announcements for some of the awards and scholarships she received during college. She allowed herself a few minutes to scroll through them and reminisce on her accomplishments. She always had goals and always worked through the precise steps to achieve them. She never failed. And finding the person who killed Alyssa Cable and Rachael Kline would be no different.

Brooke pulled on scrubs and hurried toward the storage room, racing against an unseen clock, but noticing everyone around her. She passed Greg, who never smiled at her or anyone else, his attention usually consumed by a personal electronic gadget. One of the delivery drivers came next. *Why is he inside the building?* Dr. Gold's rattling cough made her jump, as did Jerome's ear-piercing sneeze a few seconds later.

Does the alleged boyfriend really work here? Jerome? Paul? Dr. Draven? Greg? One of the other part-time assistants or medical examiners I haven't met? She wanted to consider all options rather than end up surprised.

Inside the storage room, she made a bee-line for Alyssa's drawer. The label still said Jane Doe.

Brooke logged into the computer and confirmed that the data still matched the label on the drawer. It did. Jane Doe remained unidentified and unclaimed.

She struggled to keep Jane Doe's real name to herself because she wanted everyone to know how easy it had been for her to discover the woman's identity.

Why doesn't anyone else know? What is wrong with people? Plenty. Probably the reason I don't have any real fondness for people in general. Hopefully Jean Thompson and the police in Cancun are just as useless at their jobs as whoever it is who should be identifying Jane Doe. But eventually they will. She raised her index finger to her mouth and bit on her cuticles. *How much time do I have? I better move quickly.*

The noisy door gave her warning before opening. She hurried to log off the computer.

"Hey." Jerome's hair was clean and combed, certainly an improvement over when she first met him.

"Morning." Brooke stood up from the table. "Do you know what happens to the unclaimed bodies?"

He ate the last piece of a donut, dropping some colored sprinkles to the floor. "They get cremated. Storage is free for the first ten days, then families are charged per day. But if no one comes, eventually the body is cremated."

"Eventually? Do you know how long?"

Jerome shrugged. "I can't remember."

The doors opened again. "Ah, there you are, Brooke." Dr. Gold leaned against the wall. "I need your help today after all. One of our medical examiners called in sick."

Brooke inspected a large, cellulite covered, abdomen. Dissecting organs from layers of fat was always a challenge. "Who was sick?"

"What?" Dr. Gold had pulled a chair over to the side of the table to supervise Brooke's work.

"You said one of the medical examiners was sick. Who was it?"

"Oh. Mya. She might have the flu."

Brooke reached for the scalpel. "Mya doesn't seem to like me."

"Hmpf. Maybe she knows what you're being paid," he mumbled.

She turned her head to him. "What?"

"Watch what you're doing."

It was clear Dr. Gold didn't want to make idle chit chat and that suited Brooke fine. She focused on the work and was fully absorbed in freeing a spleen from a labyrinth of fatty tissue.

"You always seem to be in a hurry to get through the external exam and start the internal one." Dr. Gold raised an eyebrow while he scrawled on a legal pad.

"I'm just trying to be efficient and get through everything and still leave time for your paperwork."

"This work, it comes very natural for you."

"Thanks." She hoped his comment was merely a compliment and nothing more.

The autopsy room doors opened. Jerome stepped between them and stood there in silence. After a moment, he cleared his throat. Rolling back and forth on his heels, he cleared his throat again – this time, louder.

"You getting sick, too?" Dr. Gold scowled. "I told you I don't need you in here today."

Jerome stuffed his hands into his pockets. "There's someone here to see Brooke."

"Again?" Dr. Gold aimed his gaze at Brooke.

"No—I mean. I don't—" Brooke tried to keep her focus on the spleen she cradled in her hands.

Jerome took another step inside the room. "It's the police."

Bracing herself with a deep inhale, Brooke peered in the direction of the door. An attractive woman dressed in civilian clothing stood behind Jerome.

"Is this about the missing girl again?" The Chief Examiner glowered at Brooke.

"I don't know." Brooke placed the spleen on the scale.

"Brooke will see you in the family meeting room in a few minutes." Dr. Gold sighed loudly enough for everyone to hear. "Even though she's in the middle of something."

"Okay. I know where the room is." The detective turned and disappeared from sight.

"Hurry up and take care of whatever it is," Dr. Gold mumbled.

"I will." She resented the look he gave her, like the interruption was her fault.

"Jerome, I'll need you to help me until she gets back."

"Okay." Jerome stood up straighter. "I just have to finish something I was doing. I'll be back in five."

Brooke removed her latex gloves and dropped them in the trash. She scrubbed her hands vigorously while she thought about the woman waiting for her.

Was it another private investigator? A detective from Cancun? Would the Cancun authorities send someone all the way to Connecticut? I'm not really a suspect, right? No one would ever suspect a studious young woman of killing two strong young men. The police only need to know what I saw, right? What should I say? Or is this about a different matter entirely? Maybe it has nothing to do with the two guys on the beach. Maybe it's about Rachael Kline again.

She forced out an exhale and turned off the faucets.

"She's waiting for you in the family room."

"I know, Dr. Gold. Thank you." *I'm really starting to hate the family room.*

She walked down the corridor, deep in thought, her eyes roaming without taking in her surroundings.

Brooke entered and the woman stood from the couch. She was about the same age as Jean Thompson, mid-thirties. Unlike Jean, this woman was lean, like she worked out hard and only ate grilled chicken and vegetables. She wore plain gray slacks and a white top, professional yet business casual. Her sleek brown hair was pulled back in a ponytail just like Brooke's, but not as long. A hint of shimmer coated her lips.

Brooke made the first move by extending her hand. "Hi. I'm Brooke Walton."

The woman shook Brooke's hand. "Detective Lee Merrik. I'm with the Connecticut State Police. I was asked to speak with you on behalf of the authorities in Cancun."

They only sent one detective. Whatever they think I know or did, it must not be a priority for them. "Oh, sure. What can I help you with?"

"Two men were murdered in Cancun. Americans. Your family was vacationing there during that time. I'm sure you've heard about it."

There is no one right way to respond, she reminded herself. *Everyone processes disturbing news differently.* "Of course. So terrible." She added a slight back and forth movement with her head for emphasis. "And frightening. My mother said the police found the key we lost. And it was near where someone found human remains. Was that the two men who disappeared?"

"It was. The key seems to have been involved in whatever happened there."

Brooke opened her eyes wide, acting like this was big news and it frightened her. Which it most definitely did. The rush of blood through her eardrums and her clenched stomach proved it.

Are my fingerprints in the blood? Is the detective going to print me?

The detective pressed a button on a small hand-held device. "I'm going to record our conversation for the authorities in Cancun."

"Oh, okay." Brooke tried not to show alarm. *Is it acceptable to say no? I mean, I can't, I wouldn't, it would be suspicious, but still . . . could I?*

"Tell me everything you can remember about your run on the beach, the night you lost the key."

"Sure." She sighed. "Let me see. We had just arrived, and I'd been sitting all day on the plane and in the car, so I really wanted to go for a run when we got there. It was already dark. My parents didn't want me to go, my mother anyway. She didn't think it was safe. And, as it turns out, she was right."

"You went out for a long run by yourself at night?"

"Yes, I did. That's not unusual for me. I left our resort, Casa de Royale, and turned left when I hit the beach. I ran until my phone alarm went off. I'd set it to ring after forty minutes. So, that would put me about five miles out when I stopped. It was past all the resorts and pretty secluded. I guess I should have been warier, but I was just thinking about how peaceful it was. I stopped to stretch. The key was in the pouch on my running belt. That has to be when I lost it."

"What makes you think you lost it then?"

"I probably unzipped the pouch to get a tissue. I guess that's when the key fell out. Because that's the only time it could have happened unless I lost it back at our resort when I first put it in my pouch, after I got my cap from the car. Well, I guess it's possible I didn't zip the pouch all the way, and I could have lost it any time during the run. But I'm pretty sure it happened when I was stretching halfway out."

"Did you see the two young men, the Americans, when you were running or stretching?"

"I really couldn't say. I passed a lot of people walking along the beach. Couples mostly, and a few groups. I'm sort of in my own world when I'm running, so I'm like aware people are there, but I'm not really seeing them, you know?"

"I'm a runner too. I get it. You're in the zone."

Brooke nodded.

"So, you're saying you ran ten miles that night?"

"Give or take a bit."

"You do that often?"

"Yes."

"Hmm." Detective Merrik reached into her bag and removed a picture. "This is John Peters and Rico Vega. The two men who were murdered in the area where your key was found. Have you ever seen them before?"

Brooke stared at the picture without touching it. Two sets of big brown eyes. Yes, she remembered those eyes well. They were both grinning in the picture, exactly like when she met them, when they were still excited about having their way with her, before they realized they had picked the wrong girl.

She shook her head. "I'm sorry. I mean, their pictures were on television before we left Cancun, so I've seen them, but I never saw them on the beach, not that I'm aware of. They look like strong guys. I heard the authorities suspect it was a gang?"

The detective tilted her head. "Perhaps it was. Did you see anyone on the beach that night who sticks out in your memory?"

Brooke lifted her eyes to the ceiling and pressed her lips together. "No. Not that I can think of. Like I said, I really didn't pay much attention to anyone else."

"According to your father, you met up with a few other young people after your run and were hanging out with them." Merrik's gaze moved toward the open door. "Hold on. Someone is out there. We should have closed the door."

Brooke spun around, craning her neck to catch a glimpse of whoever the detective had seen in the hallway.

Merrik strode the few steps to the door and closed it. "Just someone walking by." She turned back to Brooke. "So, do you remember who you were with?"

"I joined a few girls who were hanging out." Brooke glanced back to the door and rubbed her hand over the back of her neck. "This was on the way home. Almost back to our resort, really. I was walking at that point, part of my cool down. I could tell they were American. They offered me a beer, which I declined, but it was nice of them. They were going for a swim and I went in with them for a bit."

"Can you tell me their names?"

"Hmm. One was Katie. One was Morgan. I think. There were two more. I never got their last names. I never saw them again. I think that was their last night there. They had just graduated college together. Michigan. Or Michigan State." Brooke bit down on her lower lip. "Sorry. I know that's not much, but it's all I can remember. We weren't together long."

Detective Merrik switched the recording device into her other hand. "I'm going to—"

A thin film of sweat formed on Brooke's skin. She wrapped one clammy hand around her waist, the other gripped her opposite shoulder. Her stomach heaved with fear. *Oh my God. She's going to ask for my prints!*

"—give this recording to the police in Cancun. I'll have to tell them you really don't know anything that could help them. If they have follow up questions, I'll call you." She turned off the recorder and placed it into her bag.

Brooke's shoulders dropped as the tension drained out of her. *Of course there wouldn't be any usable prints. Not with all the sand. Because wouldn't sand destroy prints? I panicked over nothing.*

"Just how long have you worked here, Brooke?" There was something different about Merrik's tone. Her voice channeled a vice principal, carrying a quiet, measured edge with a hint of condescension.

"Just a few weeks. I started the day I got back from Cancun. It's just for the summer."

"And what do you do here, exactly?"

"Data entry. I enter data from reports into the computer system and file paperwork most of the time."

"The men who were murdered, parts of them had been cut off. Hacked up at the joints with a small blade." The detective cocked her head and waited for Brooke's reaction. Her expression remained neutral, indicating nothing of her feelings.

"And?" Brooke tilted her head to one side.

"Sort of a coincidence, don't you think? Considering you work here?" Her tone was almost pleasant. She could have been commenting on the weather.

"I don't hack people up, detective. I make precise incisions and do meticulous stitching."

"So, you don't just do data entry, then?"

Why did I say that? Why didn't I keep my mouth shut? A tremor of fear coursed through her body. "Occasionally I help out with the exams."

"I know. I saw you a few minutes ago. And you've finished your first year of medical school. All the first years take gross anatomy, don't they?"

Brooke swallowed. "Yes."

"I thought so." Merrik removed a business card from her pocket and handed it over. She took a few steps toward the door as Brooke glanced at the card and tucked it inside her lab coat.

Hopefully this will be the last of her.

Merrik turned halfway around. If she noticed Brooke's unfriendly expression, she didn't let on. "You know, I wonder what those young men were up to, to deserve such a terrible fate . . ."

"Uh—"

"Thank you for your time, Ms. Walton. We'll be in touch."

Brooke's nostrils flared as she watched the detective walk away.

Chapter Twenty-Four

The conversations with Detective Merrik and Jean Thompson hung in Brooke's head like unpleasant odors that no amount of disinfectant could remove.

She worried through her exercise classes. During glute work—*is Jean delving into my past?* Throughout abdominal crunches—*is there anything else for Merrik and the Cancun police to discover?*

The meeting with Merrik had been especially strange. She didn't like the detective's smile. It seemed to teeter on the edge of a smirk. *Merrik knows something, something she's not sharing.* The pressure to enact Brooke's plan and be freed of suspicion weighed against her every thought and deed, worse than the stress of final exams, thanks to the detectives and the private investigator who apparently had nothing better to do with their time than harass her. Didn't they have real criminals to catch?

Less than an hour of daylight remained by the time she finished teaching. With a protein bar in hand, she sat down at one of the tables in the Peak Fitness lobby and opened the browser on her phone. Frowning, she poked at the screen.

Those detectives are trying to ruin my life . . .

A tap on her shoulder made her jump. "Jeez!" She bolted upright and slammed the phone face down on the table.

"I'm sorry, I didn't mean to startle you. Great workout. Thanks." Courtney rarely missed any of Brooke's evening classes.

Brooke rubbed her forehead. "You're welcome."

Courtney jaunted off, ponytail bouncing. "See ya tomorrow, Brooke."

Brooke waited for her to walk away before picking her phone up and retyping the address for Holly Gardens, where Alyssa Cable supposedly lived. It wasn't too far. She polished off the last bit of her protein bar and three ibuprofen, put on her backpack, and stepped outside. In the growing darkness, she jogged to Holly Gardens, ignoring her concussion. She wasn't planning to do anything that risked another head injury, only a long run at an easy pace.

As she breezed past empty office buildings and closed stores, the temperature dropped. Gusts of wind batted against her, a sure sign of a coming storm. The houses grew closer together, declining in size and quality until modest homes gave way to ones with sagging roofs and peeling paint.

The Holly Gardens apartments began where the most dilapidated homes ended. All indications suggested the complex had seen better days and more caring tenants. A large black crow picked at the rubbish on the ground surrounding a metal blue dumpster, only partially concealed by a rickety fence.

A tower of mailboxes graced the entrance. A brown dented one had "Cable" written across a piece of tape above the number seventeen.

Alyssa isn't the smartest to put her name on there. Brooke wiped sweat from her forehead with the back of her hand and searched the apartment fronts for number seventeen.

Doors in the two-story complex opened to the outside, like a motel. On one end of the building, spray-painted graffiti zig-zagged across dirty siding, more angry mess than an art form. The smell of something foul filled her lungs. A dead animal in the bushes? The front yards were mostly dirt scattered with clumps of weeds. Broken children's toys and other debris lay haphazardly on the ground like the aftermath of a hurricane. It wasn't clear which toys belonged with which unit.

Maybe Alyssa had a child.

A plant with a graying stalk and brittle brown leaves sat in a ceramic pot on the front steps of apartment seventeen. Decaying insects hung in the air, caught in a sturdy spiderweb stretching from the pot to the side railing.

Brooke stared at the ripped screen door. What would she do if Alyssa's boyfriend or a parent answered? She stepped back and scanned the area. Across the street, a black Mercedes was conspicuously out of place parked between an ancient Honda with garbage bags taped over the rear windows and a small, rusty pick-up truck, more patches than original metal. When she turned back to the apartment, she caught a glimpse of someone inside. The shadow of a man's figure passing through the hallway. She backed away from the door and hurried down the stairs. *I'll just look around.* While keeping an eye on Alyssa's apartment, she walked around the complex in search of information.

A gust of wind sent twigs and leaves spiraling through the air. Her ponytail whipped against her cheek. Thick, ominous clouds held all the signs of an imminent downpour. She inspected the length of the apartment complex. *What can this place tell me? What should I do next?*

She'd found nothing helpful by the time the first drops of rain fell.

Oh great, I'm going to get—

The door to unit seventeen opened and she stopped walking.

Not wanting to be seen, she bent over, pretending to fiddle with the chain tethering a rusting motor scooter to a pole, her head turned slightly. She held her breath.

Act like you belong here.

A man wearing khaki pants and a long-sleeved navy shirt with a hood stepped out of Alyssa's apartment and closed the door behind him, knocking over the dead plant in the process. He glanced at the pot, but not long enough for Brooke to see his face. In one hand he held a black rod about a foot long. The other clutched what appeared to be a white handkerchief or rag. He wiped it around the door knob.

That's not normal. A spark of excitement shot through her. Something else about him, something she couldn't yet place, set off a red flag.

The black rod snapped open, blossoming into an umbrella, and blocking her view. He hurried, head down, toward the black Mercedes waiting across the street. The umbrella obscured most of his upper body.

What was he doing inside the apartment? Is he Alyssa's so-called boyfriend, the dealer? A pimp? A family member? Whoever he is, he apparently pays attention to weather reports. I wish I had done the same.

The skies opened, and the rain rushed down in torrents. She was soaked by the time he reached the Mercedes.

His car's head lights illuminated sheets of falling rain before the engine roared to life and the car sped away. She had no chance of following on foot. When the last glimpse of tail lights had disappeared, she trotted over to unit sixteen. Swiping drops of water from her eyes, she knocked.

"Hold on," came a woman's voice from inside.

Brooke stared at the sky and winced, the cold, heavy drops pelting her. A tired looking young woman opened the door halfway, wearing a tank top and holding a fat baby against her hip. A toddler tiptoed to the woman's other side, wrapped his arms around her leg, and stared at Brooke. Cute except for the green-tinged snot dried across his cheek.

"Hi. Sorry to bother you. I'm looking for Alyssa Cable. Your neighbor."

"Yeah." She hoisted the baby up a few inches on her hip. "So am I."

Brooke edged into the doorway, so she was out of the rain. "You are?"

"Damn straight. She owes me money. She borrowed twenty dollars last week. I look like I got twenty dollars to spare?"

"Oh. No. Not really." Brooke glanced into the room beyond the front door. Dark colored walls, a blue shag carpet covered with toys, white stuffing bursting from a very visible hole in a purple couch. Crates lined one side of the room. Brooke's place wasn't much nicer, but at least it was meticulously clean. And it didn't smell like dirty diapers.

"Do you know who her boyfriend is?"

"Is that where she's at?"

"Maybe. That's what I think. Do you know him?"

"Don't know who he is. But I know where he lives."

"Really?"

"Had to pick her up there once. She called me, sobbing in the middle of the night. Got my kids out of bed, put them in my car and went and got her. She gave me gas money. But look where it got me, being a good neighbor. Cuz next thing I know, she asks to borrow money and now I'm out twenty dollars."

"Do you remember where it was?"

"Sure do. Some fancy condos across the city. I can even tell you the address cuz she texted it to me."

Brooke's pulse quickened. "Here, I'll give you some money for your trouble." She removed a bill from her pocket. "Here's a ten. It's all I have." She held the money out.

The woman snatched the money out of Brooke's hand and spun around. "I'll get you the address."

Brooke did a mini victory dance, dripping water on to the worn carpet. The toddler smiled.

The young mother returned with her phone, pressed a few buttons, and held it in front of Brooke's face. Brooke struggled to read the number through the spider web of cracks and scotch tape. She snapped a photo of the broken screen with her own phone as the baby opened his mouth and wailed. The woman jostled him against her side. "She called me back a few nights ago, but it was in the middle of the night again, so I didn't answer. I figured she wanted another ride from somewhere. Tell her I need that money back. Money don't grow on trees 'round here. Not for me it don't."

"I'll tell her. Thanks."

"Why do you need to find her anyway?" The woman narrowed her eyes. "She owe you money, too?"

"She's going to do me a big favor." Brooke snorted. "She just doesn't know it yet."

The woman sniggered.

Brooke left and jogged back to her apartment in a sopping wet shirt and shorts, drops of water flinging out of her shoes with each stride.

She had an address.

Chapter Twenty-Five

All day she'd dealt with Dr. Gold's paperwork, stealing glances at the clock as the hours crept along. Now, thanks to the instructor who agreed to teach her exercise classes for the night, she was back at her apartment and ready to track down Alyssa's killer. But first, there was something else she had to do. A voicemail from her mother had been waiting since noon. It might be nothing, or it might be another update on the situation in Cancun. She couldn't put it off any longer; ignoring it wouldn't make the situation go away. She pressed play.

"Hi. It's Mom. Have you heard from the police yet? Be sure to call us if they talk to you. Are you following the story on the news? The police don't seem to have any leads, which is just awful. How is your internship going? Maybe you could come home for a weekend soon. Your father could come and pick you up. It was nice having everyone together when we were in Cancun. Okay. Call me when you have a chance. Love you."

The tension in her shoulders dissolved with her relief. She deleted the message.

She placed her new knife in her running belt and zipped it closed. She reached for the doorknob but stopped, turning, and racing back to her bedroom.

From underneath a row of neatly-folded socks, she grabbed a small box with a tiny silk purse nestled inside. She dumped the contents of the purse into her palm.

I can't believe I almost left without these.

Earrings.

Rachael's earrings.

The ones Rachael wore every single day right up until the night Brooke killed her. Brooke had always known there was a reason to hold onto them, she just didn't know what the reason might be. Now, their objective was clear. If her plan worked, the earrings would provide clinching evidence that whoever killed Alyssa had also killed Rachael. She would find the killer's house tonight at the address Alyssa's neighbor provided. Because wasn't the spouse or lover always the most likely suspect?

Well, not always. Not with Rachael. And not with Jessica at Everett. And not with my professor at Cedarhurst. But most of the time.

Now she was ready.

The address was about seven miles from Brooke's apartment. Taking an Uber and creating a record of where she had gone was out of the question. Which reminded her that according to Alyssa's neighbor, Alyssa had called for a ride in the middle of the night, which was quite an imposition to say the least, rather than take an Uber or taxi. Why would she do that?

Jeff wouldn't have a problem lending Brooke his car, but he'd ask where she was going and possibly offer to keep her company. She'd have to make up a story and remember every lie she'd told. The more lies she told, the harder it became to keep them all straight. Which next one might bring everything tumbling down? It wasn't worth the risk. She couldn't have anyone else involved. Running was the best option for keeping her business to herself. No one who knew her would be surprised she went for a long run. Her head still hurt when she engaged in strenuous exercise, so, as challenging as it was for her, she'd again have to keep it slow.

She jogged on busy city streets toward a more suburban area with less traffic and newly renovated homes and neighborhoods. A few miles in, breathing steadily with drops of perspiration appearing on her skin, she reached into the pocket on her waist band and stroked the earrings with the tip of her finger, making sure she still had them. When the sidewalk ended on one side of the road, she crossed to the other side, casting a shadow as the sun dropped in the horizon. Eventually, the sidewalk ended again, and she had no choice but to run on the road, closely flanked by woods.

A car sped by, jolting her from her thoughts. She leaped from the broken pavement to the tall grass.

"Hey baby!" The driver laid on the horn. "Looking good!"

The tail lights disappeared and the unkempt, gravelly shoulder kept her eyes focused downward.

A minute later, just after she had rounded a bend, she spun around at the sound of another engine, but saw no one. A prickling sensation traveled across the back of her neck. For several paces, she twisted her head from side to side, certain someone was watching her. But there was no one. She shuddered and stayed close to the edge of the tree line for the rest of her way, remaining alert rather than succumbing to the rhythm of her breath and steps.

Her top was drenched with sweat by the time she saw the elegant sign for Chatham Grove gracing the entrance of her destination, well-maintained townhomes with pristine yards surrounded by dense woods. A huge improvement over Alyssa Cable's digs. It wasn't where she pictured a pimp or drug pusher living. Too upscale and trendy. But admittedly, she knew little about pimps and drug pushers.

She headed straight for the mailboxes again, rows of shiny black slots nestled inside a stone wall. None of the boxes listed names, only numbers. She jiggled the handle to number sixty-four, the unit Alyssa's neighbor gave her, but as she expected, it required a key to open.

Townhome number sixty-four was the last home in a row toward the back of the neighborhood. Bushes and trees surrounded the side, allowing additional privacy. Taking sidelong glances, she approached the building. It was dark enough for homeowners to have switched on their interior lights, but the inside of number sixty-four appeared unlit. She walked with purpose into the back yard, so if she was seen, they'd think she belonged there. The back yard consisted of a grassy area and a paved patio, made mostly private by a fence and the woods behind it. When she stepped onto the patio, a sudden noise caught her attention.

Was that a door clicking shut?

She scanned the dark patio area, straining her eyes and ears to find the source of the sound, and failed to see the small step in her path. Her body flew forward and hit the ground with a slap and a thud, inches from an outdoor firepit. She managed to stifle her gasp.

She jumped off the ground and hovered in a crouch, listening, and peering into the darkness. Her knee burned. Rubbing her fingers gently over the abrasion, sweeping off tiny pebbles, she held her breath. In the woods, birds chirped and insects screeched, and from the front of the townhome, a vehicle rumbled closer.

She stood and wiped her palms against her shorts, transferring a chalky substance onto the fabric.

Is it?

A glance at the firepit confirmed her suspicion. Ashes. Just like the powdery gray substance she'd found on Alyssa's back.

Yes! Yes! Yes! If all detectives were as capable as me . . . I'd be on death row by now.

Grinning with determination, she opened an unused tissue from her pocket. She scooped up a handful of the ash and deposited it into the center of the tissue. She folded it in half, folded it again, and stuck it into her pouch.

The next few minutes happened in a blur. Her head was jerked back as someone yanked on her hair. Caught off guard and confused, she stumbled. Her shoulder blades smacked against the metal edge of a large grill. With a grating squeak, the grill slid away from under her weight and smaller metal objects clattered noisily to the ground. She landed hard on her backside, but immediately scrambled to her feet, ready to fight or run. Something surrounded her neck and tightened, preventing her escape. She struggled to relieve the pressure, clawing her fingers under the cord, thrashing in panicked desperation.

"If you scream," a male voice hissed from behind her, "I'll pull this so hard you won't be able to breathe." The cord cut into the soft skin of her throat. It tightened further when he grabbed her wrists, forcing them together behind her back. Her heart raced as panic electrified her senses.

"Didn't hear me coming, did you?" He let out a humorless laugh. "What the hell are you doing here?" He jerked on the cord. A burning pain flared around her neck.

Brooke remained silent, choking against the noose. Her breath came short and fast through her constricted trachea. She flailed her arms in front of her, searching for an object she could use as a weapon.

"I could shoot you right here for trespassing. Make it look like an accident because you were following me. You are. Aren't you?"

She struggled to get the words out. "No. I don't even know who you are. I swear it." Her voice was a mere whisper and every tiny movement made the piercing pain worse.

"Yeah, right. You're obsessed with me. Just like she was." He sniffed, once, twice, and then let out a piercing sneeze. The cord tightened.

Brooke's hands flew back to her neck, tearing at the cord to relieve the tension before it cut off her air supply and crushed her esophagus. He stepped backward. She had no choice but to step back with him. She still hadn't seen his face. He opened the back door and pushed her into a kitchen. Artsy black and white landscape photos on a light gray wall whirled across her vision as he spun her around. She gasped for breath. He opened cabinets and banged something down on the marble countertop while holding her face pressed against a stainless-steel refrigerator. The steel reminded her of the cold storage units at the Medical Examiner's Office, which reminded her of death. Images of cadavers flashed through her mind.

The tension around her neck finally loosened just as he pressed something against her nose and mouth, cutting off the little oxygen she had. A sharp and familiar smell hit her nostrils. Darkness crept around the edges of her vision. She fell to the ground.

Her eyes fluttered open and darted from side to side. She only saw blackness.

Where am I?

Her cheeks and lips stung. Her best guess—duct tape. Her tongue pressed against a wad of fabric that had been stuffed in her mouth. She grunted, producing an insignificant, muffled sound. Her parched throat teetered on the edge of spasming. She couldn't inhale enough oxygen. The inhuman, frantic snorting of her breath sounded like a creature in a horror movie. Her mounting terror threatened to overwhelm her thinking.

A magnified pulse pounded like a jackhammer deep inside her brain—boom, boom, boom . . .

Focusing her mind on the air entering and exiting through her nose, she forced her panic into submission.

Calm down, calm down, calm down!

Her hands were heavy and numb, secured together behind her back. Rope bound her arms to her sides. She closed her eyes and waited for her pulse to steady. She managed to relax her throat and repress a gag.

She counted to twenty and her fear subsided enough to concentrate on her current reality.

Carpet touched her bare calves. She stretched one leg out from underneath herself. It hit a wall before it was fully extended. She tipped right, and her shoulder hit the opposite wall.

An empty closet?

The smell of her sweat and fear permeated the small space. She scooted to her right and felt her running belt catch on something protruding from the wall. *Phew—he didn't take my belt.* But it felt unusually light. *He took my phone!* A burst of anger returned some of her strength and determination.

She jerked and winced as her running belt broke free of the protruding object. She scooted around and touched it, something sharp with two prongs that would leave an impression the same size as the indentation on Alyssa Cable's lower back.

Is this where Alyssa died? A disturbing chill spread from her gut.

She extended her other leg forward until it reached one of the confining walls. A door moved slightly in its frame. She pushed it again to be sure and it rattled against a lock on the other side.

Oh no. She stopped moving. *I don't want him to know I'm conscious.*

Too late. Within seconds, quiet footsteps approached. Someone was standing just on the other side of the door, listening. She tried to hold her breath. *Can he hear my heart hammering against my chest?*

I have to do something.

She pressed her back against the wall, braced her feet, and pushed herself up to standing, ready for whoever was coming.

The lock turned. The closet door wrenched open and with it came enough light for her to see.

A man stared back at her. He took a deep look into her eyes and exhaled as if he too had been holding his breath. She thought she might have seen him before, there was something vaguely familiar about him, but she didn't know him.

One of the guys who works the night shift? One of the drivers? Is it Paul? Think!

She'd handled two strong men in Cancun. This was only one, although he was bigger. She chambered her leg and kicked, aiming for his crotch. But he was quicker. He jumped back before she made contact, striking his back against a piece of furniture. A picture frame fell forward and smacked the top of the dresser.

"Shhh!" He raised a finger to his mouth and froze in hunched silence. Brooke studied him, planning her next move. Seconds passed before he spoke in a voice she could barely hear. "Wasn't sure you'd be alive." He stared at the raised, raw line of skin around her neck. "I'm helping you."

His eyes darted back to the bedroom door. "I don't know when he's coming back. We've got to get out. Now."

Brooke cocked her head, perplexed by his unexpected words and tone. *This isn't the guy who threw me into the closet? Where have I seen him before?*

"Brace yourself." He pinched an edge of the thick tape covering her mouth and tore it off in one fast move. Brooke gasped at the sudden pain. She opened her mouth and pushed out her tongue to dispel her gag.

"Sorry," he whispered. "No other way."

Coughing and spitting onto the carpet, she tried to rid her mouth of an awful taste.

He made a little circle with his hand. "Turn around."

She wasn't about to turn her back on him. She didn't know if he could be trusted. Pretending to help her might be part of some demented game.

"Hurry up. We may not have much time."

She angled to the side enough for him to access the cords around her hands, watching him over her shoulder. He took out a pocket knife. With a firm but gentle touch, he grasped her hands in his and sawed back and forth until her tether gave away. Shoulders squared, she faced him.

Who is he? The boyfriend? Did he kill Alyssa? If so, why is he untying me now?

Tattoos covered his muscular arms. He didn't look much older than her, but deep lines etched his face.

"Who are you?"

He moved across the room in silence, in spite of his size. He edged into the hallway, extending one arm across Brooke's midsection to hold her back. "Let's go."

As they hurried through the house, he kept his voice low, "Do you know who did this to you?"

"I thought you did."

He frowned at her.

She stopped and slipped her hand into her running pouch. Her knife was there, but the ash sample had disappeared along with her phone. The earrings were still inside the pocket of her shorts.

He waved her forward. "Hurry.

Brooke raised a finger. She dashed back to the bedroom.

The stranger caught up to her, his voice urgent. "Let's go." He grabbed her arm, but she twisted free. She opened a box made of cherry wood on top of the dresser and tossed the earrings inside.

He pulled on her elbow. "What was that about?"

She ignored his question and they both ran down the hallway, through the kitchen, out the back door, and around to the front of the house. She kept up with his long strides until he reached a motorcycle. He grabbed the handle bars and swung a leg over the seat. "Get on."

Brooke stopped a few yards from the bike.

"Whoever tied you up might be back any minute. You know that, right?"

"How do I know it wasn't you?"

"It wasn't. It also wasn't me who tried to back into you with that Mercedes. Okay? Get on."

Her jaw dropped. "How do you—? That was an accident."

"Yeah? Didn't look like an accident to me. And the same car that hit your bike a few days ago just drove out of that garage right before I went inside to find you."

Brooke stared, processing the information. She didn't appreciate discovering she'd been clueless. "Either it was you, or you're spying on me."

He tossed her a helmet. "Guess I'm a spy who just saved your ass. Get on."

The absence of her phone created a strong sense of unease, the same vulnerability she'd have running home naked. And if the stranger's words were true, someone wanted her silenced.

She took a last backward glance at the townhome.

No one would ever accuse her of being risk averse. She threw all caution to the wind, put on the helmet, and swung her leg over the bike.

Chapter Twenty-Six

He revved the engine before Brooke was fully seated. She wrapped her arms around his waist and they raced away from the townhomes. He was as muscular as Xander. Through his T-shirt, she could feel the hard delineation of muscles along his back and sides—distinct segments of teres major, teres minor, and latissimus dorsi. She ignored her instinctive reaction— to dig her fingers in and separate the fibers.

Who is this guy? Do I know him from the gym?

The bike slowed to a normal pace once they merged onto busier streets, blending in with the city traffic. Her mother's words, *be careful,* echoed through her brain. Her head throbbed and her neck burned, but she was alive with no permanent damage.

A few blocks from her apartment, they slowed to a stop in front of a Starbucks. He parked the bike.

"Figured this is your kind of place." He tilted his head toward the store.

She jumped off, removed her helmet, and pushed aside a few wisps of hair. "I don't drink coffee, and I wouldn't pay Starbucks prices if I did."

A smile spread across his face, beautiful, confident, the kind that could sell toothpaste in commercials, one that let the world know he was more than comfortable in his own skin, yet there was also something slightly dangerous about him.

"Who are you? I know I've seen you before."

"Funny, I was expecting a thank you about now. You know—for saving you?"

Brooke stared at him and crossed her arms.

"Maybe I'm your guardian angel."

"I don't need a guardian angel." *The last thing I need is someone watching me. At least I haven't done anything wrong lately, not since Cancun.*

"You needed one tonight."

"Tell me, really, why were you there?"

He lowered his gaze to his scuffed boots, then met Brooke's eyes. "Guess I was looking out for you. I didn't have your name or number. I guess I was waiting for the right opportunity to, you know, rescue you from a closet."

A snort escaped her lips. "Seriously? You're a stalker? Mind telling me why you didn't intervene before I was choked and duct taped?"

The man cracked his knuckles. "I came around the corner and saw him pulling you into the house. I didn't know if—it might have been some messed-up sex game."

Brooke frowned. "I don't see how anyone could think that."

"Yeah. Things didn't add up. He left the house and I went in to check on you."

"How did you get in? Was it unlocked?"

"I have my ways." He grinned.

Her throat was dry. She coughed for several seconds before she could speak again. "How do I know you?"

"You don't. Not yet."

"I've seen you before."

"You came to the Goodwill and bought a chair a few weeks ago."

She held her hands out, palms up, and shrugged.

"I carried the chair inside. Found you a price."

Of course! The guy Jeff called a sexy ex-criminal, or something like that.

Her nod turned to a scowl. It was true he had most likely saved her life, but he'd also complicated things in a big way. He knew she'd been in the townhome. And unless he was a bumbling idiot, which he did not appear to be, he knew something was up. Everything about the situation was far from normal. At least, he wasn't a cop. And for that she was extremely appreciative. She had enough cops poking and prodding into her life already. "So, you work at Goodwill?"

"No. I just happened to be there dropping things off. Spring . . . summer cleaning. The guy working there wanted to put my chair, I mean, *your* chair, in the store. I offered to carry it for him."

"So, I bought your old chair?"

"Yep." He scratched his neck. "Made me think twice about getting rid of it, too. I hope you're enjoying it."

"So, what do you do for a living then?"

"I work for a tech firm." He averted his gaze for a second. "Can I buy you a drink?"

"You mean a coffee?"

"You said you don't drink coffee. We can go to a bar for—"

"No, thank you. I'm okay."

"How about just a water then?"

Normally she would have said no. But she needed to know more about this guy, now that he knew too much about her. And the gag had left a bitter, pungent taste in her mouth, an irritation in her parched throat. "Sure. I need one."

He led the way into the Starbucks. While he ordered an espresso, she pulled the elastic band out of her hair and redid her ponytail.

Once he had the drinks, they sat down at a table. He watched her place her lips around the straw and suck down the water from her plastic cup. She held the straw between her fingers and straightened up, meeting his gaze. "Thank you for saving me."

"About time." He smiled and settled back into his chair. "You're welcome. Mind telling me what that was about back there?"

"I'm not sure."

He toyed with his keys, sliding them back and forth on the table, his eyes never leaving her. "You must have some idea what you were doing there."

"I'm not even positive who lives there." She sighed. "Well, I'm pretty sure, but I didn't see him. Whoever it is, I think he's responsible for the recent death of a young woman."

"A friend of yours?"

"I like to think my friends wouldn't stuff rags down my throat and try to strangle me."

"I meant the woman who died."

"Oh. No, she's not a friend. I only know of her because I work at the Medical Examiner's Office. Just for the summer. I guess you know that if you've been following me."

"Yeah. What do you do there?"

"I'm just a summer intern. I'm in medical school. Now how about you, Mr. Mystery? Why are you following me and—"

"Nope. I didn't get abducted. When you save me from death in a closet, I have to explain why I'm there. Go on. You're an intern for the medical examiner. And?"

"First off, I wasn't going to die in the closet. I was about to get out when you came along." She frowned. "And the dead woman is a Jane Doe. A prostitute, allegedly. A drug-user, supposedly. Tox reports aren't back yet.

No one else seems to care about her. She's still unidentified, as far as I know. I wanted to find out the truth. I guess I was sleuthing, okay? Not that different from spying, is it?"

"Touché." He flashed a smile. "It seems someone doesn't care for your sleuthing. I hope you realize that even if you don't know for sure who hurt you, he knows who you are."

Brooke gulped. *And my phone doesn't have a password.*

"So." He twirled his keys. "What are you going to do about it?"

"I . . . don't know yet." *Why am I even telling him anything?*

"Wanna call the police?" He said this in a casual manner. One might think he was asking her if she wanted a refill of her water. In fact, he was handling the evening's events with remarkable calmness.

She knew almost nothing about the good-looking tattooed guy beside her. Only that he probably had better furniture than she did, drove a motorcycle, and had been spying on her. Somehow, he understood that her current situation was beyond the law. Oddly, he seemed to be okay with it.

His question hung in the air, unanswered.

"I lost my phone. He took it."

He reached into his pocket and set his phone on the table, pushing it across to her.

She shook her head.

"Yeah." He grinned. "Didn't think so."

"You're sure you aren't the police?"

He smirked.

"What's your name?" She twirled her straw around.

"Charlie."

"You don't look like a Charlie."

He raised his chin with a laugh, sitting upright. "You can call me Charles if you like it better. Back to what happened tonight, did you find what you were looking for?" A slight smile lingered on his lips.

"I might have found something."

"And you honestly don't know who attacked you?"

"I'm not positive. So, I have to find out for sure who lives there."

"I can help you with that."

"How?"

"Give me your phone number." He picked up his phone. "I'll find out and tell you tomorrow."

"Seeing that I don't have a phone anymore, that's not going to work. But I can give you my email."

"Okay." He tapped his phone. "Ready?"

"It's surgeontobe@gmail.com"

"Got it." Charlie leaned forward, his T-shirt sleeve moved up on his arm.

Brooke stared at the tattoo on his upper arm. Her eyes grew wide. "Hey. I've seen that before."

"Seen what?"

"The design on your arm." She pointed. "That one."

"I doubt it. Maybe you've seen something like it."

"No, not just something like it. That exact design."

"Only a few guys from my unit in Afghanistan have this exact one."

"My boyfriend has the same one. He was in the military too. In Afghanistan."

"Your boyfriend?"

"Xander Cross."

Charlie slapped the arm of his chair. "No way!" Two women at the next table turned to look at them. "Xander Cross. Of all people, Xander Cross!" He covered his mouth with his hand. "Seriously?"

"Seriously. We're both in medical school. We share an apartment. Well, he's away for the summer, in Chicago, but once he gets back."

"What's he doing in Chicago?"

"He has a summer job doing research at a PTSD clinic. With psychiatrists."

Charlie dipped his head. He probably understood why Xander might be involved in medical research with PTSD. "Well, that is one hell of a surprise. And I mean it when I say that you could not be with a better guy."

Brooke nodded.

"Come on. I'll drop you off at your apartment."

"Because apparently you know exactly where I live."

"Sorry, but yeah, I know a lot about you. Part of the job."

"Which is…"

"Going to remain a mystery for now." He got up from his chair. "Need to use the restroom?"

Brooke rolled her eyes. "What, are you my teacher now and we're going on a field trip?" She stood. "But actually, I do. Give me one minute."

She reached for her empty cup, but Charlie grabbed it first.

"I've got it. I'll throw it out. Meet you outside."

Chapter Twenty-Seven

Brooke opened her apartment door as she held up Jeff's phone. "Thank you, Jeff. You're the best."

He waved his key at her. "Just be quick. And if anyone calls with an ID that says 'Chris from Nolens,' you bring me that phone immediately, hear?"

The door clicked shut behind her. She called Xander and told him everything.

Well, not everything.

She told him Jane Doe could have been Rachael's twin and her body was found in Greenwood Circle, reminding him Rachael's pocket book had been discovered in the same location. That's why she had set out on her own to uncover Jane Doe's identity. She emphasized how no one else seemed to be doing anything about the matter. No one at all seemed to care about poor Alyssa Cable.

"I'm proud of you for caring, Brooke, but I don't want you getting hurt—"

"Wait, there's more." She minimized the near-death part of the evening, continuing to speak right over him while he repeated, "What? What?" She didn't lie exactly, she simply failed to mention the most disturbing and relevant events.

"Charlie Ballard! Are you for real? Is this all a big joke?"

"That's kind of what he said, too. He couldn't believe it when I told him you were my boyfriend."

"Charlie has some mad skills. Hand to hand combat, stuff like that. He is one person you do not want to cross."

"I wasn't planning on it."

"Also, the one person you most want to watch your back if you're in a dangerous situation. He's a really good judge of character too."

"He works for a tech firm now."

"Really? I thought . . . I heard . . . well, never mind. He's brilliant, you know."

"Really?" She scrunched up her nose. "I didn't get that impression."

"He is."

She opened her fridge and scanned the shelves—refilled water bottles, eggs, natural peanut butter, vanilla almond milk, and two apples. She selected the almond milk.

"Considering what happened, I'm glad he was there."

"Right." She opened the freezer and took out the frozen bananas and kale.

"The guy that threatened you might not have anything to do with Rachael, but he's someone dangerous. Maybe one of those nut jobs who hates trespassers and was just waiting for one to set foot on his property. What did the police do?"

She raised the milk to pour it, but halted, letting it hover in the air. "Um, I haven't...

"What? Why not?"

"Um. I just—"

"Brooke. Call the police. Now. Let them handle this."

"But I was trespassing, so, I mean . . . that's not okay. And I still don't know who it was, I didn't see him. Who do you think it is?"

"How would I know? Who do you think?"

"Someone who needs money. Someone who was using Alyssa Cable to push drugs or to get him new clients. There's this one guy who works at night. I haven't met him yet. Paul. He's an assistant. Probably doesn't make much." She pressed the mix button on the blender.

"What's that noise?"

"Nothing. Sorry. Almost done." She pressed stop. "One of the guys I work with says Paul has a kid and that's why he has to work at night. Kids cost a fortune, you know. And this house, it was fancy. Maybe too fancy for someone like Paul."

"Anyone who chooses to work with dead bodies is suspicious, if you ask me."

"Hey!"

Xander laughed but cut it short. "This isn't anything to laugh about. I feel sick thinking about what could have happened to you. You need to be more careful."

"Always."

"You're not careful at all. I mean it. Call the police as soon as you hang up with me."

"Okay, I'll call them."

Eventually.

Charlie had just opened a beer in his kitchen when Xander called. He took a long drink and set the bottle down on the counter before answering.

"Xander. Hey. I was going to call you."

"Don't give me that crap. You had my number. Aside from a few group emails, you've been a ghost."

"Me? You had my number, too. At least your girl talks to me. That's a start."

"Yeah, she told me about your shared adventure. What gives?"

Charlie doubted Brooke had told Xander everything. "Talk about mad coincidences. This was some messed up stuff, but it's going to be okay now. She won't be having any more trouble."

"So—she said you were following her?"

Charlie laughed, giving himself time to come up with an excuse. "Sort of. I was going to ask her out. And if you guys ever break up, I'm totally hitting on her." He hated that his excuse made him sound like a weird guy who followed beautiful women around. Would Xander even buy it?

Xander snorted. "Good thing I trust you like no one else. Anyway, what are the chances? I'm in Chicago right now, but when I get back we can go out and grab a drink together. It will be good to see you. I . . . I was having some issues, flashbacks from Kandahar. I'm supposed to talk about it with people who will understand."

"We'll grab a beer any time, no worries."

"Brooke said you're working for a tech company now."

"I am. It's a big change for me."

"What do you do there?"

"We have special projects and contracts, as needed type of stuff for companies when they have a problem. I just help make it all happen. Tell me what you're doing."

They talked about Xander's internship and some of the guys from their unit for another ten minutes before saying goodbye.

Charlie understood how Xander fell for Brooke. She was hot, smart, funny—who wouldn't? But there was far more to Brooke Walton than met the eye. Did Xander have a clue? Or was Brooke that good at fooling even those closest to her? He'd have to find a way to break them up. Eventually.

He glanced at the clear, plastic Starbucks water cup sealed inside a plastic bag on his counter. Pretty soon they would know for sure.

Chapter Twenty-Eight

Brooke woke to a painful tenderness around her neck. For a second, confusion reigned. Once she was fully awake, she remembered exactly why she hurt. She jumped out of bed, more resolved than ever to push forward with her plan. Keeping her normal routine was imperative; otherwise, someone might get suspicious. She would go to work and pretend the ordeal from last night never happened.

At work, Mya, who usually avoided her, gave Brooke a strange lingering look as they passed each other in the corridor. The stare was rude, but Brooke had more pressing concerns. With all that happened the previous evening, something Charlie told her was just now registering. He'd said the incident with the car in the back lot wasn't an accident at all. She wasn't sure if she believed it. Why had someone wanted to hurt her? She needed to figure out the who and the why.

Inside her office she sat down and logged into her personal email server.

A new message from Charlie Ballard waited. She opened the email.

The friend you met last night is named Morris F. Draven. You need anything, you let me know.

Brooke touched her fingers to her chin. *Of course, it's Draven.*

She'd always thought so, but she had done her best to be open-minded, to anticipate the unexpected.

His behavior during Alyssa's autopsy made total sense now. The way he had rushed in the room and offered to take over.

She deleted Charlie's message, jumped up, and hurried to her office door. Anyone with an access card could open it, but there was an old-fashioned dead bolt on the inside. She slid the bolt into place and jiggled the handle to make sure it couldn't be opened. Turning, she leaned her shoulders back against the door.

Draven knows where to find me. Will he come looking? Not likely. Surely, when he discovered the empty closet, he imagined the police were on their way. Probably he grabbed the first flight to Mexico. That's what a normal person would do. But is he normal?

And why did he kill Alyssa Cable?

She could think of plenty of reasons. Drugs. Gambling. Greed. The need to silence her.

But do any of those things justify a murder? He's a physician. Doesn't he have other options?

Someone might have said the same thing to her about the guys in Cancun, or about Jessica or Rachael – or even her professor at Cedarhurst. Draven might have a great explanation for Alyssa Cable's demise, even if it didn't appear that way to others. In any case, his explanation was irrelevant unless it helped with the execution of her plan.

Rachael's earrings were now inside his home. Unfortunately, two other people, Draven and Charlie, knew she had also been there. Both had to know she wasn't entirely innocent of something, or she would have called the police.

What a mess. And somewhat amusing, if only my future wasn't at stake. So. . . who should I talk to first? Jean Thompson? No, not yet. Jerome? He has a thing for me, but how well does he know Draven? Xander? Definitely not.

He'll insist I call the police. Charlie? She knew Charlie the very least, but for reasons she couldn't explain, she trusted him the most. He didn't seem to be a play-by-the-rules sort of guy. He found her tied up in a closet and hardly asked any questions. He hadn't tried to pressure her into calling the police.

Yes, Charlie can help me. If and when I need help.

And meanwhile, I'll act normal and do my job. Data entry seemed unbearably mundane, even more so than usual, relative to her own pressing plans.

A knock on the door startled her. "Um, hold on. One second." The knock was immediately followed by a beep—the access card machine allowing entry. The knob turned. The bolt prevented the door from opening.

Her stomach sunk. "Just a minute."

Dr. Gold grumbled, rattling the knob. "Why is this door locked?"

She scrambled to release the bolt and open the door. "Sorry. I spilled something and just needed to change my—never mind, what do you need?"

"I need you in the autopsy room." He was walking away before he finished his sentence.

"Sure. Coming. I need to change first." Before leaving, she signed off her computer and scanned her office from corner to corner, although she wasn't sure why. She walked to the locker room, checking her surroundings the whole way.

After changing into scrubs and grabbing a lab coat, she paused outside the autopsy room to compose herself. She was jumpy and nervous, not at all like her usual self, when she needed to be calm and thinking clearly. *I've done nothing wrong. I'm granting the whole city a favor by finding Alyssa's killer.* A certain fortification of will always arose when she recalled the purpose driving her actions. With a swell of confidence, she swiped her card and entered the room.

She halted when she saw the three men staring back at her: Gold, Jerome, and Draven

Yikes!

Jerome's gaze moved to her neck. So did Gold's.

She covered her throat with her hand, flinching when she accidentally touched her tender skin, and walked into the room.

"What happened to you?" Jerome pointed to her conspicuous welt.

She forced a short laugh. "You wouldn't believe it if I told you."

"Try us."

"It was just an unfortunate accident."

"Looks like you were choked with a rope or something." Jerome furrowed his brow.

"I'm thinking erotic asphyxiation, and someone didn't hear her safe word." Dr. Draven muttered with a grin, but his knuckles were white from gripping the edge of the table.

Dr. Gold's eyes remained on the blazing red scars while he scowled.

"So, why are we all here together?" A cheerful tone came easily due to her nerves being on edge.

"We have a sudden backlog." Dr. Gold placed his cane against the wall and positioned one of the dictation microphones over his head. "And since Dr. Draven showed up again today," he grumbled, taking a quick glance at Draven, "we need a few assistants." He consulted a hand-written list and rattled off the names of the two bodies he wanted from the storage room.

Jerome and Brooke left to retrieve the bodies. Draven followed them.

Fidgeting with his hands, Jerome walked beside Brook. "Um, there's something I've been wanting to ask you since you met with that detective a few days ago. Sorry 'bout this, but I kinda overheard that you lost a key near a murder scene in Cancun. I searched for it online. It's in the news. The two American guys."

"Hmm. I'd also be interested to hear what you know," Draven murmured.

"There's nothing interesting about it." Brooke pressed her lips together. "What happened was terrible. And if you want to satisfy some morbid curiosity, you can google it to your heart's content." She turned to Dr. Draven. "And how are you this morning, Doctor?"

"I had an unexpected guest, which made for an unusual night."

"Oh, really? I did too. An unusual night, that is." She traced her finger along the lower edge of the rope burn on her neck.

Mouth hanging partway open, Jerome stared from the doctor to the intern.

Dr. Draven unlatched a door and yanked out the drawer inside. "Brooke can assist me. We haven't had the pleasure of working together yet."

"Uh, whatever you say." Jerome shoved his hands inside his pockets and shuffled back toward the autopsy room.

The intercom bell rang, indicating a delivery had arrived at the back door.

"Take care of that." Dr. Draven spoke to Jerome without looking at him.

Jerome left the storage area to sign in and help move the new arrivals. Dr. Draven and Brooke each rolled a body into the autopsy room.

Mrs. Murphy, the part-time receptionist, spoke over the intercom system. "Dr. Gold. There's a family waiting to speak to you. What should I tell them?"

He grumbled, removed his gloves, and pressed the intercom button. "Tell them I'm coming."

"Of course." The intercom left a trail of static before clicking off.

"I'll be right back." Dr. Gold left Brooke and Draven alone with the cadavers.

Brooke glanced at the sharp tools laid out at the end of their table, an equal distance away from her and Dr. Draven. Only the constant rush of the air conditioning and the sound of the zipper peeling open the body bag filled the silence. Together, they removed the body.

Draven pulled the overhead microphone towards him and began dictating cursory observations for the external exam. He didn't ask Brooke's opinion or pause to hear what she might have to say. After a few minutes, he spoke directly to her. "Hand me the Stryker saw."

Her hand hovered over the tray of stainless steel objects gleaming in the overhead lights. Sharp scissors. Pointed probes. Deadly scalpels. She picked up the Stryker saw, passing it to Draven.

He grasped it, his eyes challenging hers from behind his goggles. "Why were you trespassing at my house?" He switched on the saw and lowered the rotating blade into the skull.

She raised her voice to be heard over the high-pitched grinding. "I didn't know I was at your house. Not until this morning."

"Hmmmf."

"It's an excellent set up you have going here."

Draven set the saw down and placed his fingers on the skull cap, prying it away and exposing shiny lumps and curves of brain. "What are you talking about, Miss Walton?"

"You know. Edna Jones, for example."

"Who is Edna Jones?"

"You signed off on her autopsy. Said you'd done one when you hadn't."

He grunted.

"Falsifying data is a lot easier than getting your hands dirty completing an autopsy, isn't it? Or did you really confuse Violet Simpson's stab wound with a natural cause of death?" She raised an eyebrow. "Perfect set up here, with Dr. Gold unwilling to deal with the computers. You can do whatever you please, can't you? Easy money."

A vein pulsed in Draven's forehead. His fingers dug deep into the brain tissue, expelling cerebral fluid. He yanked the brain from the skull cavity with a sickening squelch. "Sever the brain cord."

Brooke did as she was told, anxious to get it done and step back away from Draven. "It makes sense. Quick money. You must need it for something. But what about Alyssa? Why did she have to die? There are enough bodies needing to be examined without creating your own supply."

The doors swooshed open and Dr. Gold reentered, grumbling.

"No need to answer." Brooke lowered her voice. "I'll figure it out on my own."

Draven turned red as he gritted his teeth. "By the way, Miss Walton, I found a phone on the floor in the refrigeration room. I believe it's yours."

"Where is it now?"

"It's on the computer table in the storage room."

"Why, thank you. I can't imagine how I ever misplaced it." She poured out the sweetness and charm. "I think you can finish the autopsy yourself, Dr. Draven, if that's all right with the Chief. I've got lots of paperwork that needs my attention. You wouldn't believe the errors I find." She stepped back from the table, peeled off her gloves, and walked backward to the storage room so as not to take her eyes off Draven as he clutched the scalpel and watched her go.

Her phone sat next to the keyboard. If only she hadn't disabled the password function last year. Constantly typing it in had wasted too much of her time. Now, she wished for a do over on that decision and wondered what Draven had seen. She snatched it from the table, holding it at arms' length like it was contaminated with a deadly disease. At least the Medical Examiner's Office had no shortage of disinfectants. She grabbed a bottle from a shelf in the autopsy room.

She raised her phone and the bottle when she passed Draven on the way out. She spoke so only Draven could hear her. "Disinfecting this to be safe. In case you have Hep C." She flashed a grin. Hepatitis C couldn't be spread from casual contact, but it was the first insult that came to mind.

Why am I going out of my way to piss him off?

She'd said too many things that couldn't be forgotten.

She hoped she wouldn't regret it.

Chapter Twenty-Nine

Draven ordered a Tequila shot at the bar to stop his hands from shaking.

Not gonna show up early and appear anxious.

He drained his glass and passed a few more minutes, tearing his napkin to shreds before heading to the back of the club and down the stairs to the private basement room.

Nothing compared to the deep thrill of taking a seat at the poker table wearing his game face, silently assessing his opponents, and reviewing his plans to outsmart them. A rush of smug satisfaction accompanied his first win. Elation blossomed inside him when another followed. He felt invincible, like he was flying down a wide-open road in a Ferrari, nothing and no one to stop him. Smarter. Stronger. Unbeatable. Everything was going his way. And as always, when he reached that height, he upped the stakes.

He didn't let the sting of his first loss show, nor his second. He kept his face calm and still, a placid lake offering no reflection. It happened. Everything worth doing had ups and downs. He was back to breaking even. *Stay calm.* He'd never let a few small losses keep him from playing big. No one ever won big by playing it safe. How many people quit and walked away, never knowing how close they were to unimaginable success? He vowed never to be that person, the one who walked away right when they were on the verge of victory. He possessed the confidence required to wait out the minor bumps. His next hand would be the one to turn his fortune around. Had to be.

Losses continued to mount. His face turned pale and perspiration coated his skin. His stomach turned sour. Now he had to play just to earn back his money. He slapped a pill onto his tongue, gulped it down, and used his balled-up fist to stop his leg from bouncing under the table. His despair spiraled deeper into that dark, forsaken place he hated to visit but couldn't manage to avoid. Spoiled luck greased his way down and he began to worry there might not be a bottom this time.

Like a broken record, his familiar regrets began: *What have I done? Why did I come? Why didn't I quit when I was ahead?*

He took a deep breath.

It's not my fault. I'm an addict. I have a problem.

He stood up to go, muttering curses, watching everything he had go into the pockets of the others at the table.

This is not how things were supposed to go. And not just today's game. His whole damn life. The great existence to which he felt entitled had washed away with wave after wave of unlucky cards.

Outside the club, he was surrounded by a crowd that was waiting to enter. He had to weave around and through their cool, uppity attitudes to get away. Most of them were young, probably a quarter of them underage with fake IDs. Their confidence, most of it pretense, stoked his bitter rage. They had no idea what it was like to endure his burdens. He should have so much, and instead, he had nothing. He trudged along in the dark. Alone. What was he going to do now? Brooke Walton, the arrogant, screwed-up, summer intern, had not only come snooping around his home in search of who the hell knew what, but she'd also stolen away his extra source of income. He had a good thing going faking autopsies until she came along. And with Alyssa gone, how could he buy and sell drugs? He wouldn't stoop to be a dealer on the street. Not yet, anyway.

His rage and disappointment needed a target. Brooke. What was up with her? She was not what she seemed.

He shook his head, running a sweaty hand through his hair.

Stupid intern distracted me, forced my eye off the ball. It's her fault.

He shivered, laughing like a maniac.

She's not going to get away with it.

Chapter Thirty

Standing over her bathroom sink, Brooke finished massaging vitamin E into the crimson line circling her neck. She angled her head to the left, pleased with the thin cords of muscles forming a V from the base of her throat. She loved everything about her body— its strength, endurance, grace, and coordination. It excelled in all she asked of it—mentally and physically, powering through her concussion and work-outs that would make a Navy Seal collapse.

Yet she rarely considered her outward appearance.

Her beauty made life easier, it influenced the way people treated her, but aside from appreciating that perk, she didn't waste time dwelling on her looks.

Her phone rested on the back of the toilet. Draven had deleted all her text messages and voicemails. He had probably read and listened to them first, so she tried to remember their content. Xander's messages were slightly embarrassing, since he often made his attraction to her explicitly clear. Several of her mother's texts referenced the incident in Cancun and their conversations with the police. If Draven had read them, he knew more about her than she wanted him to know. What might he do with that information? That was the question.

With a nagging sense of suspicion, she picked up her phone and turned it over in her hands. She'd created a password earlier in the day. A little too late, but lesson learned.

Could he have put a bug inside my phone to eavesdrop on my conversations? Was that even a real thing someone could do?

Her phone vibrated. She glanced at the screen and cringed. An unknown number. The detective working on Rachael's disappearance? Or the detective helping on the Cancun case? Neither would be a welcomed call. For once, she hoped it was the ridiculously cheerful automated lady who called a few times a week offering help with her school loans, a woman she would happily strangle to get her to stop calling. *"Hiii. This is Christina! I have good news about consolidating your student loans, but you have to act fast."*

Without answering, Brooke tossed her phone onto the chair. From her closet, she grabbed a scarf and draped it loosely around her neck before walking across the hall to Jeff's apartment. She pressed the doorbell. "It's Brooke."

"Come in," Jeff yelled from inside.

He stood in front of the stove, stirring a pot. "Why are you wearing a winter scarf?"

"I'm making an effort to be fashionable."

"It's *not* working."

"Oh, well." She shrugged. "Can I borrow your phone again?"

"Sure. It's on the table. Password is 4345."

"Thanks. I'll be right back."

Back inside her apartment, with two phones, she scrolled through her own list of recent calls. She found a local, unfamiliar number. It had to be Jean. She keyed it in on Jeff's phone, just in case Draven was listening in on hers. Probably a ridiculous precaution, but better to be safe than sorry. Her finger hovered over the green circle that would connect the call.

What should I say? Would it be better for the tip to come from an anonymous source? I could pretend to be someone else.

She pressed her fingernail against the side of the phone.

Do it now. I need that PI to get on this right away.

She connected the call and Jean answered immediately. "Hello. Jean Thompson speaking."

"Hi, Jean. This is Brooke Walton. We spoke last week about Rachael Kline's disappearance. You came to the Medical Examiner's Office?"

"Of course. What can I do for you, Brooke?"

"Well, you said if I thought of anything, I should call you."

"Yes. Absolutely."

"I think I might know something after all, something I remembered. It's probably not important, but—"

"Go on." Brooke could sense the edge of anticipation in Jean's voice, like Jean had been watching her phone, willing it to ring, hoping for something just like this to happen.

"Well, while it may be nothing, I'm concerned enough for my own safety that I'd like to ask you to promise not to share with anyone else that the information came from me."

"Well, that could depend on other factors, but I'll do my best not to involve you. Especially if you have reason to believe you could be harmed. What have you remembered?"

Brooke savored her sense of control over the situation. Jean sounded desperate.

"See, it's been awhile since anyone has asked me about Rachael, and this time, when I was talking to you, I felt like I knew something, like something was bothering me, but I couldn't pinpoint what it was."

"And?"

"I hadn't been working at the Medical Examiner's Office long when I got this nagging feeling. Actually, it may be your questions that made me remember."

"What did you remember?"

"I think Rachael was seeing one of the employees here before she went missing."

"Who?"

"Dr. Morris Draven."

"Does he work there still, I mean currently?"

"Yes. Mostly at night. I've only seen him a few times. She probably met him at the hospital, or maybe through her volunteer work."

"Why didn't you mention Rachael was seeing someone before? It never came up in the interviews that she was seeing someone other than a fellow student."

"I don't know in what context she was seeing him. We see lots of doctors in scrubs and lab coats around the medical school campus. It's hard for anyone to stick out. But now I'm pretty sure that's why he seemed familiar when I first saw him at work."

Carefully-crafted lies spun from her mouth like a spider building an intricate web. No one ever told the whole truth. People embellished and exaggerated. And witnesses of the same crime might report ten different statements: the perpetrator had dark skin, the perpetrator had white skin, he was average height, he was tall. Who was to judge her version? And so what if it contained a slight variation from actual events?

There was a pause, filled with scratching noises. Jean was writing.

"Again, please don't mention you got this information from me. For obvious reasons, I don't want his rage directed at me, you know, like if you end up talking to him. I think he's got some serious anger management issues."

"Oh. I don't see any reason to tell anyone where my tip came from at this time."

"I know it's really unlikely that anything will come of it, but still, you asked me to call, and I guess I just feel better knowing that I've told someone, rather than keeping it to myself."

"I appreciate your call, Brooke. Sometimes it's those gut instincts that provide the best leads."

"So, will you, you know, check him out?"

"I will do a bit of research. Yes."

"And could you let me know if you find something? I mean, if you find any reason to believe that he is a dangerous person."

"If I were to find something of concern, I could do that."

Brooke leaned forward, clasping her hands. It was a start. She imagined Jean was already typing Draven's name into her internet browser and asking her police department friends for investigative favors. The ball was in motion. She would wait patiently for just the right time and then give it a whopping kick.

Draven was about to join her in the unpleasant world where detectives swarmed, breathing down your neck with their invasive questions.

Chapter Thirty-One

Jean tapped her pen on a stack of overdue bills, waiting for her ancient computer to wake up. She was in dire need of a lead, and now she had one, but that didn't mean it was a good one. On the positive side, Brooke Walton appeared to be an intelligent woman with her act together, a credible witness. Maybe, hopefully, there would be something to her recollection. Jean said a silent prayer, logged into her investigative software, and began a background search on Morris Draven.

Draven's social media accounts held nothing more than a few pictures. In his profile photo he wore a Hawaiian shirt in a tropical setting with palm trees. His smile revealed bright white teeth against a deep tan. The most recent photo on his page was two years old, Draven wearing aviator glasses with three other men in front of a small plane. The few other pictures in his public account had been posted by others. In each, he posed with attractive women, mostly in black-tie attire and holding up fancy drinks. An air of arrogance surrounded him. Morris Draven appeared to be a lucky man who enjoyed luxuries and had the money to buy them. Jean had a negative net-worth and had never once attended a black-tie affair. Disliking him was almost instinctive.

Scrolling through her PI app that pulled info from various online locations, she carefully read over information related to his college, medical school, internship, and residency. When his medical education was complete, he worked for a short time as a family physician in a group practice. Nothing Jean could find hinted at why he left, or if he had left of his own accord. She didn't expect to learn those details online, unless he'd done something significantly terrible enough to lose his license and make the newspapers, which he had not. Currently, he was listed as one of the coroners in East Dalton. Changing from a family practice doctor to a coroner struck Jean as an unusual step for a young physician. Less income, less prestige. Why would he do that?

She located his address, drove to his townhome, and pressed his doorbell. She waited, fiddling with the cross around her neck and taking in the homes. None of them needed repair, unlike most of the houses in her neighborhood. How nice it would be for Millie to live somewhere as clean, quiet, and safe. Unfortunately, Jean's inconsistent income as a PI would never allow it. She punched her finger into the doorbell a second time.

A woman in tight workout clothes walked past. A pink bow flopped around on her miniature dog's head. Jean gave up. She turned away thinking about grabbing some fast food for Millie's dinner, when the door opened. She spun around. "Dr. Morris Draven?"

"Yes?"

She recognized him from his social media pictures and had to ignore a wave of resentment. At first glance, he was neat and trim in appearance. Closer inspection revealed his bloodshot eyes and the slight tremor in his hands before he stuffed them into the pockets of his jeans. She recognized the signs of a user.

Maybe that's why he switched out of family practice. And why he only works on dead people now.

"I'm Jean Thompson." She flipped her ID open and closed it just as fast. "I have a few questions for you. I'm hoping you can help me with an ongoing investigation."

He winced, holding a hand up to block the sunlight. "Sure, uh, usually I take follow up questions at work. I'm just waking up. I work unusual hours." He made clear his irritation regarding her visit, yet he kept mumbling on. "But, what can I help you with?"

"Did you know a Rachael Kline?"

He tilted his head. "Never heard of her. Wait, are you a police officer?"

"I'm a private investigator. You've never heard of her?"

He sighed, shaking his head and closing his eyes. "No, I've never heard of her, okay?" He rubbed his eyes. "Listen, Miss . . . "

"Thompson."

"Yeah, I think even a low rent PI like you can understand, I examine hundreds of deceased individuals every year. I don't focus on names. That shouldn't be hard to comprehend. You'll need to make an appointment with the Medical Examiner's Office if you need more information."

He pushed the door closed. Jean extended her hand to keep it from shutting and then pushed it open again. "Rachael Kline was never on your examining table and everyone around here has heard of her. She disappeared from her dorm at Rothaker Medical School six months ago—"

"Oh, that Rachael Kline." He blinked a few times. "I didn't know her. Why are you asking me?"

"It's come to my attention that you might have known her, before she disappeared. That you and she might have been having a relationship."

"What?" He raised his eyebrows. "That's not . . . that's preposterous. Look, I have dated a few medical students from Rothaker in the past, and maybe I don't remember all their names, but if I'd had any sort of relationship with Rachael Kline, I would remember. I can assure you."

"Were you here in East Dalton when she disappeared last November?"

"Are you serious?"

"Yes. If you were working somewhere else at the time, if you weren't even in the city, that would end my questioning right now."

Dr. Draven ran his hand through his hair like a claw. "You're asking me to recall where I was, what, six months ago?" He huffed. "Look, lady, I told you—"

"Jean Thompson."

"Whatever. I don't know Rachael Kline. I've never met her, I've never seen her or talked to her before. What are you accusing me of?"

"I'm not accusing you of anything. I'm just following up on a lead here. Doing my job."

"Do your job elsewhere." Draven slammed the door before Jean could protest, leaving her on his doorstep with her mouth hanging open and thinking, *innocent people don't behave that way.*

Her phone buzzed. She read the new message while walking back to her car. It was the after-school program. Millie had just suffered another asthma attack.

Draven's abrupt end to the conversation now seemed like fortuitous timing. She wanted to be by Millie's side as fast as possible. Her daughter was tough as nails, but her asthma attacks always left her exhausted and shaken. The message served as another reminder of why Jean couldn't have a full-time job working for anyone other than herself.

Jean tucked Millie into bed with a movie and a snack. From Millie's nightstand, she removed a legal pad from under a pile of nebulizers, empty inhaler boxes, and antihistamines. She flipped over pages covered with writing until she found the current page, half-full already, where she wrote down the day and time.

"Get some rest, sweetheart."

Millie pulled her sheet up to her chin. "Mommy?"

"Yes, Millie."

"I'm sorry I get sick so much."

"Oh, sweetie." She hugged her daughter. "No. This isn't your fault. None of this is your fault. You're the bravest girl in the whole world and you make me so proud."

Millie smiled and snuggled under her blankets. "I love you, Mommy."

"I love you more, Millie." Jean held back the tears brimming in her eyes. "I'll just be down the hall. I need to make a phone call." Jean gave Millie another hug and held on until her daughter squirmed out of her arms.

At the kitchen table, she needed a few minutes to compose herself before she was ready to call Draven's former employer.

A woman with a sing-song voice answered. "East Dalton Family Practice. Can you hold please?"

"Sure." Jean grabbed the coupon section from Sunday's newspaper and started cutting. *What's my best approach here?*

A minute later, a different woman with a deeper voice picked up the line. "East Dalton Family Practice. How can I help you?"

"I'm calling to ask about Dr. Morris Draven."

"Oh...um, Dr. Draven he got—I mean, he doesn't work here anymore. He left the practice a while ago, a year maybe."

"I see. Can you tell me why he left?"

"I'm sorry. I can't discuss that with anyone."

"Can I ask if it had anything to do with his behavior, I mean...."

"I'm sorry. I couldn't tell you, I mean, I'm not allowed to talk about it."

Jean had a feeling she could not ignore. Sometimes, what people didn't say, or the way they spoke indicated more than what they actually said. Jean had heard enough to bolster her suspicions. Dr. Draven had skeletons in his closet. But what kind of skeletons? And did they include the disappearance of Rachael Kline?

Chapter Thirty-Two

As Brooke trudged toward her apartment, Jeff stepped out of his. "Hey, sunshine. Wanna go get something to eat?"

Her stomach growled. "I do, but I want to take a hot shower more. I'm beat."

He stepped behind her and rubbed her shoulders. "Rough day?"

"I just taught ultimate conditioning and then strength training. I'm drained."

"Speaking of ultimate conditioning, when was the last time this hair saw a stylist?" He lifted a few long strands away from her ponytail and let them drop slowly. "I see a few split ends."

"Stop. I'm going to shower, slip into one of Xander's cozy t-shirts, and just veg tonight."

"Which, for you, means getting a head start on next year's curriculum, I bet. Well," he walked backwards as he departed. "Shoot me a message . . . "

"Okay, thanks. You're the best."

Maybe I'll finally get the TV connected and watch some news, see what's happening in the world outside East Dalton. But . . . probably not.

The pungent combination of chemicals from the Medical Examiner's Office and sweat followed her into her apartment. She removed her phone from her running belt and tossed it on her chair. On her way to the fridge, her doorbell rang. With an irritated sigh, she backtracked and opened the door. "Jeff, I—"

Draven charged in, knocking Brooke backwards. He slammed the door, pressing his back against it.

Brooke glared at him. Her fingers curled around the hem of her tank top, pulling it lower down her hips. "What are *you* doing here?"

"I came to talk." He glanced around without losing sight of Brooke. "Like I promised."

Wearing a yellow windbreaker with a golf club insignia and khaki shorts, he didn't look like a crazed killer, but his determined presence inside her living room was unsettling.

"You left something behind." He opened his fist. Rachael's earrings rested in his palm.

"Those aren't mine."

He closed his hand tight around the earrings and dropped his arm back to his side. "They weren't there before you showed up. I vacuumed every inch of that space after I . . . after . . ."

"After what?"

He glowered. "Why the hell did you put them on my dresser?"

Brooke rolled her eyes. "Don't you have bigger worries?"

Draven moved closer, positioning himself between Brooke and her chair. A muscle under his eye twitched in a way that both fascinated and revolted Brooke. She squared her shoulders and held her ground.

"You aren't even afraid. And you haven't called the police. What exactly is wrong with you, Miss Walton? Are you some sort of sociopath? Way off the grid of normal?"

"Ha! You're wondering what's wrong with me?" *Careful. Remember, he's crazy, demented.*

"Wouldn't that be something, a sociopath who could be on the cover of the Sports Illustrated swim suit edition. Mental illness doesn't discriminate, but who would ever suspect?" He glared at her, but a hint of amusement was visible in the slight upward curl of his lip. "You've got some questions to answer."

She eyed her phone, sitting just beyond him on the chair cushion. "Okay." She stepped sideways toward it, trying to appear casual. "Try me. What questions?"

"To start, why are you going above and beyond to ruin my life? Why are you gleefully reporting my mistakes to Dr. Gold?"

"Mistakes? Pfff! Interesting choice of words. Let's not play games with each other. You and I both know those weren't mistakes."

He slammed his fist down and winced. Her countertop was fine, but his hand had to be killing him. "Why did you do it?"

"At the time, I thought the Medical Examiner's Office had an incompetent employee, and I have a strong intolerance for incompetence. Now, I believe that employee has a drug addiction or a prostitute addiction, maybe a gambling problem, something to make him desperate, maybe all those things."

Dr. Draven snorted. "Why were you snooping around my house?"

Brooke held his gaze but didn't respond.

"And after you escaped from my closet, why didn't you call the police?"

"Why don't you just consider yourself lucky that I didn't?"

Draven pointed a finger at her. "Does your unusual behavior have anything to do with a couple of murdered tourists in Cancun?"

"Jerome." She curled her fists.

"That drooling moron? Please. He aired your dirty laundry, yeah, but it was your mother who first clued me in. Left an interesting voicemail asking if you'd heard from the police again." Draven slipped the earrings back into his pocket. "An investigator came to my house asking about a disappearance that happened months ago. Rachael Kline. Know anything about that?"

"No."

"I think you do." He strode toward her, one hand in his jacket pocket. "I had zero problems before I met you."

"Oh, I doubt that."

Draven lunged to grab her. "You're coming with me."

"I don't think so." Brooke scrambled out of reach. She noticed the pulse in his neck, throbbing under his skin. "My boyfriend is going to be home any second."

He barked out a laugh. "No, he's not. I know you live alone." Without taking his eyes off her, he withdrew his hand from inside his jacket. He stood with his legs apart, blocking her path, and raised his arm, a syringe in his hand.

Brooke snorted. "No one is ever going to believe that I was doing drugs." She inched slowly toward her phone.

"I don't care what they believe."

"And everyone will be looking for who did it."

He moved closer. "For who did what, exactly?"

"Whatever it is you think you're going to do to me. You're not going to get away with it."

"Sure I will." He laughed, another twitch thumping below his eye. "No one is looking for Jane Doe."

"Jane Doe? Is that what this is about?" Brooke sneered. "So, are you going to show up for the forensic exam when they find me? Why not, right?

You can collect the money without doing an autopsy, since you'll already know what happened to me."

"Shut your mouth," he hissed. "You think you're so clever, but you don't know everything."

He rushed forward, forcing her into the corner. She kicked at him, her fists flying. He kept coming as she pummeled him, ignoring her strikes, cursing like he was angry enough to kill. With a single stroke, he managed to plunge the needle deep into her shoulder. She tried to jerk away. The needle ripped through her skin but pressure from Draven kept it in place. He slammed her against the wall, using all his weight to pin her there, until the syringe was empty.

A deep and powerful fear gripped her heart with talons and spread like wildfire. An unknown drug was seeping its way through her veins and there was nothing she could do to stop it. Blood drizzled from the tear in her arm and hit the floor in splattered drops.

What did he give me?!

She'd never experimented with drugs in her life, she had zero acquired tolerance. She also had a high metabolism—would that help or hurt?

Is it enough to kill me? Is this how Alyssa Cable overdosed?

The room spun ever so slowly, like a merry-go-round just getting started. An alarming warmth spread throughout her body, permeating every cell. Her legs grew weak. Dr. Draven gripped her arm, smearing her blood onto his coat. She tried to stay strong and resist, she fully intended to make a grab for her phone and then lock herself in the bathroom. Instead, she sunk to her knees. Draven yanked her back on her feet like a rag doll, tossing one of her arms over his shoulder. Against her will, she sunk heavily against him. Barely able to move and terrifyingly aware that her control was ebbing away as her dizziness escalated, she was incapable of resisting when he dragged her out of her apartment.

Is this the end? Is this how I'm going to die?

Her head flopped back and she stared up at the night sky.

Bright stars. Millions of light years away. Thank God it's nighttime or I would be gawking at the sun and frying my retinas. She laughed and jerked her head forward.

A couple exited a car and walked toward them. They stared straight at Brooke, not bothering to hide their amusement.

I've seen them. They live here. But usually he's just in one dimension. I mean, three dimensions. Not so many dimensions. Stop. Stop. Pull it together. This is serious. This is serious. Help. Help. "He . . . he . . ." is all that came out of her open mouth.

The man laughed and kept walking.

I will find you, slit your chest open and tear out your heart for laughing at me, for thinking I chose to be some drunk, stumbling, helpless . . . Laughter rang out, strange snorts an animal would make. With revulsion, she realized the inhuman sounds were coming from her own throat.

"Excuse us." Draven shook his head. "She's had one too many celebrating."

Again, she tried to call for help. Slurred, non-sensical words emerged. For the first time in her life, she felt stupid. Her worst nightmare had become reality—she wasn't in control.

Draven pressed forward through the parking lot and somehow her feet stumbled one after the other as he dragged her along. When he opened his car door, she tried to press against the roof, but her strength had disappeared, her muscles weren't responding. He easily plucked her weak grip from the top of the car and pushed her inside. She collapsed against the seat as he tossed her legs in.

She had ideas of what she could do to turn the situation around, but her body wouldn't cooperate. The urgency she desperately needed simply didn't exist. Her breath and heart beat slowed to a sluggish, drawn out rhythm. She was unable to summon the anger and determination that had always been readily available for her at a second's notice. For once, her body was useless.

Draven ran around the front of the car and got in on the driver's side. He leaned toward her, grabbing her hands. She attempted to snatch them out of his reach, but they floated above her legs like two limp noodles. He tied them together with ease. She struggled to keep her eyes open but eventually succumbed to the powerful drugs. Her head lolled forward, and she lost all awareness.

The car stopped with a lurch, throwing her forward. Brooke forced her eyes open in time to watch Draven turn off the car and drop his head against the center of the steering wheel with a thud. According to the clock on the dashboard, over two hours had passed. Had they been in the car all that time? She did a mental check of her body parts to make sure everything was intact, and nothing felt violated. She wasn't in any pain, far from it, most likely from the drugs. Her hands were still secured together in front of her. A gag now prevented her from screaming.

Again with the gag. A dash of wry amusement now accompanied her predicament. The fact that she was still alive a few hours later served to dispel some of her fear.

Outside the window, she saw familiar rundown apartments and the woods beyond them. Holly Gardens. He'd taken her to Alyssa's neighborhood. Whatever he had in mind, she had no idea what it was. Perhaps he didn't either.

The drugs were wearing off. She wasn't one hundred percent, and that alone frightened her, but her awareness had returned. Her muscles responded when she flexed them. Draven didn't need to know. She sagged to one side in her seat, pretending she was still totally zonked out.

Draven lifted his head and opened his door a crack, illuminating the interior. His face reflected determination, or resignation, like he'd finally decided what must be done. Tiny red capillaries stretched through the white of his eyes. He shivered, in spite of the perspiration on his forehead. "Time to go."

He pulled Brooke out of the passenger seat and away from his car, holding her tightly against him while he pressed his key fob to lock the doors. She trudged beside him on to a narrow path through the woods behind the apartments, passing a discarded couch, broken chairs, and a rusted stove. Tree canopy blocked out the stars above, making the ground indistinguishable from the darkness. With her hands tied, she could do little to prevent the mosquitoes from feasting on her body.

Great. If he doesn't kill me, I'll probably get the Zika virus.

After walking slowly for about five minutes, she noticed an orange-yellow flame flickering through the branches to her left. A faint buzz grew louder as they continued walking, until it turned into discernible shouts and conversations. People were partying around a bonfire.

Without warning, two teens, a boy and a girl, emerged from a cluster of bushes. The girl stared down at her own chest, buttoning her blouse. They froze at the sight of Draven and Brooke.

Draven stopped moving, temporarily rooted to the spot.

The girl bore an embarrassed look. For one second, the boy's eyes met Brooke's and she thought he registered her situation. With a gag over her mouth and her hands tied together, it should have been obvious to anyone that she was in trouble. But the girl tugged at his arm and they ran off, their laughter echoing after them.

Draven changed direction and Brooke staggered alongside him. She'd given him no reason to believe the drugs had worn off.

They kept moving forward on the path, him pulling and her stumbling, until the once boisterous shouts from the bonfire party grew fainter.

Draven stopped in a small area cleared long ago by a fire and surrounded by trees. "Good a place as any." He pushed her onto the damp ground. "We're going to talk. Do you understand me?"

She let her chin roll and drop towards her chest. *Why here? Is he just trying to scare me?*

"Wake up!"

She opened her eyes and blinked.

"You've become dangerous to me."

Brooke closed her eyes again.

Draven tore the tape off her face and waited while she spit out the rag and inhaled deeply through her mouth. "That was just a small dose I gave you, but I have more than your body can tolerate." He pulled another syringe from his pocket and waved it from side to side in front of her face. "You're going to answer my questions."

She slurred her words. "Or you'll kill me like you killed Alyssa?"

He paced around and shook a fist in the air. "I didn't kill Alyssa. God damn it! I didn't kill her! I've never killed anyone! Alyssa loved me. That was the problem. She misunderstood our arrangement. But I never would have hurt her. She overdosed. By the time I found her, it was too late. All I did was get rid of her body. There wasn't anything that could be done for her."

"How do you know?"

"Because I'm a physician!"

"So, doctor, everyone should take your word for it. It wasn't in any way your fault."

"It wasn't!" He swung his head around, making sure they were still alone, and lowered his voice. "She was dead when I woke up. She passed out on my patio and I dragged her inside and put her in the closet. I panicked. I wasn't thinking straight. But I didn't hurt her."

"Then why didn't you call the police? Why did you move her from your house and dispose of her in Greenwood Circle?" She'd said too much too fast. Would Draven notice?

"I told you, I panicked. Look, you were right. I faked a few autopsies because I owed money to some people who have no patience. If I didn't pay them off, I would have been killed. I can always do autopsies for free some other time to make up for it. It was never a big deal, faking the autopsies of elderly people. You shouldn't have made it one. Who cares how they died. They were still dead no matter what the cause."

Brooke did her best to look lethargic, slumping away from Draven into a tree and staring out at nothing. She didn't agree with him. A job should always be done well. Expectations were to be met or exceeded. Draven didn't deserve to be a medical doctor.

"Listen, you've got issues, too. Maybe more serious than any of mine. Why don't we work out some kind of deal to stay out of each other's business from now on?"

"Hmmmm," she moaned.

"Because . . . if we can't reach an agreement, well . . . I can't really let you go on messing up my life, can I?"

He's not going to kill me, or he would have done it by now.

"You can't talk yet, huh?" He rubbed his shaky hand over his head with a harsh movement. "That's okay, you'll be feeling more like yourself in a few minutes. I just needed to subdue you. We can wait. We've got all night. We'll wait until you're ready to talk. And if you aren't up for cooperation, then you leave me no choice." He waved the syringe in front of her face.

She peeked around, her gaze intentionally unfocused. Satisfied no one could see or hear their exchange, she closed her eyes and slumped to one side again. "I'm really tired." She dropped to the ground like a big sack of potatoes and took long, slow breaths, intently listening.

Twigs snapped and leaves crunched as Draven paced nearby, muttering to himself. Peeking out from barely lifted eyelids, she saw him remove two more syringes. More than enough to stop her heart, if they were full. A surge of panic wiped out a few layers of her confidence.

I underestimated him. If he injects me again, I won't be able to defend myself out here.

He put two of the syringes back into his pocket but kept one in his hands.

Silently, she began counting.

He stepped close to her face and lifted an elbow away from her body. She fluttered her eyes open to offer a sign of resistance, allowing her arm to fall limply back to the ground.

When he walked away, she rolled slowly onto her side and drew her legs into a fetal position. She remained still until crunching leaves signaled he was close. Her eyes opened a tiny crack. He was squatting down beside her.

She rocked back and thrust her legs out swift and hard. Her shoes connected with his nose in a sickening crunch. The syringe fell from his hands, dropping by her feet. Draven stumbled backward, eyes wide and mouth hanging open, blood pouring from his face.

Brooke scrambled to pick the syringe off the ground, clutching it between the tips of her fingers.

She hurried off the path, moving away from Draven's furious curses. She strained to be silent, running on the tips of her toes, barely touching her feet to the ground, but she couldn't help kicking up fallen branches and crunching decayed leaves. Saplings scratched her face and arms like tiny knives. Shrubs cut into her legs with thorns and briars. She bashed into a tree trunk, whacking her nose and forehead. Gritting her teeth against the sudden sharp pain, she wanted to scream and kick something. She raised her tied hands in front of her chest, protecting herself from the next unseen tree.

A swath of moonlight escaped the clouds and made it through the trees, illuminating a cleared path to her right. On it, she moved at a faster, quieter pace. Where the path split in two, she stopped and leaned against a tree, sweating, heart pounding, and listening for any indication that Draven had followed.

Certain she was alone, at least momentarily, she dropped the syringe at the base of the tree, where she would be sure to find it. Wiggling her back, she used the tree trunk to shimmy her pouch around to her front. When it was just below her tied hands, she unzipped it millimeter by millimeter until she grabbed her knife between her finger tips.

A gust of wind howled through the branches above, signaling a brewing storm.

A stomping, crunching sound made her spin around.

She popped open the knife and froze, holding her breath, poised to run. Somewhere off in the dark woods, or maybe just a few yards away, she pictured Draven standing as still as a statue, just like her, craning his ears for clues to her location.

After a few seconds without another unusual sound, she squatted down against the tree trunk and clamped her knees tight around the knife, trapping it with the blade up like a vise. Back and forth, back and forth, she jerked the rope against the blade. She kept at it, fast as she could, until the rope fell apart and she could separate her hands.

With a glint in her eyes, she gripped the knife in one hand and picked up the syringe with the other. She didn't know if her racing heart pounded from exertion or excitement. "Morris. Oh, Morris." She cackled. "Can you hear me? I'm ready to talk now."

She walked on the tips of her toes, placing each foot down with care, alert for the sound of his approach. A twig snapped. She held her breath.

Silence.

A nearby THUNK—perhaps a shoe striking an exposed tree root—made her turn slowly around. She crept backward and flattened herself against a large tree trunk.

"Where are you?" Draven's voice rang out, but not loud enough to carry as far as the bonfire. Good. She didn't want anyone coming to save her now.

A dark form passed a few yards away, unless it was just her imagination. She took a chance, leaping from behind the tree, grasping for any body part. But Draven lunged in her direction. His hands shot around her throat and squeezed. A shock of fiery pain emanated from her recent injury. Her struggles intensified the pain and she grew weaker. Shadows crept around the edges of her vision, threatening to spread like a black curtain. Her body grew limp, but she held onto the syringe with a death grip. When she had lost all her strength, and all her oxygen, he released his hold. It was only a bit, but it was enough for her to drive her shoulder into his chest, sending both of them sailing to the ground. She scrambled to one knee and jabbed the needle into his throat, plunging the drugs through his skin.

Brooke jumped up, gasping, and gulping down air.

Draven stood and stumbled backwards. "You bitch!" He staggered to the side, reaching his arm out to support himself against a tree.

Brooke circled him.

His eyes glazed over. Moving in slow motion, he sank to the ground on one hip.

"What's the point of this?" He was already slurring his words.

Earlier, Draven had emptied an entire syringe into her neck and it hadn't killed her, just rendered her temporarily useless for a few hours. He was bigger, and he probably had an acquired tolerance for drugs and alcohol. At best, assuming it was the same drug, some sort of narcotic, she didn't have much time. His strength was ebbing away, but it would return.

Moving toward him, she easily avoided the unbalanced jabs he aimed her way. He ineffectively tried to resist when she grabbed the back of his coat and pulled it off.

"You weren't messing with me." She felt a wave of awe and a little respect. "You brought enough drugs to stop my heart. Enough to subdue a tiger." She removed the other two syringes and cradled them in her hands, behind her back. "They're mine now."

She stared down at Draven, waiting to see what he would do. He could try to run, but he had zero chance of eluding her now. She knew just how he felt—dizzy, lethargic, his muscles turning to jelly.

She came closer, readying the syringes, her voice a mere whisper. "If you were telling the truth, it's really too bad you didn't go to the police when Alyssa died. Now, no one will ever know what really happened."

Chapter Thirty-Three

Determined not to make another costly mistake like losing the key in Cancun, Brooke sat down near Draven's lifeless body to formulate a strategy.

It wasn't the best time for thinking clearly; the drugs had dulled her sharp edges, leaving her brain in a fog, although her adrenaline had countered much of the sedative's remaining effects.

Her instinct was to run all the way back to her apartment and go to bed, leaving Draven in the woods and avoiding any connection to the events of the evening. She could act just as surprised as everyone else when they learned of his demise. Although, who would care really? He wasn't very useful to anyone as far as she could tell. But without her statements, how would he be implicated for Alyssa's and Rachael's deaths? There had to be a way. But she didn't have much time to figure it out. Waiting to see if the police put two and two together would be unbearable.

Besides, people had seen them together—the people at her apartment, the teens in the woods. So, as tempting as it might have been, sweeping her involvement under the rug wouldn't work for a multitude of reasons. If she didn't report the abduction, it could come back to haunt her.

He had abducted her, that was an indisputable fact, so she could have killed him in self-defense. But there was the Cancun investigation to consider. She didn't want Detective Merrik learning she could hold her own against a dangerous grown man. Thanks to her mishap in Cancun, she needed the police to underestimate her until the end of time.

She brainstormed ideas while Draven sprawled on the ground nearby, as still as a stone.

He had too many demons closing in on him.

He knew from the private investigator and Dr. Gold that I had suspicions about him.

He broke into my apartment, drugged me, and took me to the woods.

The more she thought, the more her confidence ballooned, until she said aloud, "Yes. That sounds good." She laughed. "Thanks for the input, Draven. You've been very helpful."

She pulled her tank top off over her head and used it to wipe down each of the empty syringes. Holding the fabric to prevent transfer of her prints, she lifted Draven's lifeless hand and pressed his fingers around the plastic before dropping them by his side.

She put her shirt back before checking his pulse and heartrate, making positively sure they didn't exist. She briefly entertained the idea of taking him somewhere and cutting him open. She wondered if his alcoholism had progressed to the point of cirrhosis in his liver. With longing, she imagined fibrous scar tissue covering the organ like warts on a toad.

Don't be greedy. There was too much at stake to give in to her scientific curiosity. And this time, there would be no mistakes. To make it all work in her favor, she'd have to run out of the woods screaming like a helpless victim whose life had just been spared by sheer luck. She hated presenting herself that way. Hated it with a deep passion. She was no one's victim. But it was the best plan. The only plan that made sense. There were a few loose ends, but she would figure those out later. She refused to let her pride be her undoing.

After pressing her finger against his carotid one more time—his pulse wasn't going to return, but she felt oddly compelled to recheck—she was ready. With the same misgivings she once experienced before finally leaping from the high diving board for the first time, she plunged into action.

"Help! Help!" She tore through the woods towards the bonfire flames flickering in the distance. "Help me!" she yelled, getting close enough to see people.

Curious, surprised voices met her cries.

"Did you hear that?"

"Who is it?"

"What the hell?"

She stopped when she reached the edge of the crowd. The teens ceased laughing and chatting to stare at her. They resembled goblins and demons, their features lit ominously by the glow of the flickering flames. She recognized fear in their faces, fear of the unknown. She toned down her reaction, not wanting to scare them off. Covering her mouth with her hands, she feigned terror, clutching her arms and rocking her body forward and back. She needed to elicit compassion, something she would never feel for others, although she could fully understand the concept.

"I've been kidnapped." *Damsel in distress, lots of blinking, if I wasn't going to be a surgeon I could surely be an Oscar winning actor.* "I need someone's phone. Please. He might come after me again."

In their attentive expressions, she saw initial surprise give way to the realization that something interesting and unusual, involving a gorgeous young woman, was now happening in their midst. Their excitement and curiosity hung heavy in the air.

Several of them held out their phones, but a tall and muscular young man with a buzz cut and an East Dalton High School football jersey was the first to step to her side. "Are you okay?" He placed his arm around her and scanned the edge of the woods.

Brooke nodded, hugging herself. "Yes. I think so. I think I will be."

"I'm Drew." He turned to another teenager. "Is this the girl you saw with the thing over her mouth?"

"Yeah. That's her all right."

"Nice of you to do something about it," Brooke muttered, although she was immensely grateful the boy had not had the courage or the sense to step in and save her from Draven. Who knows what might have happened then. Everything was going just fine now.

"She had that fanny pack." The teen pointed to her waist.

Brooke gritted her teeth and tried not to shoot daggers at him. *It's a running belt, idiot.*

Someone turned off the music. All eyes rested on her, anxious to see what would happen next, how the surreal scene would unravel. Some of them moved closer, engulfing her, until Drew pressed them back with an outstretched arm and a glance everyone seemed to obey.

So many witnesses. Brooke kept her glee from showing by wiping a tear from under her eye and holding a trembling finger over Drew's phone keypad.

She had considered calling Jean Thompson and handing her the spotlight, the PI obviously needed to solve a case. But without her own phone, she didn't have the investigator's number handy. Instead, she pressed three numbers. She only had to wait a second for a response.

"911. What is your emergency?"

Chapter Thirty-Four

D rew led Brooke out of the woods, lifting aside errant branches and holding them back, keeping a close watch on her and their surroundings, like he was a hired bodyguard protecting a princess. Behind them, teens finished their joints, stuffed their mouths with mint gum, and followed. Males commented on her looks in ways that disgusted her. The party-goers streamed out of the woods and milled around, waiting for the police, obviously thrilled with the evening's unexpected entertainment and anxious to see how the situation would unfold. A group of loud and chatty girls emerged and huddled together, stealing glances at Drew and eyeing Brooke suspiciously. Every few minutes, one of the girls would shriek and claim to have caught a glimpse of the insane kidnapper. To them, Draven was now akin to Freddy Kruger and Jason rolled into one.

Blaring sirens signaled the arrival of emergency vehicles. Apartment doors flung open and people stepped outside to see.

"Over here." Drew waved his arm. "Sergeant. Over here."

"Drew Conrad!" The cop hurried over. "I hope no one tried to mess with you. We're counting on you for another state championship."

"No one messed with me or any of my friends. I just happened to be here. This is —" He turned to Brooke. "What's your name?"

"Brooke Walton." She was grateful Drew's protective posture made her look more helpless. His credibility as some sort of local high school star athlete probably worked in her favor as well.

"These two also saw the guy." Drew pointed to the boy and girl who had snuck out of the bushes earlier.

A cop waved to Brooke. "Step over here, ma'am." He spoke with her first, then individually questioned the couple who had seen her with Draven. All the teens were herded toward the parking lot—told to go home—and three cops headed into the brush and trees. The commanding officer told the two remaining ones to keep a lookout at the edge of the woods to prevent Draven's escape.

Brooke refused an ambulance trip to the hospital. The police took pics of her injuries, all minor, before allowing the paramedics to clean the cuts and scrapes and the torn puncture wound in her shoulder. They shined a pocket light into her eyes, and finally left with a sample of her blood. Drew stood by her side for all of it, telling her everything would be okay.

Of course it will be okay. Inside her head she was rolling her eyes, but she feigned an expression of gratefulness mixed with just the right measure of fear.

As the first drops of rain splatted her arms, a patrol man handed her a coat to cover her tank-top and escorted her to the backseat of a police cruiser. Drew hugged her goodbye and she let him.

"Thank you sooo much for everything." She batted her eyes before closing the door on him.

She waited on the ripped leather seat, tired and insanely hungry. *How long will it take them to find Draven?* In a matter of minutes, rain pattered against the windshield and dripped down the windows. A police officer hurried into the car and wiped rain out of his eyes. "We're going to leave for the station in a few minutes. You okay?"

She nodded and pulled the coat tighter around her shoulders. "Did you find him?"

"Ah, not yet. Listen, is there someone we can call to come down and be with you? Family or a friend?"

She thought about it. "Um, no. I don't think so." She pretended to be slightly in shock, although she felt more like a zombie, so tired she could barely keep her eyes open. The persistent drumming of rain over the roof of the car had a lulling effect. Looking out the window, she watched the last of the teens rush away, until the rain beat down so hard it was impossible to see. Rain or no rain, they weren't going to see Draven fleeing from the woods tonight. His days of running and hiding were over.

The police headquarters were outdated and unattractive by most business standards, but still a step up from the Medical Examiner's Offices. Sections of fresh paint, royal blue stripes over gray, stood out as failed attempts to spruce up the decor. The air was stale and smelled faintly of cigarette smoke, which made Brooke's blood boil with anger. She scanned the room to see if anyone was smoking inside. *Half a million deaths attributed to smoking each year. That's a lot of people choosing to die and spending good money to do it. Really makes me wonder why there was so much fuss over each person I killed.*

Brooke sat on the lobby couch and continued to act the way she imagined someone should act if they had survived the situation she described to the police. A cop randomly offered her a package of peanut butter crackers.

Brooke devoured them, savoring every crumb, but they only stimulated her gastric enzymes. She imagined acid burning a little hole in her near-empty stomach, yet she knew a normal person might be too distressed to eat, so she didn't want to ask for anything else. She accepted coffee but tossed it after a few miserable sips. She missed having her phone like she'd left a body part behind.

Have they found him yet? And the empty syringes?

Uniformed police walked in and out and around the offices, talking to each other in hushed tones and loud-mouthed shouts over the stacks of folders and papers towering atop their desks, answering the phones that never seemed to stop ringing in spite of the late hour, and keeping an eye on Brooke. No one told her anything, aside from repeatedly mentioning that someone would be with her shortly. The men offered plenty of reassuring smiles, and the women shot her sympathetic looks, until Brooke saw a detective she knew: Merrik.

Wearing a tailored dark pants suit, her hair gleaming in a ponytail, Merrik stood out from her colleagues, more like a high-powered management consultant than a detective. All her movements conveyed a confident, athletic ease. She stopped to speak to Brooke. "Lots of excitement tonight, I heard"

Hardly appropriate words to comfort someone who had just been drugged and abducted. Brooke tried to convey timidity and fear with a lame nod, unable to suppress a yawn.

"Try not to fall asleep." Merrik waved over her shoulder. "I'll see you later."

"Get your hands off me!" A slovenly, drunk man passed by, attempting to twist out of an officer's grip.

Brooke's anger grew. Her forehead still throbbed with a rhythmic pain from hitting the tree—just what she needed after a concussion—and she'd have a headache the next day from being up half the night and not eating. Eventually, as her adrenaline receded, and the events of the long day and the drugs took their toll, she nodded off to sleep.

Her head snapped forward, jolting her awake.

The cycle of drifting off and jerking awake continued its course until, finally, a man in civilian clothes tapped her arm and told her to follow him into a room. She stood up and stretched her arms overhead before following him. They were standing at the table when Detective Merrik joined them.

Brooke fidgeted with her hands. This was not the time for her to be poised and professional. That would seem unnatural. "Did you find Dr. Draven?"

"First, introductions. I'm Detective Pispani." He was middle-aged with graying hair and a wiry beard that needed a trim, but it was his unusually large pores that interested Brooke. He lowered his hefty body into a chair opposite her. "And this is Detective Merrik, our psychiatrist. She has an interest in this case." Merrik sat down beside him.

Discomfort stirred inside Brooke's empty stomach. "You didn't say you were a psychiatrist when we met before. You didn't introduce yourself as a doctor."

"No, I don't usually." Merrik crossed her legs.

"She's humble like that." Pispani glanced at Merrik with a quick smile.

Brooke's eyes darted between.

"We're recording this." Pispani glanced at the device on the table. "Have a seat and tell us what happened." His voice was firm, but not harsh.

Brooke sat down and studied her twisting fingers, channeling her best I'm-so-upset-I-can barely-hold-it-together act. "I've already told the police what happened. It's all because . . . I should have just minded my own business."

"What business? Start from the beginning." Pispani moved the recorder a few inches closer to Brooke.

"It's complicated. I . . . I'm not even sure where best to start. I really angered Dr. Draven."

"How long have you known Dr. Draven?"

"Not long, and I barely know him. I just met him a few weeks ago."

"Start from the beginning then."

Brooke let her words rush forward in a frightened voice. "Dr. Draven was faking autopsies at the Medical Examiner's Office where I'm working."

"Why would he do that?"

She chewed on her lower lip. "To get paid without doing the work."

"I see."

"I discovered discrepancies in the computer system."

"Were you searching for them?"

"No. It's my job to enter data for some of the medical examiners." Brooke glanced at Merrik and caught a slight smile. Amusement? Or was it condescending? She tried not to let Merrik distract her. "I told the Chief Medical Examiner what I found. I think word got back to Draven that I'm the one who brought the issue to the boss's attention. That's what started everything."

"Everything?"

"Him losing it. It gets worse. Much worse." She let out a quiet moan and briefly covered her mouth with her hands. "At first, I thought it was just too many coincidences, but everything pointed to Draven."

"You thought *what* was too many coincidences?"

"We found a Jane Doe. She reminded me of Rachael Kline, a classmate who went missing in November."

Pispani dipped his chin. "Everyone here is quite familiar with the Kline case."

"They looked so much alike." Brooke shook her head, for effect. "And Dr. Draven was acting really strange, not wanting us to complete the examination and find the correct cause of death. I knew he was somehow responsible. And that's when I remembered seeing him with Rachael. So, I called the detective working on Rachael's disappearance—"

"A detective from our department?"

"No, I mean, she's a private investigator. Jean Thompson. I really didn't think my tip would add up to anything, but I had a gut feeling and I really wanted to help Jean's investigation, since I knew Rachael. See, when I met Dr. Draven, I was pretty sure I had seen him before, and then I remembered it was with Rachael. I begged the investigator not to say the tip came from me. I don't know if she betrayed my confidence or not, but he suspected I tipped her off. He wanted to kill me." She opened her eyes wide and then dropped her head into her hands. "Excuse me, I need a minute."

"It's okay, take your time."

She knew she would be recounting her story over and over again. This was just the spill-it-all-out version, but she needed to get it just right.

Brooke took a deep breath. "Last night, I had just returned from my other job—"

"Which is?"

"She teaches exercise classes at Peak Fitness." Merrik answered before Brooke.

"Um, yes." *Why does she know that?* "I had just walked in the door, when he broke into my apartment—"

"He broke in?"

"Sorry. It was unlocked. Burst in is more correct. He drugged me, tied me up, and took me to the woods." *Plenty of witnesses to corroborate my story.*

The detective nodded.

"I'm not sure what happened after he put me in the car. I couldn't stay awake. I tried, but the drugs . . . they must have been sedatives."

"We'll know soon enough," said Merrik.

"When I woke up, a few hours had passed. I guess he was driving around all that time. I really don't know." *I really don't.* That thought made her nervous. "I could tell the drug's effect had worn off a bit, but I pretended like I was still really out of it, so I could get away if I got the chance."

Detective Pispani nodded. Next to him, Detective Merrik's strange knowing half-smile hadn't budged. *Must be a psychiatrist thing.*

"He talked non-stop after that. I guess because he didn't expect I would be alive to tell anyone. He said he had too many demons hiding in his closets and they were starting to come after him. He told me he killed Rachael and our Jane Doe, her name is Alyssa. I don't know why he killed her. He said he owed money to people with no patience. He said his problems were all closing in on him because of me. He—" Brooke stopped her sprint of words, taking short, fast breaths, like she was close to hyperventilating.

"Take a deep breath. Slow down." Pispani patted the air with his hand.

"I begged him to turn himself in. I told him my boyfriend would be looking for me. I tried to make him see that killing me wouldn't help him, it would only make his situation worse. He had one more syringe with him and told me he was going to use it, and then," she choked down a sob, "God, I don't know what happened. I guess he just changed his mind. He started crying and he let me go. I have no idea why he let me go, but I'm just so grateful." She let out a deep sigh. "I wasn't sure how to get out of the woods. I ran into a bunch of teens who were out there partying. I asked for a phone, and I called the police. I stayed with them until you came. I was so afraid he would change his mind and come bursting through the trees any minute."

Yes! Mini fist pump. She had delivered her own convincing version of events in a frantic rush as if it was the God's honest truth.

Pispani nodded. Merrik's strange smile was really getting on Brooke's nerves.

Brooke could tell they had found Draven by the look on Pispani's face—a hint of satisfaction and understanding rather than determination, a tired resignation related to all the paperwork that lay ahead.

"Have you found him? Please say you have him," she pleaded.

Pispani and Merrik exchanged glances.

"Do you have him in custody? I live in an apartment alone right now. I don't think I'll ever feel safe with him out there. Will he be arrested?"

Pispani stared into her eyes. "You don't have to worry about him finding you. He's dead."

She sat up straight, opened her eyes wide. "You killed him?"

"We can't disclose any further information at this time."

"But you're sure?"

"We're sure." Pispani nodded.

"So, just to be clear, when you left him, he was alive and crying about his current troubles?" asked Merrik.

"Yes." Brooke closed her eyes for a second. "I guess I should say I'm sorry, but I'm not. I really thought I was going to die tonight, just like my friend Rachael and like poor Alyssa Cable. I'm not sorry he's gone. I'm relieved." She choked down another sob and raised her eyes to the ceiling.

It's going well. Really well. But I don't like the way Merrik studies me. "You have to call Jean Thompson. She'll want to know he killed Rachael. She's been trying to find out who did it."

"We would have found out eventually," said Detective Merrik. "Killers always make mistakes. Always."

Brooke nodded. "That's good to know." *So tell me, who was Jack the Ripper? Even if killers make mistakes, that doesn't mean they get caught.*

There were only two reasons Brooke's plan could ever backfire– Xander and Charlie. Both knew she'd already visited Dr. Draven's apartment and been tied up in his closet. If they told the police, it would ruin all her credibility. But if she told Merrik and Pispani now, the obvious question became—why hadn't she called the police after he locked her in his closet? *Darn. Darn. Darn.* There was no way of avoiding it. She had to tell them everything. She had to.

"What happened to your neck?" Pispani rubbed his beard.

"Maybe you should take a break now—" Merrik said.

"There is something else I have to tell you." Brooke shifted her weight in her chair.

"You don't need—"

Brooke interrupted Merrik a second time. "Something else I did set him off. Something I regret. It has to do with the burn around my neck."

Merrik leaned back in her chair and glanced at the ground.

Brooke coughed to clear her throat. *I have to be careful not to insult them. I need them on my side. It's not their fault they aren't as smart as me.* "Could I get some water, please?"

"Sure." Pispani typed into his phone. "We'll get you some water in a minute. Go ahead."

Here goes. "The day after we autopsied Jane Doe, she was still unidentified. I just really felt sorry for her. I mean, she had to have friends and family out there somewhere. We had reason to believe she might be a prostitute, so I did a little sleuthing on my own." She lowered her gaze to acknowledge that it might not have been the best idea. *But there's nothing illegal about what I did.* "She just reminded me so much of Rachael . . ."

When she finished her story, she sat back in her chair, exhausted.

"That's quite a story." Pispani stood up. "Excuse me. I'll see about that water and be right back."

Merrik shut off the recording device and leaned forward. "I'd love to hear your reason for not calling the police." Her voice was barely above a whisper.

Brooke didn't answer. *Crap! I knew that was coming. Why didn't I prepare an excuse?*

Detective Merrik kept a calm, steady focus on Brooke. "Whenever you're ready."

There was one short knock before a uniformed officer opened the door. "There's someone here for Brooke."

"Dad!" Brooke's hand flew to her chest when her father emerged. A stab of fury hardened her gaze for a second then disappeared. Brooke hadn't called anyone, but the detectives had done it anyway. She didn't want her father involved with any of this.

Her father rushed into the room, his face full of anguish and concern. He wrapped her in his arms. "I came as fast as I could."

The pent-up tension and stress racking Brooke's body rushed forth. She sobbed and shook in her father's arms. Genuine tears ran down her fair skin. Though incapable of remorse, she was constantly aware of how much she had to lose if she made another mistake, and it was a large burden to bear.

Merrik appeared to study the father and daughter while they embraced. "Why don't you go ahead and take her home now." She nodded to Mr. Walton. "She's been through so much. I'm sure she's exhausted."

Chapter Thirty-Five

Mr. Walton drove Brooke from the police station to her apartment. Weary, yet with a shaky, low-blood sugar sensation inside her veins, Brooke collapsed into bed and fell asleep immediately, leaving her father to figure out what to do with himself.

She woke up confused with a slight headache, wanting to stay under the covers. Someone was snoring lightly in another room. Then she remembered. She tiptoed into the living room. Her father was lying on the floor under a blanket, a folded towel functioned as a pillow under his head. He must have sensed her standing there because he rolled over and opened his eyes.

"Morning. How are you feeling, Brooke?"

"Okay. I've been better."

He sat up. "Do you want to go out and get something for breakfast? You can show me your favorite places."

"Okay." She gently rubbed the tender spot on her forehead, testing just how much it would hurt.

"You've got a bruise there."

"I'm starting to feel like a prize fighter, with all my injuries."

Mr. Walton stood and stretched. "I think the floor might have been good for my back." He ran a hand over the hairs sticking straight out of his head. "Don't let me forget, I've got a container of protein powder and a case of protein bars for you in the car. Your favorites. Your mother threw them in the trunk right before I left. She won't be happy with me if I forget to leave them with you."

"Thanks."

"Are you ready to go? Because I can be ready in a few minutes."

"I've needed to take a shower since . . . way too long. And I have to call a few people. I can't have them find out about last night from anyone else."

His phone rang. He glanced down. "It's your mother. I'll let her know what's happening here. Of course, she'll want to talk to you."

"Can you tell her I'm in the shower? I'll call her a little later."

He nodded.

"Thanks, Dad."

Brooke took a quick shower and stepped back into her bedroom. Smelling clean and fresh, her hair still wet, she called Xander first. It was only a matter of time before the police would call him and Charlie to corroborate her story about the first time Draven tied her up, if they hadn't already done so.

"Good morning, gorgeous. It's a little early here for a Saturday. Did you already run?"

"No. My dad is here. He stayed with me last night."

"Nice. Tell him I said hello. Is he okay with us, you know, living together?"

"I told you, he's fine with it. He's a professor. They're very liberal, don't you know?" She laughed. "In fact, both my parents are glad I won't be alone. They won't worry as much about me. But he's not here just for a visit. There's something I have to tell you."

"Oh. Um, do I want to hear this?"

"It's actually good news, kind of, but I know you'll freak out." Brooke took a deep breath and told Xander everything she had told the police.

Xander listened without interrupting before asking her several questions. "I feel sick thinking about what could have happened."

"Don't. I'm fine. And if you're going to flip out, I'm not going to tell you things. So . . . I'd like to speak with Charlie. Did you have his number?"

Xander forwarded Charlie's contact number and she called it immediately.

Charlie's phone rang and rang. No one picked up and it never went to voicemail.

"Darn." *I need to talk to him before the police do. I should have called him last night, regardless of the time.*

"Dad, I'm just going across the hall to see one of my classmates. I've told you about him. Jeff."

"No matter how capable you are, you'll always be my little girl, you know. I'm so proud of you."

Brooke smiled at him and turned away when she thought she saw sentimental tears brimming in his eyes. "I'll be right back."

"Take your time. I'll shower while you're gone."

Even if the police couldn't officially attribute Rachael's disappearance to Draven, once Brooke shared Draven's confession with Jeff, the seed would be planted, and it would quickly grow. Jeff would share the story with everyone from school.

When she finished speaking to him, after answering an incredulous flurry of questions, and returned to the apartment, her father was in the living room setting up Xander's television. He wiped dust off the top and screen with a dish towel.

"Sorry, Dad. That took longer than expected."

"No problem. I was thinking . . . I'm planning to stay another day. I know the police want to see you again today. I'll go with you."

"Thanks, but it's not necessary."

"Listen, Super Woman, you're a little beat up. Let me worry about you in person, okay? Just one more day. It's that or a hundred calls and texts from your mother. And you know she'll do it."

Brooke laughed.

"Maybe we can see a movie tonight? Take your mind off things."

"Sure. I haven't been to a movie theater in ages." She smiled at him from the kitchen. "Thanks for coming. In the middle of the night, no less. I'm really glad you're here."

"Of course. After all you've been through, it's the least I can do for you." He gave her a hug. "Do you want to come home with me tomorrow? Just for a few more days? Until things settle down."

"I'll think about it. Getting back to work might be the best way for me to move past all this."

At that very moment, Draven might be laying inside a drawer in the Medical Examiner's Office. One lucky examiner would get to study his liver and everything else inside him. If only . . . but once everyone at work found out about her involvement, helping with Draven's autopsy would be out of the question. Something about it smacked of unprofessionalism, at least her colleagues would probably think so. And they would bombard her with questions. Even tight-lipped Mya and oblivious Greg, who had yet to have an actual conversation with her, might want to hear all the details.

The restaurant Brooke chose was a favorite of Rothaker University students, located near the main campus on a street lined with cafes, bookstores, and ice cream shops and bustling with students. A server delivered a stack of blueberry pancakes and Brooke devoured them. They tasted so delicious she could have licked the plate.

She swiveled from side to side on her bar stool. "I haven't eaten anything that didn't come from my own kitchen since Cancun."

"Looks to me like you haven't been eating much at all."

"I guess I haven't lately." A gaping space existed between her waist and her size two shorts. She could almost pull them up over her hips without unbuttoning them. Her abs were usually flat and hard, but now, even after the tower of pancakes with syrup, they were sunken in below her ribcage.

"The police wanted to see you at noon and it's only ten. How about we go to Target and pick up some things for your apartment while I've got the car here? We'll throw in a few pints of ice cream too. You need it."

"Sure." She smiled. "Just excuse me for a second, I'm going to the restroom."

Inside the restroom, she gripped her phone with white knuckles and called Charlie. Getting in touch with him before the police did had become an obsession. He didn't answer, and it still wasn't possible to leave a message. She scuffed her shoe into the ground with frustration. *Where is he and why isn't he answering his phone?*

At Target, her father tried to pay for her groceries and necessities. She thanked him, but insisted she had enough money from her internship. He insisted too and ended up paying. When they finished putting away the groceries, it was time to go to the police station.

In the lobby, Brooke sat down next to her father, carefully thinking over what she'd told the police and what had really happened—which were not quite the same. The cops got everything they needed to reach the proper conclusion in the case: Draven had committed suicide. But she was nervous about Detective Merrik. Something was up with that woman. She couldn't tell if Merrik had whole-heartedly joined Brooke's group of admirers, the ones who had bestowed her with accolades, awards, and scholarships over the years, or if Merrik didn't like her at all. If the psychiatrist knew something, why was she holding it back? What was she waiting for?

Stop being paranoid. Maybe that's just how Merrik acts all the time. You've handled this perfectly. Everything is going to be fine. Better than before. Much better. Perhaps Merrik is just jealous. That makes sense. She wouldn't be the first woman who envied me.

Multiple police sirens started up like fire alarms, wailing away from the station. Detective Merrik entered through the main doors. "Hi, again." Everything about her greeting appeared warm and normal. "How are you feeling?"

"A little shaken. But I'll be fine. Thank you for asking."

"Of course." Detective Merrik walked away.

"She's been especially nice to you, that detective." Mr. Walton extended his hand toward Merrik. "She asked me questions about you last night."

"She did?" A coil of dread snaked through Brooke's gut. "When?"

"On the phone. While I was driving here."

"What did she ask?"

"Mostly about your school work, I told her you were valedictorian in high school and again at Everett. We talked about your dedication to fitness. I told her about the time you ran a half marathon in Orlando one day and then a full the next. She was impressed and seemed sincerely interested. Oh, here comes the other detective." Mr. Walton stood up.

Pispani waved and walked over. "Thanks for coming back in. Just a few more things to go over with you." He turned to her father. "Mr. Walton, I need you to wait out here. I'm sorry. We won't be long. She'll be in good hands."

Ian Walton nodded. "I'll be right here." He squeezed his daughter's shoulder before he sat back down.

Detective Merrik was waiting in the interview room when Pispani led Brooke inside.

Of course, she would be here, too.

At Pispani's request, Brooke repeated most of her story with great care and attention to the details she had previously told them.

When he finished asking a few questions, it was Brooke's turn. "Can you tell me anything about what you've been doing on your end?"

"Yes." He glanced at the file in his hands. "First off, the drug you were given last night is most likely triazolam. It's a sedative, but its short lived. It puts people to sleep for a few hours. There shouldn't be any lingering effects."

"Makes sense it was triazolam. I do feel okay now. Pretty much."

Merrik placed her hands on the table. "We've been busy gathering evidence to support your story."

"We found the women who identified Alyssa for you." Pispani placed the file down. "The street walkers. One of them identified Dr. Draven as the man Alyssa was seeing. He was pushing her to sell drugs for him."

Brooke nodded. *Excellent.*

"We also located the people who saw you being taken from your apartment to the parking lot."

"I remember them, vaguely." Brooke rolled her eyes. "They thought I was drunk or drugged, by choice. I wish they hadn't jumped to that conclusion."

"Believe me when I tell you they feel terrible. At least, they saw you before you were gagged. On the other hand, the two teenagers who saw you in the woods with Draven, they saw the gag and they saw your hands tied together." Pispani shook his head.

"The future of our country . . ." Brooke rolled her eyes.

"Hmm. Right." Pispani removed a photograph from a folder. "There's something we need to show you. Draven had a pair of gold earrings in his pocket." He held up a picture of Rachael's earrings. "Do they belong to you?"

"No, they're not mine."

The detective put the picture away.

Brooke scrunched up her face.

"What is it?" Pispani tilted his head.

"They're not mine, but they look familiar."

"Familiar?"

"Can I see them again?"

The detective took out the picture again.

"I think . . . Rachael Kline used to have those same earrings. I mean, maybe lots of women have those same ones, but she wore the same ones every single day. I'm positive." Her voice rose to a high pitch. "Ask her parents. See what they say."

"We'll do that. We're speaking with them shortly," said Merrik. "Odd he would be carrying her earrings around in his pocket, don't you think?"

Brooke pretended not to hear Merrik's question and faced Pispani. "Is that enough to prove he killed Rachael, like he told me?"

"Probably not, but it's not all we have." Pispani turned his head to the side to cough. "We also found samples of Rachael Kline's hair in his apartment.

Brooke tried to mask her shock. "You . . . you did?"

Pispani nodded. Beside him Merrik seemed to be studying Brooke.

The room was silent for several seconds while Brooke wondered if she'd heard correctly. *Why were Rachael Kline's hairs in Draven's apartment? Had Draven actually known Rachael?* It was good news, of course, but also incredibly confusing. She quickly pulled herself together. "I'm so glad he's gone and there's not going to be another Rachael or Alyssa."

Because there isn't. Going forward, I'm going to control my actions. This will not happen again. I'm so done with the exhausting hassles that follow. I can't wait to have it all behind me.

Pispani's phone chimed. He turned it over. "Excuse me. I have to take care of this." He got up and left the room, but Merrik stayed.

Brooke scooted forward on her chair. "Can I ask you something?"

"Anything." Merrik kept her gaze steady.

"I've been following the investigation in Cancun. The one you spoke to me about."

"Yes."

Brooke rubbed her fingers outward across her cheeks and pressed them against her temples. "What I want to ask is, after all I've been through here, please don't let my name come up in anyway related to the Cancun investigation. Please keep me out of it. I've seen what can happen to someone who tries to help. If there's a killer out there, I don't want him to think I saw him, because I didn't. But he doesn't know that."

"I understand." Merrik nodded. "We can accommodate that."

Really? She'd expected a response telling her there was nothing that could be done about it. She continued with the speech she had practiced anyway. "Enough is enough. I need to focus on medical school and becoming a surgeon."

"I assure you, it won't be a problem. And there's something else I want to share with you."

"Yes?" *What's up with her amused expression?*

"Somehow, the rental car key—your rental car key—disappeared from the evidence room in Cancun."

"It disappeared?"

"Yes. So it won't be of any use to the investigators." Merrik stood up. "You know, I've had an interesting time researching your background."

"You have?" *What does she know?*

"I'll be speaking with you again soon." Merrik walked away.

Brooke found her father waiting in the lobby. He put his arm around her. "All done? How did it go?"

"Fine, I think." Merrik had left her feeling unsettled again.

On their way down the steps, Jean Thompson was coming up. When she saw Brooke, she stopped to give her a hug.

"You poor dear." Jean kept her hands on Brooke's shoulders. "I'm so sorry this happened to you."

"It's okay. It's over." Brooke crossed her arms. "So, um, now that Rachael's disappearance has been solved, what will you do now? New case?"

Jean dropped her hands to her sides. "Actually, I'm going to be returning to the police force in a few weeks. An internal position, working with detective Pispani. He just happened to need someone, a very flexible position, and I was here at the right time. Thanks to your tip and what happened . . . Rachael Kline's case may have been my last as a PI."

"Oh. Well, congratulations. If you hadn't followed up on my lead . . . who knows what would have happened." Out of the corner of her eye, Brooke saw a couple she recognized, even though they walked looking down at the cracked pavement.

"Thank you, I'm really—"

Brooke grabbed her father's arm. "Sorry, we have to go. Good luck with your investigation." She hurried him off in the opposite direction of the couple.

"What's going on?" Her father took long strides to keep pace.

"Nothing. I just really want to get away from this place. I've had enough."

Jean leaned forward while speaking with the detectives and the Klines. "I went to see him. The day he committed suicide."

"How did he react to your visit?" Detective Pispani leaned forward in his chair.

"I asked him a few simple questions. He got angry and slammed the door in my face."

Detective Merrik uncrossed her legs and shifted her weight. "Did you tell him Brooke had given you the tip?"

"Of course not. I had a feeling he might be dangerous. I'd done some research into his past, and the kind of people he was involved with. I told him nothing regarding the source of my information. I never mentioned Brooke's name."

"I know you found Rachael's earrings," said Mr. Kline. "Those were hers, no doubt about it, we gave them to her. And you also found strands of her hair, proof she had been in his home. But do you have any concrete proof he killed her, besides what he told Brooke?"

Pispani knocked on the table, using his fist like a gavel. "What we have is more than enough to convict someone, if he were here to stand trial."

"Did he tell Brooke what he did to Rachael?" Mrs. Kline's face was blotchy from recent tears. "How she died? Anything?"

"According to Miss Walton, he didn't give any specifics." Pispani's tone was gentle. "I'm very sorry."

Mrs. Kline pressed her lips together. "Brooke Walton is lucky she wasn't seriously harmed."

Detective Merrik turned to the side. She placed her hand against her temple, shielding her face from view.

Jean swallowed, pushing away the question she'd asked herself repeatedly. *Was Brooke drugged and kidnapped because I confronted Draven? Was it my fault?*

"But we'll never find Rachael's body now." Mrs. Kline's words caught in her throat.

"We still may . . ." Pispani nodded toward Jean. "And our newest colleague might have some extra time in her new position to pursue open-ended cases just like yours."

Chapter Thirty-Six

Early Monday morning, Brooke left a message for Dr. Gold. "This is Brooke Walton. I'm not sure how much you know or have heard about what happened with Dr. Draven, but I'm still planning to come into work. I'll be there in a few hours."

Her father had already left, and she had the apartment to herself again. Happy to be rid of her concussion symptoms, she ran to work, hard and fast, like she was racing toward a finish line.

When she arrived, Jerome was waiting for her inside the lobby. He hesitated before coming forward and giving her an awkward hug. "Glad you're back."

Brooke braced herself, pushing her discomfort aside, and hugged him back. "Sorry, I'm pretty sweaty." She stepped back. "So, you know what happened with Draven?"

"Uh, yeah." He opened his eyes wide. "Dr. Draven's in a drawer right now."

"Who did his autopsy?"

"Greg."

"Greg with the earbuds?"

"Yeah. Hey, um, Dr. Gold wants to see you. He told me to let him know as soon as you arrived. But, first, can I show you something?"

"What is it?"

"It's this way."

Brooke followed Jerome down the hall. He wrinkled up his nose and sneezed on the way.

"Allergies again?"

"Yep."

Before they reached her office, she saw her bike outside the door, looking good as new except for the scratched-up paint.

"I had it fixed for you. I know a guy . . ."

"Wow. That was really kind of you."

Jerome blushed. "It was nothing. Let's go tell Dr. Gold you're ready."

"I need to take a quick shower and change into scrubs. I'm really sweaty. Please tell him I'll be there in a few minutes." She walked back down the hall and disappeared into the women's locker room before he could say another word.

She wasn't sure what to expect when she talked to Dr. Gold. Would he want to hear her story? Would he be disappointed because he'd lost one of his medical examiners? Or would he appreciate the fact that he didn't have to fire him now?

When she came out of the locker room, looking freshly scrubbed, her cheeks still pink from her run, Jerome was standing outside in the hall, playing a game on his phone. He saw her, quickly ended the game, and slipped his phone into his pocket. He walked alongside her to Dr. Gold's office. Brooke had the sensation of déjà vu and realized Jerome's protective behavior reminded her of Drew, the young football player from the bonfire.

When Dr. Gold saw her, his eyes lit up. "Brooke, thank goodness you're okay. I've been so worried."

"You were?" She suddenly saw him in a whole new light. He seemed kind and concerned, a Yoda-type character, giant wrinkles and all, rather than the grumpy man she'd become accustomed to working for each day.

"I just spoke with your friend," said Dr. Gold. "He feels terrible about everything that has happened. And of course, so do I."

"What do you mean?"

"I knew Draven was having some problems, I hired him as a favor to his father, my wife's cousin. I had no idea he was a danger to anyone besides himself. Truly, I did not know."

"Oh." *That explains a few things.* "But what friend did you talk to?"

"Robert Mending. Perhaps you should call him, and he will explain. Go ahead and take care of whatever you need to do. I'm sure you have a lot to deal with." Gone was Dr. Gold's usual annoyance, replaced by a tone of reverence and respect.

Brooke had several missed calls from Robert. But so many people were reaching out to her lately, she'd mostly ignored all of them. She sat down in her office and called Robert.

"Brooke! Are you okay?" Robert made raspy sounds into the phone.

"Yes. I'm fine."

"Thank God. I feel so responsible."

"Why would you feel responsible, Robert?"

"I set up the internship for you. Told them it was for you alone. Remember you told me it would be the ideal place to work?"

"Really?"

"I had no idea it might put you in close proximity to Rachael's killer. No idea. I'm so sorry. Really, I can't even believe it."

She wasn't entirely surprised by Robert's admission. It explained many things: the sudden and generous stipend, the reason only a few others were granted interviews, the initial resentment from Dr. Gold. The Chief Medical Examiner must have thought she was a spoiled girl with no skills and no chance of getting an internship on her own—which couldn't be farther from the truth. Well, at least she had dispelled that notion and earned his respect.

"Thank you, Robert. I mean, what happened was terrible, but in hindsight, I'm so grateful I got this job. It's been a real life-changer in more ways than you can imagine. And being part of catching the man who killed Rachael—it's just been so gratifying."

"I'm sure it is. God, I can't believe you were working with him!"

"It's amazing how things happen." Brooke's lips curled up in a smug smile. "Like it was meant to be. So, thank you, Robert. Really, I can't tell you how much I appreciate what you did for me."

"You're welcome. You know how I feel about you. At least I hope you do. I'll do anything I can to help."

"Thanks again." It was all she could think of to say at the moment.

Finally, with Rachael's killer gone, that whole mess was behind her. From now on, she would be so careful. She wouldn't let anyone else get to her.

But there was still one loose end that needed to be closed—the incident in Cancun.

Chapter Thirty-Seven

When she arrived home from the gym, Brooke sat down in the chair she now thought of as Charlie's cast-off, logged inher laptop and typed: *Vega and Peters, missing in Cancun.* Due to the ongoing police inquiry, Brooke had been too preoccupied over the past few days to check up on the Cancun murder case. Getting up to speed on the latest news suddenly seemed imperative.

The search returned pages of links. The most recent was a news clip filmed earlier in the day. In the video, a beautiful Latina woman with sleek dark hair gripped her microphone. "Is the search for the murderer of American tourists Rico Vega and John Peters over?" The reporter seemed to be staring directly at Brooke, asking her the question. "The American Embassy has been pressuring the Cancun police for weeks, but the investigation was going nowhere. Now, there appears to have been a major break-through in the case. We have a clip from Cancun's Chief of Police, who had this to say."

The screen filled with the image of a tired and harried-looking middle-aged man standing behind a podium. He clutched the edges of the wood platform and slowly let his gaze travel over the reporters in front of him. "Thanks to the cooperation of our wonderful citizens, we now believe we have caught the killers of Rico Vega and John Peters, members of the Black Shadows. We believe the gang is also responsible for the death of other local citizens over the past years. We're still collecting evidence, but the good news is that we firmly believe we have taken ruthless killers off the streets and Cancun is once again a safe and relaxing destination for tourists and locals." The sound of polite applause rang out around him.

The reporter returned, staring with that same intensity. "We'll bring you an update as soon as we have one, but for now, one Mexican resort community—so many local citizens who depend on tourism for their livelihood—and everyone who loves to vacation there can breathe a sigh of relief that the killers have been apprehended. Signing out for Channel 44 News, this is Anna Rodriquez."

Brooke stared at the screen, dumbfounded. *What? How? What evidence could they have possibly found?* She shook her head, momentarily forgetting all else. On the one hand, she should have been thrilled, but the news didn't make sense. Maybe to everyone else it did, but not to her.

A knock at the door startled her. She set her laptop aside and crossed the room. Out of caution due to her last unexpected visit, she peered out the peephole first.

"Xander!" She flung open the door.

"Surprise!" He spread his arms wide.

Jeff stood behind him, grinning. "I guess I'll let you two catch up."

Xander turned. "Thanks again, for picking me up at the airport."

"Anytime." Jeff waved goodbye and left.

Xander stepped inside, dropped his bag on the floor, and kicked the door closed. He scooped Brooke into his arms and twirled her around.

"It is so great to hold you."

He set her down and kissed her, drawing her in close. Finally, they moved apart, and he gazed around the apartment. Brooke studied him, appreciating his solid build.

"It's nice."

"You think so? Because Jeff says I don't know the first thing about decorating. Which is true." She chuckled. "I would have organized things a little more if I knew you were coming."

Xander laughed and turned his attention back to Brooke. "The only thing it needs to look amazing is you in it." He wrapped her in his arms again and she hugged him back, pressing her hands against the solidness of his shoulders.

I wonder if he'll unpack today so I can finally be done with having to see his stacked boxes against the wall. And maybe he'll make a trip to one of the large markets, make us a decent meal, and the refrigerator will be more full than empty for once. Or perhaps he'll eat the food I have, not that there's much at all, but he must eat a ton, and I'll regret agreeing to live with him.

"How long are you going to be here?"

"Just three days. We'll need to make it count." He smiled suggestively. "I can't believe everything that's happened to you. I mean, I'm glad they found Rachael's killer, the bastard." Xander's hands tightened into balls at his hips. "I wish I could have strangled him with my own hands. But it makes me sick that you crossed paths with him, too. I knew the morgue would be full of weirdos. I told you that. I knew it."

Brooke didn't know if she should laugh or be offended so she settled with jabbing him playfully in the arm.

"I'm just glad he's gone." Xander hugged her again. "Too bad he's probably not the only crazy in the city."

"Probably not." Brooke bit on her lower lip. "Anyhow, what a surprise. You're here!"

Later that night, Brooke watched Xander move the chair in front of the television and log into his movie streaming account. He hadn't even been there a full day, and already the incessant buzz of political and sports commentary coming from the television grated at her nerves. Apparently, he liked to leave the TV running, even when he left the room for an extended period.

"We need to buy a couch," he said.

Brooke sighed. "Couches are expensive."

"Don't worry. I'll figure it out and get one before I go. I want you to be comfortable."

"I'm fine."

He beckoned her with his finger. "For now, you can sit on my lap."

Brooke remained standing.

"I'm binge watching Game of Thrones, finally. I'm on the fourth season. It's addictive."

"Never seen it. I don't have time."

"We make the time for things we love. Come on. I'm hooked. You'll love it. Or maybe you won't."

"Okay, now I'm intrigued. If you like it so much, why wouldn't I?"

"The bad guys seem to be the ones who make out the best. They don't always get what they deserve. And some of the best characters get decapitated when you least expect it. It's massively unfair. Some people can't handle it."

Brooke moved closer. "That's life. Rarely is it fair. And I think I'll give your show a try." She sat down on the floor next to Xander, using his legs for a back rest. She tried to focus on the show but had no idea what was going on. Her swirling thoughts and incessant planning made it near impossible to concentrate on the action unfolding before her. It was almost a welcome distraction when her phone buzzed. Until she glanced at the screen and felt a little sick.

Xander hit pause on the remote, freezing a young king's face with his mouth open in the middle of a haughty laugh. "Are you going to answer it? Is it Charlie?"

"No. I still haven't spoken to him since the night we met. Can't even leave a message. For all I know, he hasn't heard anything about what happened to Draven. Anyway, it's not Charlie. It's the police again."

"Go ahead and take it. I'm not going anywhere."

She accepted the call but hurried into the bedroom and closed the door before saying hello.

"This is Detective Lee Merrik."

"I know." Brooke bit down on her lip. "I've got your number saved in my phone."

"Good. I'm calling because we need to meet tomorrow."

"About what?"

"We have a few more things to work out with you. I'll pick you up at your apartment at 7:45 am."

"I can meet you at the police station."

"I know you don't own a car and I'll be out anyway. It's no trouble. I'll pick you up."

"Okay." Brooke tried to sound upbeat and cooperative despite her nagging, bad feeling about Merrik.

Xander hit pause when Brooke returned. "What was that about?"

"I might have to meet with the police again tomorrow." She didn't say the meeting was definite because Xander might insist on coming with her and his presence would complicate things. She could just imagine him unknowingly contradicting her statements in his effort to be helpful.

"I'll go with you if you go."

Brooke shook her head. "Not necessary. And I do have to go into work for a few hours tomorrow morning. I promise I'll leave early and come back as soon as I can."

"Okay." He turned around and unpaused Game of Thrones.

Chapter Thirty-Eight

From the kitchen came a clattering noise, a shout of "Ow!" and then laughter. Xander was already awake and busy doing who knew what. She rolled onto her side and pulled the sheets higher around her shoulders, wanting to remain comfortable in bed for at least a few more minutes. Thanks to Xander, and what he humbly called his "bedroom skills," she felt calm and relaxed, like she'd already finished a tough workout and had a massage.

She stretched a leg diagonally across the bed—languishing in the coolness of the space she had recaptured now that Xander was gone. The tempting smell of sizzling bacon wafted into the bedroom. Not wanting to miss out, she got up and went to the bathroom for her morning routine, which only took a few minutes. A container of Xander's PTSD medication rested on the counter next to his toothbrush and razor.

She joined Xander just as he transferred scrambled eggs onto a plate.

"Oh, good." His eyes lit up. "Just in time." He grabbed another dish and made her a breakfast plate identical to his own. "Your toaster oven isn't working."

"I know."

They ate standing at the counter, with Xander humming a song and smiling between bites. Having Xander around, larger than life, full of testosterone and energy, really changed the atmosphere in the apartment.

Gone was the quiet contemplative silence she had appreciated since she moved in. But he did make a good breakfast. And last night proved he still harbored skillful surprises.

Brooke checked the time. "I have to go." She rushed to finish the rest of her food.

"I'll finish unpacking and see if I can borrow Jeff's car to go shopping for a few more things that will make your life a little easier."

Brooke crossed her arms. "Like what?"

"I made a list. A new toaster oven, potholders, a spatula, some counter stools, so you can eat sitting down, at least until we get some real furniture."

"Okay. But that's all we need."

Xander ate the last morsel of food from his plate. "We have enough white towels for an army. Why do you have so many towels?"

Brooke responded with a shrug.

"Call me when you're finished at work. I don't want to be out if you're here. Not when I have to leave tomorrow." He put his hands around her shoulders, kissed her on the lips, her nose, and then the top of her head.

Dressed casually in shorts and a T-shirt, Brooke walked outside to the front of the apartment building, called Dr. Gold, and left him a message. "The police need to see me to tie up a few loose ends today. I'm not sure if I'll make it in. I'll let you know as soon as I can." The way she saw it, since Dr. Gold had hired Dr. Draven, he was partly to blame for her troubles and could hardly complain about her absence. He'd been very considerate of her lately, so she doubted it would be a problem.

It was a beautiful morning. A few fluffy white clouds stretched across the sky. She waved hello to a man on a riding mower. The air carried the smell of freshly cut grass.

Exactly on time, Merrik drove slowly toward Brooke in a newish-model Chevy Tahoe. She was almost to the curb when a Hyundai cut her off and swerved into the parking spot closest to the entrance. A young woman raced from the car and inside. Maybe she remembered she had left her curling iron on or had a bathroom emergency. Whatever it was, she had unknowingly cut off a police officer.

Brooke walked behind the Hyundai to the Tahoe, interested to see how Merrik would respond to the incident.

Merrik didn't look the least bit flustered or put off about it. No "did you see that?" or "Unbelievable!" Just a pleasant "Good morning," as Brooke sat and adjusted her seat belt.

Riding as a passenger, subject to the whims of the driver, always made her a little nervous. *Relax.* She uncurled her fingers.

"It's supposed to be a scorcher today." Merrik pulled away from the curb. "Did you get your run in yet?"

"I'm going later tonight. With my boyfriend."

"Xander Cross is visiting from Chicago, is he?"

For a split second, Brooke's breathing halted. She didn't remember mentioning Xander to Merrik or Pispani at any time. "How do you know that?"

"Perhaps you told me."

"I didn't."

Merrik's eyes sparkled as if she and Brooke were old friends laughing about a joke. She put on her left blinker where Brooke expected her to turn right.

Maybe there is more than one way to get to the police headquarters, a better way in rush hour traffic. Brooke stared out the window, analyzing each subsequent turn until there was no possible explanation for their current route, all signs indicated Merrik was driving North when the station was to the South.

Brooke squirmed in her seat. "This isn't the way to the police headquarters."

Merrik kept her eyes on the road. "We're not going to that location today."

"Where are we going?" Brooke tried to sound calm, tried not to raise her voice and reveal her escalating unease.

"We're almost there." At the next stop light, she leaned toward Brooke, adjusting the air conditioning.

A gun bulged from a half-concealed holster under Merrik's blouse. Brooke had never handled a gun before. She didn't know what steps were required to fire one.

A public golf course, hotels, and a shopping mall flashed by outside the window. A mile passed with a pair of sneakers thrown over telephone wires on every block. Brooke pulled down the passenger side visor to block the glare of the morning sun. The console listed the interior temperature as sixty-eight degrees, but Brooke felt uncomfortably warm.

Merrik persisted with attempts at small talk, all of it having to do with Brooke's life, interests, and job. Brooke responded with short, concise answers. A nervous swirl of energy gnawed quietly away inside her. *Time to turn this conversation away from me.* "Where did you go to medical school?"

"Duke."

Brooke tapped her finger on the door. "And then?"

"I completed my residency at Rothaker teaching hospital. I met my husband in Connecticut, so I got my license and certification here and stayed."

"What made you choose psychiatry?"

"I've always been fascinated by the human mind." She glanced at Brooke, then back to the road. "Especially when it strays from what is generally considered normal." Her hands slid from the top of the wheel to the sides. "Are you considering psychiatry?"

"No. I'm going to be a surgeon."

They stopped at the edge of the city, in a corporate office park with newly planted landscaping.

"Here we are." Merrik turned off the engine. "Come on. It's all brand new and a lot nicer than the police headquarters."

Seeing no other alternative, Brooke followed Merrik through bright sunshine to the tallest building and into a gleaming corporate lobby. Merrik pressed the elevator button for the fifth floor and they rode up in silence. When a five popped up on the digital screen, an electronic bell chimed, and the doors opened to a dark gray wall. Silver letters, almost as tall as Brooke, spelled out Greytech. The company occupied the entire floor of the building.

"Hi, Ingrid." Merrik walked over to the attractive woman behind a desk spanning the entry. "This is Brooke Walton."

Ingrid had light blonde hair, ice blue eyes, and wore small elegant earrings and a single bracelet. With her cool and professional look, she could have been Brooke's sister. She flashed Brooke a genuine nice-to-meet-you smile.

A door swung open at one end of the desk and Ingrid made a graceful arc with her arm. "Go on in. May I bring you anything to drink?"

"No, thank you." Brooke tried to place Ingrid's accent. Dutch? Finnish?

"I'll have the usual, Ingrid, thank you." Merrik smiled. "Bad habits die hard."

They walked down a corridor lined with offices and conference spaces. Merrik entered one of the window-lined rooms with a large oval table and took a seat. Brooke sat down across from her and took in the modern and minimally-furnished space.

What am I doing here? An insistent voice inside her head urged her to flee the building. But Merrik was a cop. Brooke had no choice but to cooperate and, with a hint of morbid curiosity, almost like watching a scary movie, she wanted to find out what was going to happen next. *What does Merrik have on me?*

Ingrid arrived carrying a Diet Coke for Merrik. "I've let Mike know you're here." She turned to Brooke. "Sure I can't get you anything?"

Brooke noticed tiny lines around Ingrid's eyes and realized Ingrid was older than she first appeared. "Yes, I'm sure. Thank you."

"Okay, then." Ingrid left, taking smooth steps in her slim pencil skirt, tailored blouse, and heels, leaving Brooke feeling underdressed, alone again with Merrik.

"You probably don't drink soda, do you?" Merrik tapped the top of the can before prying it open.

"No, I don't." *How much longer is she going to continue with inconsequential small talk before I learn what I'm doing here?*

"It's something I'm trying to quit." Merrik laughed. "So, any other Caribbean vacations in your future?"

"No. That trip was unusual for my family. And I'm a full-time student. With a lot of debt."

"I was once in your shoes. That might change for you soon."

"What do you mean?"

She took a long chug of her drink. "I've never been to Cancun before. I have a feeling it's safe though, most of the time. Especially if you're prepared for the worst. You know, like aggressive men who can't leave an attractive woman alone."

Alarm bells rang inside Brooke's head, jolting her to an even higher level of alertness. "Why am I here?"

Merrik answered with an unnerving, serious expression, like she was finally ready to get down to business. "You're here because you're special."

Of course I am. Brooke raised her eyebrows. "Special, how?"

"As you well know, you lack the capability for sympathy, empathy, guilt, and remorse. You're also brilliant. You're a rare find. A highly functioning psychopath."

Brooke's eyes darted to the door. For once, she had no idea how to respond. As she sat in stunned silence, every muscle tense and ready to flee, the door opened and a handsome man with a crewcut entered the room.

Detective Merrik stood up. "Brooke, this is Special Agent Mike Merrik. My husband."

The introduction did nothing to alleviate Brooke's confusion.

"I'll leave you two to get acquainted. I've got things to do, but I'll be back." Merrik left, closing the door behind her.

Mike Merrik had broad swimmer's shoulders. The way his dark suit draped over his body suggested a lean, hard body. Older than Merrik, but no less fit looking, silver hairs mixed in with the dark at his temples, giving him an air of sophistication and reminding Brooke of cold steel. He sat with erect posture that mirrored her own. His expression was unreadable. "Welcome. It's come to my attention that you are ideally suited to work with a special unit I supervise."

"I'm sorry." Brooke gave a slight shake of her head. "I have no idea what you're talking about."

"I trust my wife. She's never been wrong about someone before."

"That may be, but I'm a medical student."

"And that will make you even more of an asset to us."

"What? I'm sorry. I think you might have me confused with someone else."

"I don't. We've done extensive research. I know everything about you. Everything."

Her mouth was suddenly dry, and she regretted not asking Ingrid for a water bottle. "I really don't know what it is you think I can do, or what you want me to do, but in a few weeks, I go back to being a full-time student. I can't work with you."

"I apologize, Brooke. I wasn't entirely clear. You see, I'm not asking you."

"Excuse me?"

"This isn't what you'd call a negotiable opportunity. You're going to be working for me. You'll remain in medical school and you'll work for me. One thing you'll appreciate about our arrangement is that we will pay off the considerable amount of money you owe and finish paying for your degree."

"What?" Brooke was no less confused, but at least there was something positive in it for her, whatever *it* was.

"Your past indiscretions will be swept under the rug. You may have noticed, some of them already have been. Just in time to save you from prison."

"Huh?"

"Remember the rental car key you lost? Your prints are on it. Over the blood of John Peters and Rico Vega. Try explaining that to a jury."

"I . . . I don't—" Brooke stammered.

"By the way, Rachael Kline was never in Morris Draven's house. Or at least it's highly unlikely that she was. But samples of her hair were found there and are now in the police department's evidence room. You have Greytech to thank for that."

"I don't understand."

"Besides the two men you killed in Cancun, there's Dr. Morris Draven, Rachael Kline . . . do I need to go on? All people who got in your way, it appears."

Brooke's muscles grew even more rigid. She eyed the exit and wiped her damp palms against her shorts. She desperately wanted to ask how he knew, but she managed to remain silent.

"You won't tell your family or friends or your boyfriend about your work at Greytech."

"I still have no idea what you're talking about." She was telling the truth. "What is Greytech?"

"You already know someone who works here. I'll let him explain everything." Mike Merrik typed into his phone and in a few seconds, the door to the conference room opened again.

Charlie walked in looking strikingly handsome, wearing a navy-blue suit and crisp white shirt, very different from the cyclist in the T-shirt and jeans who had rescued her from Draven's closet. He sat down next to Agent Merrik.

Brooke clasped her hands together on the table. Her eyes radiated fury. "So, this is the tech company you work for?"

Charlie nodded. "We have a lot to talk about."

"What is going on?" She glared.

"A lot of remarkable timing," answered Charlie.

"Please explain."

"If you hadn't gone into the Goodwill store, we may have never crossed paths. Fortunately for you, you happened to be the most beautiful girl I'd ever seen. And low maintenance too—buying your furniture at Goodwill." He smiled. "You said the name of your apartments when you were talking to your friend. It was easy for me to figure out who you were."

Brooke watched him, tight-lipped.

"That was when your name came up in the Cancun murder investigation." Charlie leaned back in his chair. "I asked Dr. Merrik to get involved with the case, so we'd have some control over it. And everything we've discovered since then convinced us that you were a perfect fit for Greytech."

"Hmmmf." Brooke's eyes blazed. "I really don't see how—"

Charlie held up his palm to silence her. "Your self-preservation skills are incredible. You lie effortlessly. You don't appear to experience guilt or remorse. Yet you're highly intelligent and able to manipulate people so they have no idea who and what they're dealing with. You don't seem to register pain like a normal person either."

"Yes, I do, I—" Brooke decided there was no point in trying to correct him regarding one item from his list. They knew her. She was afraid, but beyond her fear, she wasn't sure if she felt embarrassed or proud. "And I honestly thought you just wanted to ask me out. Guess one of my strengths isn't reading people."

"I'm good at what I do." Charlie sighed. "I forgot to mention your attention to detail. Nice touch with those earrings. We might have our hands full with you, but eventually you'll do good for our country." He turned to Mike, who nodded.

Brooke crossed her arms. "I'm going to be a surgeon. That's been my goal for as long as I can remember."

"You'll still do that, but you'll also work for Greytech." Mike leaned forward. "Believe me, this is the best possible situation for you. Much better than prison."

Brooke pressed her lips together. She hated not having any control over the conversation. "Okay. So, you both work for Greytech. What is it, exactly?"

"Greytech is a CIA unit," said Mike. "It's made up of individuals with specialized skills. Survival skills. Combat skills. All of them are extremely capable and dangerous, like you and Charlie."

Brooke glanced at Charlie, at a loss for words.

"No one outside the operation knows it exists. We take care of things."

"You take care of things?"

"Just like you do, except we have critical reasons." Charlie crossed his arms. "You're going to fit in beautifully here."

Brooke shot out of her seat and took two strides toward the door. Mike reached for something and stretched out his arm. She ducked out of instinct, but he didn't have a weapon. Instead, a clear plastic bag dangled from his fingers. Inside it was a familiar key, the representation of her single biggest screw-up. She stopped moving.

"I don't think you'll like the alternative." Mike's voice remained level, his gaze steady. The bag swayed from side to side above the conference table.

"How did you get that? I thought it went missing from the evidence room in Cancun." As she spoke the words, she realized what had happened, and the extent of Greytech's reach and capabilities.

"Right now, we're the only ones who know the prints on this key, in the victims' blood, match yours." Mike let the bag fall to the table. "That can easily change."

Brooke offered a barely perceptible dip of her chin, sat back down in her seat, and crossed her long legs at the ankle. "I admire tenacity; I really do. And I can see that your organization has incredible capabilities – planting evidence at Draven's house, stealing evidence from the Cancun investigation . . . But if I am what you say I am, a ruthless killer who has—according to you—murdered more than one person because they were inconvenient to me . . . why would you openly threaten such a person?"

Mike's face remained relaxed. "We're more invincible than you are. Take some time to think about your situation."

Brooke swiveled her chair around so she faced the window, staring out across the expertly landscaped view, away from Mike and Charlie.

On the positive side, they're the first people ever to know the real me, and yet they want me to work with them, rather than wanting me on death row. That alone is a bit amazing.

With a soft sigh, she turned back around, her gaze dropping to the bag with the key. "Seeing I have no choice . . . count me in." She placed her hands on the arm rests of her chair and relaxed. The corners of her lips twitched and then gave way to a beautiful grin. Teeth bared, she turned to Charlie, and then to Mike. "Here's to a successful collaboration."

NOTE FROM THE AUTHOR

Thank you for reading THE INTERN. I thought I was done with my psychopath protagonist when I wrote the second Brooke book, ROTHAKER. Readers responses to Brooke Walton were mixed. Some people can't help rooting for her and have begged for more books. Others want her behind bars for life. A few years after I left her as a first-year medical student, I started writing *The Intern*. I wasn't sure of Brooke's fate until I was almost finished with this novel, and I had the idea for a compromise that might make everyone happy.

If you have the time, I would deeply appreciate a review on Amazon, Goodreads, BookBub or elsewhere. I am an indie author, which means I am the writer, the publisher, and the marketing department. I appreciate any encouragement. If you enjoyed this book, please tell your bookish friends.

You can contact me through the contact page on my website Jenruff.com.

Happy reading!
Jenifer Ruff

JENIFER RUFF

USA TODAY bestselling author Jenifer Ruff writes dark and twisty thrillers, including the award-winning Agent Victoria Thriller Series. Jenifer lives in North Carolina with her family and a pack of greyhounds. If she's not writing, she's probably devouring books or out exploring trails with her dogs. For more information you can visit her website at Jenruff.com

amazon.com/stores/author/B00NFZQOLQ

facebook.com/authorjruff

instagram.com/author.jenifer.ruff/

tiktok.com/@jeniferruff.author

http://bookbub.com/authors/jenifer-ruff

www.ingramcontent.com/pod-product-compliance
Lightning Source LLC
Chambersburg PA
CBHW021125190726

48288CB00008B/2501